John Richards was educated in the UK and lived in London and Singapore before settling in Brisbane. He was shortlisted for the Elizabeth Jolley Short Story Award in 2021 and the Glendower Award for an Emerging Queensland Writer in August 2022. *The Gorgon Flower* is his first published work of fiction.

THE
GORGON
FLOWER

JOHN RICHARDS

First published 2024 by University of Queensland Press
PO Box 6042, St Lucia, Queensland 4067 Australia

The University of Queensland Press (UQP) acknowledges the Traditional Owners and their custodianship of the lands on which UQP operates. We pay our respects to their Ancestors and their descendants, who continue cultural and spiritual connections to Country. We recognise their valuable contributions to Australian and global society.

uqp.com.au
reception@uqp.com.au

Cover design and illustration by Josh Durham, Design by Committee
Typeset in 12/17 pt Bembo Std by Post Pre-press Group, Brisbane
Printed in Australia by McPherson's Printing Group

  University of Queensland Press is assisted by the Australian Government through Creative Australia, its principal arts investment and advisory body.

A catalogue record for this book is available from the National Library of Australia

ISBN 978 0 7022 6640 9 (pbk)
ISBN 978 0 7022 6934 9 (epdf)
ISBN 978 0 7022 6935 6 (epub)

University of Queensland Press uses papers that are natural, renewable and recyclable products made from wood grown in well-managed forests and other controlled sources. The logging and manufacturing processes conform to the environmental regulations of the country of origin.

For Dominique, Tim, Matt, Ben and Joey,
the most important characters in my own story

Contents

A Fall from Grace

One interpretation of the facts is that Jean-Michel Houvrée produced his most arresting art only after he had died.

Born in 1694 in Ariège-sur-Mentouin, a village a few kilometres north of Carcassonne, to a moderately prosperous inn-owner and his wife, he was brought up a Catholic but embraced Jansenism in his early twenties. He was educated at the local village school until the age of fourteen: an indifferent scholar in the classroom, he was an avid student of the natural world. He was a good boy, obedient to his parents, kind to his friends, open to the loving grace of God. He had big feet, thick black hair, dark brown eyes, a shy smile. Any free time he had after assisting his father in the inn, he would wander the sun-baked lanes and fields carrying cheese and bread in his bag, beneath a sky colour-washed fresh each day by his Creator.

To Jean-Michel, nature was a thin veil through which the divinity of God could be glimpsed and, if you unfurled your senses, touched. A field of corn stalks rilling in the wind as if stroked by an invisible hand. A ball of maggots frothing in the sunken stomach of a wolf-savaged ewe. Olive tree branches bowing in ceaseless supplication to the breeze. Cloud bellies roasted red by the charcoal-hot earth at dusk. All these things the boy saw, imbibed and thought upon. And then he began to draw them. But it was not the case that the Creator, *his* Creator, supported his corporeal hand in Her invisible one and guided his fingers. But nor could it be said that the patterns of expressive and sinuous lines, the deft and sympathetic shadings, were his own renderings of what he saw in the material world. Instead, it was as if they were copied by him from a master sketch which had already faithfully reproduced its subjects' divine and therefore true character – a celestial blueprint to which he alone had access, he alone could see in his spirit's eye.

His parents came across drawings left lying around. The abandoned well in the field next to the parish church, haunted by the ghosts of those who had used it down the centuries; Francine Moutard, his young cousin, her head to one side, gazing indulgently at the kittens she cuddled in her arms but with the whisper of something else – contempt perhaps – hovering on her lips; the split-second stare over his shoulder of a male osprey – and this time there was an unmistakable superiority in the bird's black button glare. Both mother and father had an untutored but instant appreciation of the boy's gift. The inn served a main road and was busy with those who had occasion to travel in those days: grain and cloth merchants, farmers' agents, tax collectors, travelling salesmen. His father made enquiries of those passing through and was given the name of a local painter living in the next town who was getting on in years and might require an apprentice.

The next week, a warm wind tugging at their hats and travelling cloaks, Jean-Michel and his father rode over to see the painter. Mathieu Géroux was desperately busy, inundated with orders from the local bourgeoisie for family portraits, religious scenes and landscapes. But cataracts were crawling slowly over his eyes; his hands and wrists were stiffening with arthritis as if made of papier-mâché, drying in the sun. Barely looking at the boy's drawings, Géroux hired him on the spot, and Jean-Michel said goodbye to his father and started as the old painter's assistant.

Géroux lived and worked alone. The boy slept on blankets in the corner of the painter's barn-like studio. When, a couple of years later, Géroux's legs became too unsteady to climb stairs, his bed was moved to the studio and Jean-Michel slept on a mattress in the vacated bedroom. The boy was kept busy: he rose at dawn, swept the studio, milked the goat, fetched the bread and eggs, and prepared the porridge before the painter arose. During winter, he had to re-light the stove in the studio.

At first, he was confined to painting backgrounds: the smoky burgundy backdrop to a portrait of the local bishop; the sunlit benchtop for the still life of summer fruits; the blue undulating hills behind the family scene of Madonna and child, the commissioner of the painting kneeling in attendance. But as soon as his talent became clear, he was invited to paint the hand-held prayer-book, the burnished platter, until before long he had gravitated to the subject of the painting itself, where he demonstrated such an intuitive understanding allied with such technical mastery (the stubble speckling the episcopal jowls, the precisely reticulated thorax of the peach-gorging fruit fly) that Géroux would stare at the finished work with wonder in his milky eyes. Within a couple of years, without any formal acknowledgement or ceremony, their positions were reversed: Géroux met the patrons and delivered the finished work of art, but the boy prepared the charcoal outline and executed the most complex and demanding elements of each work, relegating the old painter to those parts of the final picture which the eye passed over without seeing or absorbing.

Word spread of the high quality of work coming from Mathieu Géroux's studio, and the more informed amongst his clientele correctly attributed this to Géroux's young apprentice. As the fame of the studio rippled across the south of France, its products began to change hands for a value in excess of that paid for their creation.

When Géroux died from consumption nine years after the boy had come to live with him, Jean-Michel, now twenty-four, had become the son the painter never had; if he inherited, under the old painter's will, Géroux's name and property (a cottage across the yard from the studio had been replaced by a double-fronted stone-clad villa with gardens and an orchard), the studio's prosperous business was already in effect his. By this time, the household retained a small group of servants – a couple of young women for the kitchen and the house, and an older man for the grounds. Jean-Michel remained unmarried. He worked long hours, starting at dawn and continuing long into the night, the oil lamp at the unshuttered studio window a solitary twinkling light, as though a star had fallen from the heavens and landed in the black folds of the earth. But no matter the number of commissions demanding his attention, he walked the countryside for an hour each day whatever the season or weather, welcomed visits from his mother (his father having died shortly after he left home) and each Sunday worshipped at St Pierre's. If asked, he would have said he was no more than, but also no less than, an involuntary instrument by which the Creator's presence in each particle (it was too soon to think in terms of atoms) of Her creation was captured and celebrated. He would not have accepted, or even understood, the romantic idea of an artist as someone who partook of a self-motivated, self-idealised human act of creation.

The old painter had been of the Jansenist persuasion: his Bible never strayed far from a copy of Jansen's *Augustinus*. It had been axiomatic to Géroux that although life was a gift given to all, divine grace must be a gift given to less than all. How many had received the gift of faith he had not been in a position to speculate, but one could not insist on the right to be saved any more than one could insist on possessing the artistic ability of a Jean-Michel. Towards the end of his days, Géroux had joined a group of parishioners drawn from the better-educated sort who met at one another's dwellings to read and discuss the New Testament through the prism of Jansenist theology. The meetings were not secret, but they were not advertised, and attendance was by invitation only. Jean-Michel had accompanied Géroux to these meetings, and after the old painter's death he continued to attend. He spoke less at the gatherings than Géroux had done but listened more. On the evening when it was his turn to host, one of the young women closed the shutters in the front parlour, drew the curtains and lit the oil lamps before the guests assembled. Bread, cheese and wine were served and, once the theological conversation had commenced, the parsing of the Gospel of St John and the First Letter of St Paul to the Corinthians continued long into the night.

One evening in July 1725, when Jean-Michel was thirty-one, he was returning home from such a gathering, held at the chateau of a wealthy neighbour, a merchant who lived a few kilometres from his house. A warm breeze, spiced with lavender and thyme, fingered the trees and shrubs as his horse followed the moonlit track. The horse had been unsettled from the start, swinging its head from side to side as if to shake off an invisible hand on its head. About thirty minutes into the journey, as Jean-Michel was passing through a stand of oak trees, a colony of bats exploded from the branches above and with a flurry of high-pitched clicks and leathery flaps swept across the path in front of the horse, causing it to snort and rear on its hind legs. Jean-Michel was thrown to the ground, where he hit his head on a tree root. At dawn the following day, noticing the horse had not been stabled the previous evening, the groundsman set off along the path to the merchant's house. About halfway there, he found Jean-Michel unconscious on the ground, barely breathing, a shallow crater of shattered bone and greyish-purple tissue denting the back of his head. There was no sign of the horse.

A cart was fetched, and Jean-Michel was laid on blankets in the back and accompanied on his journey home by the groundsman, the physician and his servant, and the cart's owner, each of whom walked with one hand on the cart to steady its juddering progress along the stony ground – to alleviate, if only to that small extent, the discomfort and physical indignity of the injured painter. When the party reached the house of Jean-Michel, the body was placed in the front parlour and the physician told the assembled servants that the artist was no longer breathing and that he would contact the priest.

All this is agreed history, pieced together from public registries, accounts found in personal diaries, the personal recollections of witnesses, and informed and sympathetic supposition. We can say: this much was known of the life of Jean-Michel Houvrée. What follows is more uncertain: facts are contested, and interpretations disputed.

Eighteenth-century French parochial records are singularly unreliable but there are no local records of Jean-Michel's death in 1725. There is no evidence of a funeral service being held around that time, either. Instead, a Monsieur Houvrée (no first name given) is recorded in the annals of the local parish as dying from pneumonia in 1756, although again there is no record of a requiem mass or other religious service being held to commemorate the death.

In early eighteenth-century France, the cataloguing of commercial transactions was not common; the footprint left in local archives by a moderately wealthy member of the bourgeoisie was inevitably fragmentary. From the scarce records there were in 1725, however, it appeared as if Jean-Michel disappeared from the social intercourse of his community: no further evidence of attendance at church or participation in the Jansenist discussion groups existed; no further record of him purchasing charcoal, vellum, pigments or varnish from his usual suppliers has survived. So far as we know, no further visits were made to the local tailor, physician or barber and no requisitions made from his vintner or butcher. Indeed, there is no evidence that anyone ever saw Jean-Michel Houvrée in person after 20th July 1725. Finally, most tellingly for those who would argue that the painter was physically incapacitated or even died on this date, there are no more entries, whether sketches or text, after this date in those of his notebooks and journals which have come down to us. The last known entry which has survived is dated 18th July 1725, a couple of days before he was thrown from his horse.

Tales which were seed-planted in the mulch of village gossip and speculation took root and over time grew into a popular mythology that formed part of the culture and history of a region, of a country. There are accounts of sketches for portraits only taking place at night, the subject sitting at one end of the studio, illuminated by a phalanx of candles, the rest of the studio in darkness through which a phantom-like cloaked figure could be intermittently discerned. After an hour or so, the servant who had shown the person to their seat would return and see that person out. Commissions were no longer made in person, only in writing by way of letter left at Monsieur Houvrée's residence; completed works were left in the parlour to be picked up, without meeting or sight of the artist. Of course, it is difficult to know how much credence should be given to such accounts; how much is grounded in fact, how much embellished by imaginative fancy.

The evidence that Jean-Michel survived the consequences of the fall, and in a state of health that allowed him to continue working, lies in the extraordinary series of paintings which were produced in the decade or so after 1725 and which are believed to have been produced by him. The so-called *peintures étonnantes* constitute a collection of portraits, landscapes, still lives and religious pictures which, though ostensibly conventional in theme and execution, contain strange, bizarre and wondrous elements placed alongside or embedded within the ordinary and quotidian. As one art historian later commented, it is as if the nightmarish, hallucinogenic creatures of Hieronymus Bosch had invaded and taken occupation of the calm, ordered world of Vermeer; what is most striking about the *peintures étonnantes* is the cool, forensic blending of the fantastical and the formal.

The features of the tax collector in *Portrait of Monsieur Fregier* are those of a prosperous, humane, middle-aged tax collector. The painter has captured the weary self-knowledge in his eyes – and also a sinuous black tongue, forked at its tip, lolling from Fregier's half-open mouth.

In *Visit of the Magi* the traditional gifts of gold, frankincense and myrrh proffered by the kings have been replaced by a meticulously delineated sleeping bat, a pinkish-grey object veined with red threads about the length of a forearm subsequently identified by veterinary anatomists as a skinned fox, and a nacreous cloak-like object, draped over two extended arms, seemingly gelatinous in texture, which has appeared to more than one marine biologist to be a dead jellyfish. There is no hint of awareness of the incongruous nature of their offerings in the reverential gaze of the regal visitors.

It is common to include butterflies, wasps, flies and snails in still lives of flowers – see, for example, the floral still lives of the Dutch artist Balthasar van der Ast (1593/94–1657), which are festooned with a veritable cornucopia of insects. But *Still Life with a Bowl of Flowers* is dominated by a giant beetle, bigger than a human head, drawn in microscopic detail, squatting centre stage in front of the fruit bowl. Interestingly, entomologists have been unable to identify the exact species of beetle in the painting; expert opinion is divided on whether the artist made a mistake in painting the beetle or conjured its features out of his imagination, or whether the beetle was represented accurately but in the intervening years had become extinct.

Perhaps the most famous *peinture étonnante* is the most unnerving: *The Investiture of Dr Regonard*, now exhibited in the Louvre. Dr Regonard stands looking out of the canvas at the viewer with a level gaze, resplendent in blue velvet frockcoat, cream linen breeches and gold buckled shoes, caught in a shaft of cool daylight from windows to his right. Behind him and to his left is a full-length mirror in which the back of the doctor is reflected. He is blocking the light from the window, so the back of his frockcoat and his breeches and stockings are in shadow. But as your eyes adjust to the gloom, there at the bottom of the reflection, on either side of his legs, facing out of the mirror, squats a naked homunculus with eyes like black marbles, pointed nose and wide, lipless mouth, grinning at the viewer, its arms wrapped around the leg nearest to it. In an instant your eyes switch back to Dr Regonard before the mirror: did you miss them the first time you looked? But no, the imp-like creatures are not there; they can be seen only in the shadows of the reflection, their eyes fixed on you. You look again at the doctor's face to see whether it betrays any consciousness of these malevolent entities, hugging his legs in the mirror. This time you think you perceive a tightness to the set of his mouth; what seemed like calmness in the eyes now seems like deadness; and you realise there is no animating spark, no twinkle of light in these eyes; they are dark tunnels into nothing.

The overwhelming consensus currently in place amongst art historians and scholars is that the *peintures étonnantes* were indeed painted by Jean-Michel Houvrée. This thesis was first established by the publication in 1882 of Charles Gilliment's biography of the painter, which argued convincingly that there are continuities of technique, of tint and colouration, even of brushstroke, between the *peintures étonnantes* and Houvrée's earlier work that transcend any divergences in style or subject matter. The fact that no sketches or outlines for any of these artworks were found amongst Houvrée's papers was ignored, as was the fact that the pigments, oils and varnish deployed by the artist in these paintings were entirely different from those used in his previous paintings. (On this point, it is worth noting that, to this day, art historians who specialise in historical painting techniques and materials have not been able to trace where the pigments and oils used by Houvrée in these artworks were sourced – see Susan Manzer's masterly survey, 'Questions concerning the origins of materials used in the *peintures étonnantes* of Jean-Michel Houvrée', from a symposium on Historical Painting Techniques, Materials and Studio Practice held at the University of Neymoller, the Netherlands, 18th–20th September 1989.)

It is true that the otherworldly, occult and extraordinary elements of the *peintures étonnantes* constitute a radical departure in subject matter from Houvrée's previous paintings – but they constitute a significant break from most art of that time. It is tempting to exaggerate those facets which speak of a modern, even postmodern, sensibility, or which presuppose an ironic, knowing detachment on the artist's part. But equally, there is no denying that sense of a mind awakened to the discombobulation afforded by the radical reordering of reality, or the introduction of images that convey pain and despair just as much as they speak of a deracinated jeu d'esprit.

The appreciation of these striking paintings has been transformed in recent years by the publication in 1999 of Professor Aiden Cumber's *A Fall from Grace: the altered visions and living nightmares of the* peintures étonnantes *of Jean-Michel Houvrée*. His argument is that when Jean-Michel fell from his horse in July 1725, he incurred a traumatic brain injury to his occipital lobe, that part of the brain which is responsible for visual perception and visuospatial coordination. Consequently, the way Houvrée visually experienced reality and the way he formulated visual representations was profoundly altered. This accounts for the strange, exotic or incongruous objects and the disjointed sense of perspective which thereafter are a prominent feature of his work.

According to Cumber, these 'altered visions' (as he termed them) were entirely involuntary in origin and Houvrée had no control over them: once they had formed in his mind, he simply had to incorporate them in his paintings the best way he could. Cumber's thesis is that this should not be seen as a deficit: the fall did not cause any diminution of Houvrée's ability as an artist. Rather, it enhanced his artistic repertoire and expanded his mental faculties, in the same way mescaline and LSD would do for later generations of artists. This explanation has persuaded some more than others, but whatever the explanation for the radical departure in Jean-Michel's artistic vision, it clearly did not come without some cost to the painter, as the solitary, reclusive and shadowy life he adopted after his injury suggests.

Whatever the truth about Jean-Michel Houvrée's life and art after his fall, we may perhaps give him the last word as expressed in the final work he is believed to have painted. *Portrait of the Artist Sitting at a Table* is the only self-portrait purportedly produced by Jean-Michel Houvrée. It has been tentatively dated as 1754, when the painter was sixty. An even, limpid light floods the picture. He sits to the left of a round table facing the viewer, dressed in nondescript black clothes, his eyes disconcertingly gazing up at something out of the picture, just above the viewer's head. The eyes are caught at the exact moment they have flicked up, and this has an extraordinary effect on the viewer: the natural response is to look up to see what has caught the painter's eye. Whatever it is delights him; the face is expressionless, so this effect is achieved solely by capturing a gentle, joyous humour in the eyes: a stunning technical accomplishment. His hand rests palm up on the table as if ready to hold the hand of whoever is going to sit next to him – for the seat on the other side of the table, also facing the viewer, is empty. Except when examining the way Jean-Michel leans in, the way his hand is held out, more than one viewer has had the curious sensation that there is someone indeed sitting in the chair next to Jean-Michel, holding his hand, perhaps also looking up at what has caught his eye.

The Interventions

1.

It must have been around five in the afternoon in London when I got the call regarding Stuart Fairlie. It was Theo, one of my Chief Line Managers, on the phone.

'Debbie, sorry to interrupt you on your day off. We have a situation brewing with Stuart Fairlie, which looks like it's going to be eligible for intervention. That will be intervention numero five, which is why I'm calling you.'

As a Director, I am required to sign off on the fifth intervention for any of my supervisees. The fifth intervention is a serious matter because it's the last one. There aren't any more interventions to be had. Protocol dictates I can't dial in the authorisation to intervene, I can only do it from the office, so I got changed out of my scruffs and brushed Sammy's forehead with my lips before heading down to the garage. On the way into the office, behind the wheel of my Audi (standard issue for Directors), Theo filled me in on the background details. Stuart was thirty-six, married to Caroline (thirty-two) with three children (Ian (eight), Lily (six) and David (nine months)). He was an investment banker working out of London, and he had flown to Jakarta three days ago to negotiate the debt restructuring of a large Indonesian oil and gas company. Normally a job like this would be handled out of the bank's Singapore office, but Stuart was an up-and-coming star and the client asked for him to lead the team in person. Which he had been doing. But right now, it was just past midnight in Jakarta and Stuart was in a club downtown from the central business district, in drunken but nevertheless earnest conversation with a young Indonesian woman whom it appeared he had every intention of taking back to his hotel room for sex.

I asked Theo to tell me more about Fairlie. It's unusual for someone of his age – and, to be frank, position – to be already facing his fifth intervention. Most people need an intervention or two in their teens and then one every ten to fifteen years thereafter (although every person is unique, of course, and the intervention patterns of some individuals are very bespoke).

Theo read the details from the screen in front of him. 'Never knew his biological father. Brought up by Linda, his biological mother, but she died of a drug overdose when Stuart was ten. Fostered with a series of couples, each of whom found dealing with Stuart challenging. First intervention happened when Stuart was thirteen: a suicide attempt which ranked 8.35 on the Clore-Hamblin Suicide Intentional Scale. Intervention two was twelve months later. Stuart was jumped by two dealers with knives after he tried to shortchange them during a cocaine sale. Third intervention, a few months later, was to put him in the way of a couple who had a track record of turning round troubled kids. With compassion, love (some of it the tough kind) and time, they got Stuart on the straight and narrow, and when he was sixteen, they adopted him. He did well at school, exams, university, job at a bank, MBA. Successful career, married, three kids: not the outcome you'd have expected from someone who'd had three interventions by the time he was fifteen.'

'What about his fourth intervention?'

'A couple of years ago. After closing a deal, Stuart and his team went out for drinks. Instead of getting a taxi from the railway station car park, he attempted to drive his BMW home. After narrowly missing one pedestrian out walking the dog and a second pedestrian on the way to the pub, he drove his car into a dry-stone wall three miles from his converted oast house. By the time he had staggered the rest of the way home, showered and downed a couple of black coffees, he had a plan. He was going to tell the police, who were on their way, that his car had been stolen from the station car park. He'd taken a taxi home. One problem with this plan, however: the car park had CCTV. An intervention was authorised. His wife talked him out of it, and Stuart got a fine and ten demerit points instead of a prison sentence and the loss of his job.'

I supervise around five hundred individuals; at some time or another, I've read the outline biographies of each of them. But recalling the specific details is not always easy. Once I'd been reminded, Stuart's history was not unfamiliar although I hadn't personally sanctioned any of Stuart's four interventions. In the normal course, a Line Manager and above can authorise interventions one to three; an Associate Director and above, intervention four. I had a vague recollection of being consulted when the drunk-driving intervention was under consideration, but I couldn't recall what my input had been. My sense was that this was going to involve a tough call: you'd ordinarily want to keep your fifth intervention in reserve for your forties, your fifties or beyond. But sexual misconduct is complicated. It's like a luminescent green weed, rank and fibrous, festering beneath the soil, waiting for the moment to sprout and disfigure your well-cultivated lawn, your ordered plant bed.

After arriving at work, I dropped my bag off in my office, grabbed a coffee from the pantry and made my way to the control room. Normally we're in the same time zone as our supervisees: we sleep when they sleep. But Stuart being in Jakarta meant I'd had to split the team so we could cover him around the clock. Theo, Orla and the two Leonards (R and D) sat at their workstations, staring at one wall of the control room, which was covered by a huge screen that conveyed a live video feed direct from Stuart's head, as if we were watching the world through his eyes – which I guess, in a technical sense, we were. The video feed looked out onto a table in a murky raspberry-lit club, at which a young Indonesian woman sat, smiling hesitantly.

Leonard R turned to me as I walked over to his workstation: 'He's asking how much it will cost. She doesn't want to be drawn, says they'll work it out, depends on what happens, et cetera, et cetera – they're getting nowhere fast. He has little Indonesian, she has little English.'

'Has he done anything like this before? Who's reviewing his history?'

Orla spoke up. 'I'm pretty much up to date. I'd say this is out of character big time. Sexual clean sheet up to now. Go so far as to say happily married.' (Did I hear Orla putting tweezers around those last two words?) 'Only thing I'd mention is a predilection for what I believe is called Asian pussy when the boy is doing it by himself.' I winced at the phrase and saw Orla smile to herself at that.

'What about the young woman? Have we spoken to our Indonesian colleagues yet?'

'Not yet,' said Theo. 'We were waiting for you.' Protocol required that the initial contact with colleagues in other jurisdictions should be done at the level of the highest-ranking team member present. While Leonard R sourced the video feed with Jakarta, Leonard D read the young woman's bio off the screen in front of him.

'Citra Candawati. Twenty-two. Single. Lives with her mother, two older sisters and younger brother in North Jakarta. Father died some years ago. Receptionist at a large insurance company. Boyfriend is an air-conditioning engineer; he's currently in Sulawesi on tour with his local amateur football club. Which explains why Citra's at the Butterfly Club. It's a short taxi drive away from the CBD: popular as a pick-up joint with expats.'

'I'm putting Director Ismaya Muljadi through now,' Leonard R said. The video screen divided into two and the face of a woman with short, neat greyish hair and thoughtful brown eyes appeared next to Stuart's live feed. I went over to my workstation and switched on the video communicator.

'Ibu Ismaya, it's a pleasure to meet you. Thank you for your time.'

'Pleased to meet you too, Deborah, and thank you also for your time.'

'As you know, we've got eyes on one of our supervisees, Stuart Fairlie, and he's in a developing situation with one of yours. Just wanted to know whether you were at all thinking of intervening on your side?'

'Intervention? No, we weren't thinking of it.' Ismaya smiled. 'Citra is not being very honest with Nico, her boyfriend, but her behaviour is neither unprecedented nor uncharacteristic. From experience, she won't settle for less than two hundred US dollars. That's three million rupiah – roughly a quarter of her monthly salary. Last time she did something like this, she gave nearly all of it to Nico to help him buy a motorbike. Told him she'd been saving up.' She must have seen the surprise on my face. 'Look, I'm not saying we approve. There are risks in behaving like this. And there is a moral line to take, of course.'

'You're not worried about what might happen if the evening goes well, if they arrange to meet again, if, well, a relationship starts?'

Ismaya shook her head. 'I can't see that happening, Deborah. Citra has done this two or three times before: not often, but enough to suggest that if your Mr Fairlie takes her back to his hotel, she will stay a few hours then slip away shortly after dawn and never see him again. Sure, they might exchange numbers, but Citra will erase his number and block it on the way home in her taxi.'

At that moment the eyes' view video feed lurched violently. The picture began to lift and angle downwards, shuddering and swaying. The top of Citra's head swung into the picture, then a corner of the bar table with Stuart's hand pushed down onto it for support.

'Our boy's getting to his feet,' said Leonard R. 'I think they've agreed on a price.'

The video-feed picture oscillated up and down and then shakily levelled off with a view, at head height, of tables passing either side as Stuart slowly made his way towards the exit. After a few seconds, the feed swivelled round to show Citra being led by the hand, smiling as she followed him.

Crunch time, I thought. Time to earn the big bucks. I felt the familiar tightening in my stomach muscles which told me a decision on intervening was imminent. 'Looks like we're in business,' I said. 'No intervention on your end, Ibu Ismaya. Understood. That's fine. We'd better move at our end. We'll flick into FREEZETIME® and discuss options.'

'That's right, Deborah.' She hesitated for a moment. 'You

know, Citra and Nico are hoping to buy their own flat; they are saving for a deposit.' She looked at me impassively.

'Noted, Ibu Ismaya. But Stuart Fairlie is married and has three young children.'

'Of course, of course. You must do what you consider the right thing and I know you will only act after a great deal of thought. It's been a pleasure to talk with you, Deborah. My best regards to you and your team.'

'Thank you, Ibu, it's been a pleasure to talk with you also.' As she disappeared from the video screen, the view from Stuart's eyes, showing the up-close side of a bartender's face as Stuart leant in to ask for a taxi, expanded back to cover the full wall.

'Leonard R, please activate FREEZETIME® for thirty minutes and join us when you're done.' FREEZETIME® worked in thirty-minute sections: you wouldn't ordinarily put in place a localised time freeze for longer than that. The quantum energy required increased exponentially the longer you kept it on. Run FREEZETIME® for two hours and you'd need the energy generated by six net capacity 7,000MW nuclear generators over the period of a week.

I picked up my coffee and headed for the team break-out room. This was separated from the control room by a glass wall and just big enough to hold a rectangular table that sat eight. Like many Directors, I preferred to make intervention decisions away from the control room. There was no video or audio recording in the break-out room, and that encouraged frank and searching discussions. A smaller wall-mounted video screen relayed the same eyes-on feed that dominated the control-room wall. On the screen Stuart's voice, as he asked for the taxi, slurred, slowed and stopped and the picture froze as FREEZETIME® kicked in. A digital clock on the wall started counting down the thirty minutes.

When Leonard R had joined Theo, Orla, Leonard D and me at the table, I began. 'I tell you, it feels like an intervention to me, but I'd like to hear other views on this.'

2.

It was a tie-break. Orla and Leonard R favoured intervention; Theo and Leonard D did not. In the end, it's often that binary. After I had stated my position, I had mostly withdrawn from the ensuing discussion, letting the team bat around the issues, staring at the pasty, blurred features of the bartender on the video feed on the wall screen, caught in close-up as Stuart was frozen in the act of leaning over the bar to speak to him. Sure, each intervention decision is going to be unique, determined by the specific circumstances of any particular case, but when I look back at the many calls I've made or authorised over the years, certain themes recur. You might think the number of ways any one of us can consciously and deliberately mess up our life is infinite – or, at least, a very great number – but in my considerable experience it's nearly always down to the trinity of sex, drink/drugs (that's just one, by the way) and financial greed. Am I being overly reductionist? Am I indulging in the human impulse to impose structure on random events, like we imagine the threads and filaments of flowing water weaving the same patterns over and over as we stare at the stream? Oh my God, I thought, a bar-room philosopher without a bar or a drink, how pathetic. Why did I shut down the conversation when Sammy asked me last weekend if I'd thought about retiring? Suddenly I wanted to be back home with Sammy very much.

'Let me place the fingers of one hand on my nostrils while I reach with my other hand into the gutter of soiled, shop-worn clichés. I'm a believer in what happens on tour stays on tour,' Leonard D was saying as I refocused on the discussion. 'This type of behaviour is by no means uncommon amongst men working away from home – and sometimes women too.' Orla snorted, but Leonard D ploughed on, ignoring her. 'A dalliance on the side whets the appetite and revives the juices, or perhaps it's the other way round, I forget, it's been so long ... Look, he's drunk, it happens, it's done, he goes home, he feels ashamed, over time he forgets about it. Soon, it's as if it happened to another person. Why waste an intervention on something that never happens again and has no adverse repercussions on his marriage, his family? Save it for when he really needs it, like the leukaemia he develops in his early fifties when—'

Leonard D had stopped, realising his mistake. A stillness descended on the table and Leonard R, rather theatrically I thought, dropped his pencil. I had to say something.

'Leonard, you know we deal here with life-choice and life-decision interventions only. We have no jurisdiction when it comes to medical interventions. They are dealt with by the guys downtown.' Medical interventions are a whole different game of ball, believe me: separate training, separate culture, separate office design – even, it's been rumoured, separate pay, although nobody knows for certain because it is a sackable offence to disclose or even discuss one's remuneration. You're aware an individual only gets one medical intervention, right? If you think our interventions are challenging, spend a morning doing medical interventions.

Leonard D looked chastened, or gave a passable interpretation of someone looking chastened. Orla used this as an opportunity to wrap up her pitch. She turned to Theo. 'Do you have those figures from the Clore-Hamblin Sexual Relationships Study?'

Theo read them out from the laptop in front of him. 'Sixty-two per cent of married men are unfaithful to their wives at least once during their marriage. Of these men, over seventy-eight per cent are unfaithful more than once. If you commit an act of adultery, there is a just-short-of-eighty per cent chance you will go on committing acts of adultery. Goodbye, Mr One-Night Stand.'

'Thanks, Theo,' Orla said. 'Every day, we define ourselves by our actions. If we intervene now, I don't know that Stuart Fairlie won't pick up another girl next time he is working away from home – in Istanbul or Lagos or Stockport. All I know is we can't let him go ahead and do this. It's not as if he is unhappily married, lonely or sex-starved. Not that any of that is an excuse. So why is he doing this? Because he can, like the dog and his bollocks. Because his wife and his family aren't here. Because he is thousands of kilometres away from home. How dismayingly tacky and sordid, to buy sex from a girl fourteen years younger than him just because he can get away with it. I say we intervene, and I recommend a robust intervention that will frighten him so much he'll keep his dick in his pants for the rest of his married life. Not for his sake, I couldn't give a toss about him really, but for the sake of his wife and kids.'

I glanced at the wall clock. Fifteen minutes of FREEZETIME® had elapsed: time to bring this to a conclusion.

'Your recommendation is noted, Orla,' I said, 'although the manner of our intervention is of course limited by what the team Intervention Master can fashion from the circumstances in which we intervene.'

I took a sip of coffee, placed my hands on the table and leant back in my seat. 'Stuart Fairlie is a difficult case. This is his last intervention. He's on his own after this for the rest of his life.

So, we must be very sure we are justified in making his final intervention in this case. Leonard D and Theo would have us let matters take their course. This is the first time Stuart has done anything like this. They are of the view that adulterous paid-for sex with Citra Candawati, albeit a moral irregularity, is likely a one-off and will have no, or minimal, repercussions on Stuart's relationship with his wife and family, and does not therefore warrant intervention. Orla and Leonard R, on the other hand, believe that if we allow this *sordid and tacky*,' I nodded in Orla's direction as I said those words, 'sexual liaison to go ahead, Stuart will likely have extramarital sex again – and again – which will almost certainly have a detrimental effect on his marriage and his family in due course. Besides, the act itself is exploitative and morally wrong.

'Before I make my decision, I would remind all members of the team that our sole criterion for authorising an intervention is the well-being and future happiness of our supervisee, in this case Stuart Fairlie, and not that of anybody else. If another person is adversely affected by what happens *out there*,' I gestured to the screen, 'then it is those tasked with intervening on that person's behalf who must decide whether to intervene. Now, having said that, I am authorising an intervention in the current circumstances affecting Stuart Fairlie, to block him having a sexual encounter with the young Indonesian woman he has lined up for that purpose. I note for the record this is the last intervention we will be able to make in Stuart Fairlie's life. Theo, please submit the decision.'

After Theo had done the necessary, we all filed back into the control room and assumed the seats at our workstations.

'Leonard D, which of the team's Intervention Masters is on duty this evening?' I asked.

27

Leonard D tapped on his keyboard and said, 'David Pillifer.'

I inwardly breathed a sigh of relief. David Pillifer was one of the best. He'd been awarded the Most Creative Intervention Master South-East Region for the past three years. That was no mean feat.

'Please connect us, Leonard.'

Leonard D tapped some more on his keyboard. Stuart Fairlie's time-frozen image retreated to half of the screen as David appeared on the other half, his pale blue eyes staring at us from a long way back through black-rimmed glasses.

'Evening, Deborah,' he said, 'you do like to keep me on those things at the end of my feet, don't you?' He paused as he continued to work on an adjacent screen and then, having completed his task, he turned and smiled directly into the camera.

'What do you have for us, David?' I asked. 'As usual, timing is tight.'

'I have three options for you,' David said, reading from the screen adjacent to the video camera. 'First one: he gets a call on his mobile from his wife. His daughter, Lily, was awarded the class mascot at school today and wants to tell her father about it. Won't take no for an answer. In fact, she's refusing to go to bed until she's done so. Caroline wouldn't ordinarily ring him so late in the evening his time, but this is a special occasion. Caroline will put Lily on the phone. We believe that talking to his wife and six-year-old daughter will divert Stuart from his current course of action. He'll talk for around ten minutes on the phone and Citra will leave the club. I've cleared it with the respective supervisors for Caroline and Lily. In terms of spatio-quantum energy, it will use up 7.5 Rüstens on the Clore-Hamblin Reality-Bending Index. Only one problem, though.'

'He might ignore the call,' I said.

'Exactly. Second option. Five seconds after FREEZETIME®
is lifted, Amaara and Rob, vice-president and manager on his
team, enter the Butterfly Club. We believe that being seen
sneaking off to his hotel with a young lady in tow by two junior
members of his team will also divert Stuart from his current
course of action. He'll pretend he doesn't know the young
woman, shoo her away and stay and have a nightcap with them.
Cleared with Rob's supervisor; we're just waiting for clearance
from Amaara's supervisor, who's being a bit sticky, doesn't like
the idea of her being injected into an Indonesian nightclub at
half-one in the morning. This intervention has a Clore-Hamblin
Reality-Bending Index score of 8.1 Rüstens.'

'Can Rob swing by the nightclub by himself? Does he need
Amaara with him?'

'I would have thought not, except Rob's supervisor is only
consenting to Rob's arrival at the club if he is accompanied by
Amaara.'

I raised my eyebrows.

'I know, Deborah, most irregular. But we don't have time to
take it to adjudication.'

'What's the third option?'

David paused, pressed his lips together and briefly scratched
the side of his nose.

'Option three is a bit tricky, I'm afraid, although I've got
approval from all the relevant supervisors. There is a young
male–female couple sitting at a table two booths down from the
table where Stuart and Citra were sitting. They've been having a
heated argument for most of the evening. He's called Sandy; she's
called Setiawati. Sandy is very angry that Setiawati won't come
to hear the rock band he plays in at their local community centre
at the weekend. Setiawati is just fed up big time with Sandy.

She's just walked off to get a break from his incessant hectoring. Three seconds after FREEZETIME® ends, Sandy picks up his beer bottle and, in an aggressive burst of temper, throws it at her retreating back. He misses and the beer bottle sails past her and smashes against the side of Stuart's head as he is standing at the bar, causing a deep gash above his left eye which will need stitches. There's a lot of blood and confusion, an ambulance is called, Stuart is taken to hospital and Citra goes home. Sandy makes a quick getaway, I should add; permission from his supervisor for his involvement is conditional on that.'

'Wow,' I said. 'That's a bit drastic.'

'It certainly is,' admitted David. 'Unfortunately, somewhat surprisingly, it comes in at only 4.4 Rüstens on the Clore-Hamblin Reality-Bending Index. So that's a lot less dabbling in the spatio-quantum gravity field, deploying only three additional dimensions rather than the usual six – a lot less energy all round.' He seemed embarrassed. 'Deborah, as you know, we're on an energy-saving drive and our revised operating protocols dictate we must recommend the intervention option which uses the least quantum energy. Furthermore, there is an expectation that such an intervention option will be deployed unless a Director submits a Form 117N2R explaining the grounds for deviation within an hour of the intervention being authorised.'

'It's the first I've heard of Form 117N2R,' I said. 'When was it introduced?'

'Five pm this afternoon.' David checked his wristwatch. 'One and a half hours ago.'

'Well, I'm not touching option three. Our role is to ensure our supervisees emerge from situations involving life-defining moral choices having made the right decision or having the right decision made for them – without blinding them in the process.'

Across the table, Leonard R was holding up five fingers. We only had five minutes of FREEZETIME® left.

'Excuse me, David.' I looked at Leonard R. 'We're going to need another thirty minutes of FREEZETIME®. It's unfortunate but we can't rush this. Please put it through.'

Leonard R nodded, and I turned back to David. Before I could speak, Leonard R read from the screen in front of him: 'Sorry, Deborah, no more FREEZETIME®. It's been blocked. A thirty-minute cap has been introduced for all teams as of 5 pm this afternoon. Like Form 117N2R.'

Frigging hell, I thought. I could feel a bead of sweat trickle down the side of my neck like a wet fingertip running down my skin.

'Where are we on option two?' I asked. 'That's my preference: we don't have to involve Stuart's wife and daughter and we're not running the risk he might ignore the call.'

David checked the screen before him. 'What the ...' he muttered angrily. 'Now Rob's supervisor will only consent to Rob showing up at the nightclub if he's accompanied by Amaara *and* Lulu. Lulu is the team's local Indonesian team representative.' He tutted. 'Even younger than Amaara. That's seriously out of order. Let me speak with Rob's supervisor.'

'We haven't got time,' I said.

'Well, I'll be filing a complaint against Rob's supervisor in the morning. How can I offer a suite of practical, effective intervention options if people play silly-buggers like—?'

'David, I know, it's okay.' Time was running out; my options had narrowed alarmingly, but I needed to remain composed and focused. 'Let's go with option one and hope he responds to the call. I'm authorising an intervention for Stuart Fairlie along the lines of option one as presented by

Intervention Master David Pillifer at 6.28 pm. Theo, please submit the decision.'

I sat back, breathing out.

There was a pause while Theo's fingers flickered across his keys. Then, 'I can't,' he said, sounding rattled. I had never heard Theo sound rattled before. 'It's saying Caroline Fairlie is no longer available for the role of an intervener in her husband's life. That can only mean ...' He looked up at me.

'Another team is considering intervening in her life. She's been made subject to her own FREEZETIME®,' I said. 'What the frigging hell is going on? Why does she need an intervention?' I knew, of course, that no one would have an answer. For reasons of confidentiality, teams operate in strict silos and robust information barriers prevent the sharing of knowledge between teams unless cleared in advance by top management for one of a limited number of reasons.

I turned to David. 'If we are lining up Stuart's wife for an intervention in her husband's life, doesn't that make her subject to our FREEZETIME®? If that's the case, how can another FREEZETIME® take priority over ours?'

But as soon as I had formulated the question, the answer came to me. I'd been in this situation before. A couple of years ago, I was considering an intervention in the life of a highly successful bond trader, to prevent her making an alcohol-induced error in inputting details of a trade that would lose her employer millions of dollars and, more importantly, cause her to lose her job and professional reputation. The intervention proposal on the table was a phone call from her husband that would be made just in time to divert the fateful slip of her fingers on her keyboard. The team had just agreed on this approach when we were told that the team supervising the husband had slapped a FREEZETIME® on him and that he couldn't be manipulated for the purpose of our intervention. A FREEZETIME® put in place for an intervention in that person's own life would always take precedence over a FREEZETIME® put in place to induce that person to intervene in another person's life.

The purpose of the FREEZETIME® imposed on the husband was, we subsequently learnt, to thwart a scheme he was hatching with his mistress to murder his wife that evening in order to access the hundreds of millions she had tucked away in her bank accounts. Crazy, but true. In these circumstances the regulations permitted full disclosure of the husband's nefarious activities from his team to ours. The consequence: the two teams worked together. The outcome: the husband did ring her at just the right moment to forestall her mistaken entries, and on the call she told her husband she had recently altered her will to ensure that on her death her assets would be applied in furtherance of several charitable causes rather than pass to him.

But even if we were able to open discussions with Caroline Fairlie's team, there was no time for any alignments in manipulation strategies. I could see Theo mouthing the countdown to me – *sixteen, fifteen, fourteen* – in exact concurrence with the shifting figures on the digital wall clock. For a moment I was mesmerised by the synchronicity between the movement of Theo's lips and the flickering red limbs of the numbers on the wall over his shoulder as they appeared and disappeared.

I said to David, 'I hereby authorise option three. Theo, go ahead and submit, please.' As Theo pressed his return key, we all turned to the video screen on the wall.

There were five seconds of FREEZETIME® remaining.

3.

What happened next occurred so quickly that, later, we all had to watch it again half-a-dozen times to understand it. In fact, in the report I subsequently filed, I included a clip of the first ten seconds of the video feed after FREEZETIME® had ended, and this clip was shown at the ensuing inquiry.

Just before FREEZETIME® had taken hold, Stuart had been leaning across the bar to ask the bartender about a taxi. The second the picture on the screen juddered back to life, the side of the bartender's face rapidly retreated as if hurtling away from Stuart. It became apparent later this was not the bartender's face moving – instead, Stuart had been vigorously yanked backwards by a hand on his shoulder. As Stuart's vision expanded, three of the bottles on the shelf behind the bartender's right shoulder exploded in a shower of glinting fragments, like the spatter of solid water amidst a spray of amber liquid, and there was the unmistakable sound of glass hitting glass. The bar quickly swung past as Stuart's vision wheeled round and focused on a face in front of it, the face of a young Indonesian man wearing what seemed to be a black helmet with a microphone extending in front of his mouth. The man said something into his microphone. Stuart's vision feed swung to his right: two men dressed in black overalls with helmets lifted a young man from the table he was sitting at, yanked his arms behind his back, bent him over the table and put handcuffs around his wrists. Behind the table there were more men dressed in black, fanning out from an exit door at the back of the club, like hornets flying from a nest. There were shouts in Indonesian. The background music stopped suddenly. Stuart's vision swung back to his left. Citra was racing towards the entrance at the front of the club. There were men in black spilling in from that direction. One of them put his arm out to stop Citra going any further.

'What the frig,' muttered Leonard D.

Orla was the quickest. 'It's a police raid,' she said. Her fingers danced over her keyboard. 'Seems to be a regular occurrence. All the nightclubs get raided once a month. They check for drugs, underage girls, illegal gambling.'

Stuart's video feed was back on the police officer standing in front of him. 'Identification, sir,' he was saying to Stuart.

It was only then the penny dropped. 'Theo, can you trace intervention activity or is this just happening?'

A pause while Theo ran the programme. 'It's an intervention,' he said. 'Team and supervisor undisclosed at the moment.'

'Frigging hell,' I said. 'Ibu Ismaya must have changed her mind. Or she wasn't telling us the truth before.'

Stuart must have pulled his passport out of his jacket pocket because the video feed showed the police officer skimming through the pages and then handing it back.

I heard a cough. It was David, still on screen. He looked deeply embarrassed. 'Deborah, I'm so sorry. But this intervention simply wasn't available to me. There must be over two dozen police officers involved: I didn't have those sorts of resources to play with. That suggests it's an intervention put in place by a local team. But, hey, seems to have worked: and your boy is all in one piece.'

I didn't know what to say in response. It was the first time an intervention I had authorised had been undermined by an intervention authorised by a different team. A better intervention than ours so far as Stuart Fairlie was concerned, in that it involved no physical injury to his person. As the police officer stepped away, Stuart's video feed swung to the left again to fix on Citra, who, a few feet away, was showing her ID card to a police officer. When he'd made a note of it on his hand-held device, he waved her on, and she walked out of the club without a backward glance.

And that was that. We later learnt that Citra's boyfriend had returned to Jakarta that afternoon: the last game had been cancelled so the football tour had ended early. He'd gone round to Citra's mother's house and was waiting, increasingly impatiently, for Citra to return. Ibu Ismaya's team had only been alerted to Nico's premature return late in the evening, after we'd spoken (his supervisor had literally been asleep on the job). Disaster loomed. Ibu Ismaya couldn't be certain I would authorise an intervention at our end and so decided, on the spur of the moment and without recourse to FREEZETIME®, to intervene herself.

The Butterfly Club was due a visit from the police the following evening and a member of Ibu Ismaya's team had the idea of accelerating the police raid by twenty-four hours to prevent Citra accompanying Stuart to his hotel room. The quick reflexes of a police officer had saved Stuart from the impact of our well-intentioned but now superfluous intervention. The consensus was that this was an inspired piece of interventional improvisation, a view I would have concurred with were it not for Sandy. His supervisor had been induced to proffer a role for Sandy in our intervention on the basis that there would be no consequences arising from his involvement. Sandy's supervisor, entirely understandably, was furious when this wasn't the case. While the subsequent inquiry praised the ingenuity and energy-saving properties of using the police visit to the club as an intervention (only five Rüstens on the Clore-Hamblin Reality-Bending Index, notwithstanding the eighteen police officers involved), it also found that Ibu Ismaya breached protocol by not informing us of her actions. An intervention was ordered to extract Sandy from his police cell within hours and without any charges being pressed against him. In the circumstances, this intervention did not use up any of his quota: he still had all five available.

I never did find out officially why a FREEZETIME® had been ordered for Caroline Fairlie and whether an intervention had resulted. Had there been an extramarital liaison on her part? At 6.30 pm, while the children were having their evening meal? Don't make me laugh – or sob, for that matter. But of course, I couldn't ask because as of 6.30 pm (1.30 am in Jakarta) Stuart Fairlie ceased to be my supervisee. As soon as I had authorised his fifth and final intervention (and what a waste of time that was) he was dropped from our books, so to speak. I argued at the inquiry that his fifth intervention be restored on the grounds it had been negated by Ibu Ismaya's intervention, but I knew it was a try-on and the pained expressions that flicked across the faces of the inquiry team told me that they knew it too. Later, I heard on the grapevine that Caroline's intervention had been ordered because she'd been shaking baby David to get him to be quiet: there had been a fear that permanent injury was imminent. But I don't know whether this was true.

Video feeds are block-booked on a rolling three-hour basis (it's cheaper that way), so Stuart's video feed (which had another thirty minutes to run) continued to play out on the wall screen as the team collected their personal belongings and vacated their workspaces. The screen showed Stuart's swaying walk across a wet pavement stained red, blue and green by nightclub neon, the fumble with the taxi door and then the short drive back to the hotel, the back of the taxi driver's head an unmoving black oval against the windshield flaring a jaundiced yellow from the sodium streetlights. A couple of the team avoided my eye as they passed my desk. I didn't blame them. It had been far from a textbook exercise.

I sat there feeling exhausted. I barely knew Stuart, he was just one of many souls I had been responsible for, but at that moment I felt the way I did about anyone whose fifth intervention I had overseen. He was leaving me, sailing on into the many years, decades in Stuart's case, that lay ahead, alone and unwatched, like a black-sailed barque with a single lamp in the stern, slipping silently from the shore across the endless dark waters of his future, receding into the distance, the light diminishing until it could no longer be seen, only imagined.

I rubbed my face with my hands. Time to go home to Sammy. I stood up, went to the pantry to slop my coffee remains down the sink and to my office to pick up my bag, vaguely conscious that as I left the control room Stuart was now back at his hotel, stumbling around his room. When I returned, however, I pulled up short. Stuart's face filled the screen: it took me a second to realise he was standing in front of his bathroom mirror. I gasped because he appeared to be staring at me. 'I can't do this anymore,' he said. 'I don't know how.' Who was he talking to, I wondered – himself? me? God? – but the pleading look in his eyes was so intense that I found myself involuntarily raising my hand to touch his face as the image cut out and the screen went black.

The Gorgon Flower

*Being Extracts from the Journal
of Lord Tobias Henry Edmundson*

Afternoon of Wednesday 17th July 1861

A canvas awning on poles has been erected for me by the First Mate over a folding travel table on the deck and it affords me a most comfortable and accommodating location to write and sketch. The HMS *Stockport* floats about a hundred yards from the edge of the mangrove beds which line the estuary banks on both sides of the river as far as the eye can see. The estuary must be a couple of miles wide at this juncture. The water either side of the moored ship barely partakes of riverine motion; it is the colour and consistency of warm broth, with snapped-off tree branches and clods of matted twigs serving as lumps of gristle and lifeless vegetables. About a half-mile beyond where I sit on deck, this briny pottage disgorges into the Java Sea and there, by a wondrous alchemy, the water is scrubbed clean, and forms serried bands of blue water of a deeper and deeper hue as one raises one's gaze towards the horizon.

Closer to where I sit, a small settlement of huts assembled from thatched palm, banana and fig tree leaves, linked by wooden walkways, sits on stilts speared into the muddy bank. This is Lumpung, barely a speck on the maps of the locality, where we have nevertheless stopped for a few hours to replenish our stores of water and fruit and to bask in the sun, lizard-like, before proceeding up the river into the rainforested heart of this island of Borneo.

Since setting sail from Portsmouth, I have sought to execute the entries in my diary as diligently as the nausea engendered by the motion of the ship and the claustrophobia induced by the close quarters of my cabin have permitted. But looking at these pages I see that I have expended what energy I had on committing to my journal the tawdry comings and goings of my wife and her accomplices before my departure. In the early years of our marriage when the sun of our mutual love shone directly above us, the shadows cast by our fundamental incompatibility and the demands of her concupiscent nature were short and barely perceptible. But now the sun slips ineluctably towards the horizon and these shadows stretch, hideously elongated, across our lives, and we would no more spend time together in the same room than we would with a prey-starved Bengali tiger.

On board this worthy vessel, my thoughts, ensnared by the unpleasantness with Charlotte and preoccupied with its unfortunate consequences, seemed to enter into an alliance with my migraines, which, not content with plaguing me in my ordinary sphere of life, have followed me across the oceans, like a pack of ill-bred and malevolent seadogs. But now that we are nuzzling the shores of Borneo, I am of the conviction that these malodorous reflections need detain my attention no longer. She has gone from me and I from her: quite literally, you could say. That is all there is to it, and I feel myself liberated to now record in these pages my quest and the wondrous sights and delights of flora and fauna that await us.

But at this moment, even the humblest coastal breeze has appeared to desert us, and I swelter in humid air that is laced with that foetid aroma of damp vegetation and stagnant water peculiar to the mangrove.

The torpidity of the scene before me is in striking contrast to the vibrancy and bustle of Singapore, which we left barely five days ago. Captain Denton, Dr Stanhope and I had been guests of the Governor, who had put us up in style at his commodious residence at Fort Canning, where a banquet was held in our honour the evening before we departed. In Singapore, dusk falls at seven o'clock in the evening so it was already dark as we congregated in the torchlit gardens for drinks prior to dinner. Serenaded by a string quartet, we shared the lawn with an ostentation of peacocks, each of which had been armoured with a finely wrought metal frame festooned with tiny lit candles; as they strutted amongst the guests, they resembled nothing so much as a miniature fleet of blazing galleons jerking hither and thither, propelled by a breeze that enabled the ladies to take a rest from the agitation of their hand-held fans.

After dinner, we assembled on the terrace overlooking the harbour to watch the fireworks: a series of rockets fired into the night sky with a percussive whoosh, exploding, with a distant crack like the snapping of a bone, into flowers of magnesium-white light that hung glittering in the sky before dripping to the South China Sea in long, glowing streaks like shimmering hula skirts or the drooping petals of the *Echinacea pallida*.

But the Captain calls me: the account of my conversation with the Governor must be deferred until later.

Afternoon of Thursday 18th July 1861

Although an army man from India, the Governor of Singapore was an amateur botanist and possessed a first edition of my father's *Illustrated Guide to the Orchids of Java and Borneo* in his well-stocked library. He was naturally curious as to our travels in these parts, and over brandy and cigars he quizzed me in a genial but persistent manner as to the purpose of our expedition. In conformity with the approach agreed with the Royal Society before we departed, I made no mention of the Gorgon flower and spoke in a vague manner of updating my father's pioneering work. I was not impervious to a modicum of discomfort in dissembling thus but if news of our true purpose leaked, even in a place so far from London, we feared it could make its way into the hands of those scoundrels, those pits of immorality, who made their living writing for newspapers. The Royal Society had ambitious plans to announce with considerable fanfare, on our return, the induction of the Gorgon flower into the Royal Botanic Gardens at Kew – only the second time the flower has ever graced our shores; any publicity prior to this exposition would see these plans ruined as thoroughly as an Easter bonnet by a spring downpour. Since the Royal Society has made a significant contribution towards the not insignificant cost of the expedition, I do not feel myself at liberty to disregard their wishes.

I was about to take my leave when the Governor leant forward and revealed that he had met my father many years ago while stationed in Bombay; my father had been passing through. 'A most impressive gentleman and a scholar of the highest distinction,' he said, fixing me with his watery, malaria-yellowed eyes. 'I recall his discovery of that most peculiar flower, of a genus never encountered before, a flower-fungi hybrid if I remember correctly.' He paused and an ill-concealed eagerness crept into his expression. 'I seem to recall your father produced a monograph on it, did he not? It really was a most striking flower and' – he pointedly peered around, an unnecessarily theatrical gesture as we were the only persons sitting in the library at the time – 'possessed of hypnotic powers and an extraordinary carnivorous appetite if one believed the accounts. Gave rise to all sorts of stories, did it not? Ridiculous of course, and denied, as one would expect. Perhaps the fevered imaginings of Edgar Allan Poe had settled, like an invisible miasma, on a gullible public.'

A maestro at the devilish game of poker could not have maintained a more impassive countenance as I agreed that we did indeed dwell in an age in which the widespread taste for the gothic fantasies of Mr Poe and his ilk had induced in many a proclivity to grant credence to the most fantastical of stories. And with that I *did* take my leave of the Governor, wondering, as I repaired to my rooms, whether it was not too late for me to take up the cards for a living.

But I fear my scribbling must now come to an end. I sense a subtle alteration in the atmosphere and feel a stirring in the decks below me, a wakening from slumber: it is time for us to advance upstream. And in a flamboyant demonstration of that notion of activity and purpose that now hovers in the air, here come Dr Stanhope and Captain Denton, exiting at an impressive clip the hut of the Mission Officer, whom they had visited to pay for our supplies and to consult on the upstream navigation of the Jimbala River, each holding a white kerchief to his mouth and nose as they hurry across the muddy shore to their dinghy and the two boatmen waiting to scull them to the ship.

Evening of Thursday 18th July 1861

On only the second day out of Portsmouth, when Captain Denton and I were conversing on the foredeck, he asked me what my impressions were of Dr Stanhope. I replied that the Doctor and I had developed only a brief acquaintanceship but that he struck me as a most agreeable man, if rather taciturn. 'Ah, that's because he is a Fenman,' I distinctly remember the Captain saying, 'that's all you need to know about him.' Not having had much social interaction with a denizen of the Fens before, I found this categorisation of the ship's medical Doctor to mean very little.

Now, after passing two months in the Doctor's company, I can only assume being a Fenman is a synonym for a man possessing an exceptionally reserved manner bordering on shyness, which nevertheless cloaks an acute and penetrating intelligence; a placidity which is neither bovine nor indolent but rather confirmation of a confident and contemplative nature whose observations are as sagacious as they are brief, as profound as they are quietly uttered. Of his medical abilities I can vouchsafe no assessment other than that the powders he recommended I take to ameliorate my debilitating migraines afforded some relief – a state of affairs no physician I had consulted in London had been successful in procuring heretofore. But his friendship has been a benediction to me; it has been salutary to have such an intelligent companion on the journey.

Captain Denton, the only other eligible candidate for such a role, is, so far as I can tell, a highly competent seafarer and respected by the crew of the ship. If, however, he were cast outside the kingdom of his maritime knowledge, it would be a challenge to claim him an educated man: a stray reference to the histories of Suetonius or the metaphysics of Aristotle is apt to be met by a quizzical expression or a blank stare.

The ship's trinity of officialdom is completed by Mr McGuire, the First Mate, a fellow in possession of such solid height and girth allied with such upright and stolid demeanour that one could imagine him sprouting, like a vigorous branch, rough-hewn, from the solid oak planks of our vessel itself. Be that as it may, there has been, in truth, nothing inert about the cool judgement and diligent competence he exhibits in the execution of his professional duties.

Although for the most part I have accommodated the good Doctor's steadfast aversion to prolixity, even, in some instances, welcomed it, it is not appropriate to every occasion. After the hurried return to the ship of the Doctor and the Captain, some degree of garrulity on the part of the Doctor would have been welcome. But on reaching the deck from the dinghy, Dr Stanhope muttered only these words to me as he rushed past on the way to his cabin: 'Disease in the Mission. Probably upriver too. Not leprosy but leprous in nature.'

Once Captain Denton had supervised the weighing of the anchor, the unfurling of the sails and the migration of the ship from the outermost fringes of the estuarine water, the vessel caught a sufficient breeze to enable it to advance slowly but steadily upriver.

It is now ten o'clock at night, my cabin is dark, and I write within the oval of light cast by my lamp across the fold-out table in my cabin. The river is black except where embossed silver by the moon: the ship squats on the water, like a whale which has forsaken its submarine progression for the lofty realm of air, motionless except for the occasional nudge from the slow but forceful current flowing around and beneath it, its sails furled. Through my cabin window, I hear the clicks, hum and wood-sawing noise from an orchestra of chittering night insects. We are moored just over five miles upstream from Lumpung and, come tomorrow, Captain Denton believes he will not be able to take the ship more than another two or three miles further up the river. Once we have gone as far as our worthy vessel will convey us, we will continue our hunt up this brown snake of a river in the four flat-bottomed rowboats especially fitted and cargoed on HMS *Stockport* for this purpose. Half the crew will accompany Dr Stanhope, Mr McGuire and me on these boats, together with a couple of native guides we picked up at Lumpung; the other half of the crew will remain with the Captain on board the mothership to await our return. This will be the final stage of the extraordinary quest which originated on the other side of the globe, and my excitement at coming face to face, so to speak, with the Gorgon flower after all this time, after so much yearning, after so much endeavour, is like a current of that electromagnetic force so recently discovered by Mr Faraday. But this electrical frisson must yield to the beckoning arms of Morpheus, rendered more muscular by the sleeping cordial prepared for me by Dr Stanhope.

Like the gaudy curtains at the end of a Drury Lane show, my eyes sag, droop and finally close and I can write no more.

Morning of Friday 19th July 1861

At dinner last night, Captain Denton recounted to me what had transpired when he and the Doctor had paid their respects to the Mission Officer yesterday afternoon, speaking quietly so as not to be heard by members of the crew notwithstanding the privacy of the wardroom.

The Mission Officer was a Dutchman, one of the many Dutch traders and missionaries who pursued their interests along this stretch of the coast. He had received the Captain and the Doctor in the room at the front of his hut which served as his office, a dark and stifling place, pierced with rods of sunlight emanating from chinks in the palm leaf roof. As was customary in these parts, he offered his guests a thin cylindrical pipe as a gesture of welcome and then, while each in turn imbibed the tobacco, he described, deploying a crisp, fluent English, what lay ahead upriver. But the Mission Officer had appeared distracted and anxious, repeatedly glancing over his shoulder to the door which led into the room at the rear of the hut, where in the dimness could be discerned a cluster of figures: they were sitting on chairs around a bed, on which a person lay prone on a mattress of moss and leaves and from where emanated the smell of rotting flesh.

After they had discussed the navigation of the river, the Mission Officer had looked a little embarrassed, coughed and asked whether the Doctor might care to look at his son, who was not at all well. In response to this request, they followed the Mission Officer into the back room and discovered that the invalid lying on the mattress was a young boy, barely conscious, moaning softly, the blond hair on his head and his pale limbs glimmering with sweat in the dim light. His stomach had been scooped away, as if by the swipe of a jaguar's paw, exposing a knot of entrails, spongy red mottled with blue-grey tubes, marinating in gravy-thick pus. The stench hung heavy in the air. Dr Stanhope knelt by the boy and held his hand while he studied this sacrilege of the flesh. 'There is nothing I can do,' he had repeatedly muttered before taking his leave; nevertheless, on his return to the ship, he had arranged for half-a-dozen phials of laudanum to be delivered to the settlement, with strict instructions that the seaman leave them five feet away from the Mission Officer's hut.

The Doctor had not joined the Captain and me for dinner yesterday evening, an unusual occurrence which I now presume arose from his feelings of guilt or frustration at not being able to do more to assist the boy.

Afternoon of Friday 19th July 1861

It is two o'clock in the afternoon and we are getting ready to disembark the ship and proceed up the Jimbala River in the rowboats. I have half an hour to record this morning's events before we depart. Setting off at dawn, Captain Denton was able to take us two or three miles upriver before the narrowing of the waterway and the encroaching height and density of the rainforest forestalled any further progression on the part of HMS *Stockport*. The Captain ordered the anchor to be dropped at a point where the river curved around a beach of bone-white sand. All was then purposeful activity under the directions of the Captain and Mr McGuire, as the rowboats were winched down to the water and stocked with sufficient supplies for a month's onward expedition by boat and on foot: casks of fresh water; barrels of beer and rum; cases of hard tack; slabs of cheese and salted cod, beef and pork. I supervised the packing of my botanical flasks and vascula, my sketchbooks and drawing utensils, my reference books and maps, the latter ensconced in watertight folders.

Dr Stanhope had not graced us with his presence at breakfast this morning and did not do so again at lunch. I knocked on his door on the way back to my cabin, and I heard him saying from the other side, 'For God's sake, man, I held the boy's hand.'

'I am sure you have thoroughly washed your own hands since,' I responded to the closed door. 'The Captain believes we will be taking to the rowboats in a few hours. You need to start packing those items of your medical equipage that will be accompanying us.'

'You must not go up the river, Tobias. There is no knowing how widespread this disease is and what may await you. Please delay this expedition, for a month or so at least, so we can—'

'Nonsense,' I said firmly, 'we will take all precautions to ensure that this *thing*, whatever it is, does not come near us. Now please prepare for disembarkation.'

'I won't be going with you. I need to quarantine myself. Until there is no risk of me acting as a vehicle for the transmission of this infection. I told the Captain he must do the same, but he refused. Speak to him please, Tobias.'

'I will do no such thing, Stanhope,' I said, tiring of my interlocution with a shut door. 'I am sure the Captain has taken the most efficacious steps to rid himself of any infection. Please reconsider your decision; I really need your inestimable companionship and your cool judgement in the days ahead.'

I subscribe to the view that instilling in a person a sense that his contribution is critical to the success of an endeavour is the most fruitful way of securing that person's participation in such task. Confident of my success in this regard, I returned to my cabin to make my own preparations to leave the ship and to write up this entry.

Evening of Friday 19th July 1861

A moth seems to have obtained ingress into my tent and is now attempting a frenzied series of assaults against the oil lamp sitting on the corner of my writing table. It flings itself against the ceramic shade in a fit of wing-beating fury, stuns itself, falls to the table and pauses while flapping its wings, as if reconsidering the rationale for its vengeful crusade against this immovable object, only to rouse itself and renew its vendetta against the lamp with redoubled ferocity. I can see its eyes like two pin-drops of white paint on the end of a match. My old friend George Trellison, who was at Cambridge with me, is a renowned lepidopterist: he would, I am confident, be able to identify this particular specimen. But would he be able to communicate with it and convince it of its folly? That, I doubt.

It is late and I suspect I am the only member of our party still awake; certainly, I can detect no other lights in the tents scattered around our makeshift encampment in a small clearing a few feet from the bank of the river. We made camp a couple of hours ago, directing the boats to a sandy strip along the riverbank and pulling them out of the water as the light leached from the trees around us. We had made good time since separating from HMS *Stockport* shortly after three o'clock this afternoon, our convoy of four shallow-draught vessels gliding up the river, eight oarsmen in each boat pulling vigorously against the current.

Surrounded by the massive bulk of our ship, I had not truly observed or appreciated the rainforest since leaving Lumpung. But as I sat in the stern of the first rowing boat, with no cabin wall between me and the jungle sliding past on either side of the river, my senses feasted on the sights and sounds of the paradise we passed. We floated as if we were drifting through the nave of a vast cathedral with pillars of tree trunks, walls of vibrant, glossy leaves and hanging lianas, and a vaulted wooden ceiling of interlaced branches. As we slipped through the cathedralesque dimness created by the thick canopy of leaves high over our heads, we were dazzled by thick columns of radiance where the sunshine punched through the leaf cover, scattering brilliant discs of light that flickered on the water. No palisaded ranks of trees or beautifully landscaped copses here; instead, there is an anarchic profusion of trees as far as the eye can see – trees soaring hundreds of feet straight into the atmosphere, trees stunted and gnarled, trees strangled by epiphytic growths, trees half-toppled or crashed on the jungle floor, all coated by a carpet of moss, leaf litter, fungi and slime in varying shades of green. The air is viscid, syrupy; something to sip rather than breathe.

There is a ceaseless chatter of bird cry from the rainforest underscored by a constant hum from the insect life, but on the water in the centre of the river these sounds are oddly muted as if they emanate from behind a curtain: there, it is quiet, the only nearby noise the pull of the oars in their locks and the plinking of water as the oars lift from the water.

It is high time to lay down my pen. Just before I do so, let me formally record my disappointment with Dr Stanhope. Not only did he decline to accompany us on the second stage of our expedition, but he also refused to leave his cabin for the purpose of collating those medicines and medicinal accoutrements that would be of great efficacy to us. He proposed that he give me a verbal description of the items so that I could, like a pale and diffident clerk, inscribe a list and fetch them from the ship's surgery myself, but I remonstrated with him, asking him instead to prepare such an itemisation and hand it to me or, if he wanted, slip it under the closed door. When he rebuffed even this suggestion, I lost patience with him and left him to stew in the juices of his own pusillanimity and exaggerated self-caution while I raided his medical cabinets to assemble a cache of what I believed was likely to be of most value: laudanum, a jar of leeches, quinine, digitalis, bandages, splints.

My irritation at Stanhope has not abated but I suspect that over the next few days I will begin to miss his company, morose and uncommunicative as he is at the best of times.

Evening of Saturday 20th July 1861

We came across the first body within half of an hour of breaking camp and setting off upriver this morning.

We had breakfasted on fried meat and bread and then the tents and mosquito nets had been disassembled and stowed on the boats together with the cooking utensils. Boat by boat, we pushed off and slid towards the deeper stretch of the river where the men rolled up their sleeves and leant into the oars. The river stretched ahead of us, no longer resembling a lofty vault but instead an impenetrable tunnel of dank green leaves and vines, festooned on trees that crowded the banks of the river.

At first the corpse in the river resembled a tree branch stripped of its bark and propelled towards us on the current. But as it came closer, it assumed the shape of a dead human body lying face down in the water. As it floated level with our rowboat, Mr McGuire commanded the men to stop rowing and to impede the corpse's progress with a couple of oars. It was a naked female with pale skin: evidently not a member of a tribe that made the rainforest their home but rather the wife of one of the missionaries or traders who had established settlements upriver, deep in the heart of the forest. Clumps of flesh had been gouged out of her torso and legs, leaving behind craters lined with grey gangrenous tissue in which knobs of bone nestled like worms in turned-up soil. Her hair, braided into a thick rope, waved gently in the water like a black eel. A strong feeling overwhelmed me; after a moment I realised it was pity.

'Keep her away from the boat and don't touch her!' I ordered. I stared at the lifeless form for some moments and then nodded to the two oarsmen who lifted their oars to allow the body to drift away. I assumed this was the same necrotising condition that had afflicted the boy whom Stanhope and the Captain had seen in Lumpung, but I really needed the Doctor here to confirm this; as I watched the corpse being carried away by the current, I cursed his decision to remain with the ship. An air of wary unease hung over the men in the boats after this encounter, but this seemed to leach away as time elapsed and we pushed upriver.

The second body was discovered shortly after we set up camp a few hours ago. The Mission Officer in Lumpung had marked on our self-drawn map a small habitation consisting of a mission outpost and a cluster of huts, in a clearing adjacent to the river. The native guides had been scouring the riverbank in the fading light and had very nearly missed the dwelling place in the gloom thickening under the canopy. There was a small square hut which we assumed was the chapel and a handful of shelters all woven from branches and palm leaves. These structures surrounded a bare patch of earth containing a shallow pit filled with ash and small blackened rocks, where it was clear a campfire had been lit. The chapel and huts were empty, the settlement deserted: no sign of anybody having lived there recently.

The boats were moored and unpacked, and the tents and mosquito nets erected. Having eaten an evening repast of salted fish and biscuits, I was about to assume my seat at the writing table when I heard a shout from outside our encampment. A short while later Mr McGuire appeared at the flap of my tent with a lantern in his hand and suggested I accompany him to the edge of the clearing, where a dead body had been discovered by one of the men. When we reached the spot, Mr McGuire's raised lantern illuminated a naked man lying face down, sprawled across the exterior roots of a banyan tree. From his broad shoulders, sturdy back and lithe legs, I took him for a young man, fair-skinned, possibly the missionary who had constructed the chapel and introduced the natives of these parts to his God. The back of his body showed no marks of infection or wounds, but when two of the men carefully turned him over with fallen branches, we saw that his face had been eaten away and replaced by a bolus of writhing maggots. I wondered briefly whether the youth had been attacked and maimed by a wild beast, but even as I did so I think I knew already the real cause of this poor soul's affliction.

Mr McGuire gave orders for a grave to be dug and the dead body to be buried but cautioned that care should be taken not to touch the cadaver or allow it to come into contact with the exposed flesh of the men selected for this duty. Given that the men's limbs were tired after a day's rowing, this was not a welcome task: it was much to their credit that it was performed without demur or complaint. After the body had been interred, Mr McGuire, the solitary barrow at his feet, read aloud the Lord's Prayer and the twenty-third Psalm from his prayer book: these words and phrases, polished to overfamiliarity by use through the centuries, sounded alien, almost fresh, in these surroundings, but they were barely able to hold their own against the demented symphony of the shrieks, hoots and chirps of the night jungle.

But I was not really listening, for I was mentally making my own invocation: *Good God, what is this disease?*

Evening of Sunday 21st July 1861

My oil lamp sits on the corner of my writing table in my tent. A modest light, but sufficient for me to pen these words. But this must be the only man-made illumination for miles in each direction: I exclude the frenetic fireflies dancing in the dark like the sparks from a fire. What must the compound eye of the mosquito, the saucer eye of the tarsier and the dark-seeing eye of the python think of the unnatural light of my tent, a single speck in the vast darkness of the jungle?

I have before me, open on my writing desk, Father's monograph published in the 1831 *Proceedings of the Royal Society*. It describes how my father discovered the Gorgon flower when carrying out research work in Borneo between 1828 and 1830, contains a detailed exposition of the architectural structure and workings of this extraordinary plant (a description illuminated by Father's own hand-drawn illustrations), charts his dawning realisation that the properties possessed by the flower were even more striking than he had initially thought, and concludes with his speculations on the taxonomical classification of *Sthena lucidum* (as he named the flower).

Father had brought a specimen of the flower back with him and planted it in his conservatory at Hamilton Hall. The article caused quite a stir on its publication: a steady stream of visitors, some invited but many not, came to view the Gorgon flower in the flesh, so to speak. Although the exact mechanics of its reproductive system of self-pollination eluded Father, the flower prospered under his care and that of Mr Forbes-Haggard, the Head Gardener at Hamilton Hall, and himself a botanist of no inconsiderable stature. However, its sojourn on my green homeland only lasted a little over three years. One night in early 1833 – I was sixteen years old and still at school – an inferno razed the conservatory at Hamilton Hall to the ground, destroying the Gorgon flower and taking Father's life (and, incidentally, that of Mr Forbes-Haggard). The cause of the blaze was never determined although there was speculation about a smouldering cigar butt, carelessly discarded by one of Father's guests (Father did not smoke) while ambulating through the conservatory earlier in the evening.

Father had deliberately withheld from his writings the precise details of where he had discovered the Gorgon flower, referring only to it being located in Borneo – as if Borneo were a country village near Amersham rather than a landmass of nearly three hundred thousand square miles! Whatever Father's motives for shrouding the native habitat of the Gorgon flower in secrecy, with his death perished the knowledge of where it could be found. Since then, there have been no recorded sightings of the flower in Borneo – or anywhere else for that matter. Until, that is, it was rediscovered a couple of years ago by Mr Jennings, an explorer who had achieved a certain renown for discovering the rare, the exotic and the esoteric; for locating that which had previously been considered undiscoverable or extinct. (The Holy Grail remained hidden, I had heard it said, only because Jennings had not yet been asked to procure it.)

All of a sudden, exhaustion wraps its arms around me. An account of Mr Jennings's stupendous news must wait until tomorrow.

Evening of Monday 22nd July 1861

I met Mr Jennings at my club for lunch shortly after he had returned from journeying across the Malayan Archipelago, where he had spent a good deal of his time observing, writing and sketching in that industrious manner which characterises the autodidact. Over watercress soup followed by salmon and jellied asparagus, he told me that he had seen my father's Gorgon flower – had, in fact, separated a specimen and packed it in a ventilated, self-moisturising receptacle. There being no room for it on the ship taking him back to England, he had entrusted it to a Dutch frigate plying the route between Batavia and Amsterdam, where he had intended to pick it up on his way through to London. Unfortunately, the Dutch ship had been lost at sea, believed wrecked in a storm rounding Cape Colony. A tragedy – and yet all was not lost, for Mr Jennings had taken careful measurements of where the flower resided: some west-facing gullies in the foothills of Mount Taliboko in the north-east of the island of Borneo. He gave me a detailed map with coordinates confirmed by the missions in that area – a map on which our quest was wholly reliant. In return I was to make a contribution towards defraying the expenses he had incurred on his recent travels.

When Captain Denton and I had first charted the course of our expedition based on Mr Jennings's records, we had anticipated following the Jimbala River for approximately seventy miles, after which we would strike out on foot to cover the forty or so miles to the slopes of Mount Taliboko, where the Gorgon flower had been seen. Captain Denton had predicted it would take the flat-bottomed boats five to six days to cover these seventy miles, an estimation which Mr McGuire informed me this evening, after our third full day on the river, he believed to be excessive. At the pace we were pushing up the river, he was of the view we should obtain the point at which we would continue overland by mid-afternoon tomorrow, Tuesday. This piece of information was welcome to me: although the sights and sounds of the rainforest are mesmerising, sitting in cramped conditions in a rowboat for hours on end has been extremely uncomfortable even without accounting for the stiflingly humid atmosphere. Yesterday morning, I had extracted from my travelling chest a little light reading to pass the time (Julius Caesar's *The Gallic Wars* and Montaigne's *Essays*), but, after perusing a page or so, I found my attention wandering, my thoughts as flighty and flimsy as the butterflies which danced, in fluttering explosions of colour, above our heads and without, I should add, the merit of being as beautiful or captivating as these wing-borne living jewels.

I should be glad to exercise my limbs after the enforced immobility of the previous few days, but I do fear our progress will be much slower once we must hack our every step through the choking jungle like lice through matted hair.

Anyway, it is now late: time to submit to what my dreams have in store for me. The tally of dead bodies sighted today, either carried on the river current or snagged by the tree roots protruding into the water like a tangle of frozen snakes, was seven: all men, women and children of European race, all naked. I wonder that we have not come across any natives felled by this monstrous affliction and why the bodies we have encountered have been unclothed. I shared my observations with Mr McGuire, who said he had been similarly cogitating upon such matters. He postulated that perhaps European visitors to these lands were particularly susceptible to this awful disease, unlike the local tribespeople who had built up resistance and were immune to its ravages. We should proceed cautiously, he told me, a sentiment with which I unreservedly concur.

Evening of Tuesday 23rd July 1861

My fountain pen has become a baton of lead, weighing on my fingers: I am weary to my marrow, my limbs ache, my migraine pounds and I crave my camp bed. This after only a few hours trekking through the rainforest! Heaven knows how I will fare tomorrow when we commence our journey on foot at dawn.

As Mr McGuire had foretold, we reached as far as we could

go by river shortly after noon. The river had been narrowing, braided by rocks into foaming cascades and translucent ropes of water, flowing between steeper banks. Large boulders and stone terraces, polished smooth by the ceaseless motion of the river, had begun to impede our progress. Twice the men had had to unpack the boats, hoist them on their shoulders and carry them over beds of gravel and sand or rocky platforms where the water was barely a couple of feet deep. Finally, we reached the point where we could no longer use the river to penetrate the interior. The men stowed the boats on a narrow riverbank sheltered by a clump of towering ironwood trees and, after a short rest to reload the packs and eat a hasty lunch, the party set out on foot.

Before we left, there was a curious incident involving the two Dayak men who were accompanying us as our guides. Now that we were no longer following the course of the river, we were reliant on them to navigate the unfamiliar terrain for us. Mr McGuire and I had taken the two men to one side and showed them on the map where we believed we were and where we wanted to go. Mr McGuire then pointed in the direction that our compass indicated we should take. Of course, our map and compass readings meant nothing to them: they carried their own maps of the region in their heads, and it took some time for us to be confident they understood our destination.

I then showed them some of my father's coloured drawings of the Gorgon flower. Nothing had prepared me for their reaction. The elder of the pair recoiled, placed his hands over his eyes and, shaking his head from side to side, uttered a string of incomprehensible words in his native tongue. The younger one also placed his hands over his eyes and turned his back on the drawings while making a series of clicking noises.

'Good Lord,' said Mr McGuire, 'what on earth has got into

them? Do you think they recognise it?' It became clear to me that they would not take their hands from their eyes until I had put the botanical pictures away. Even after I had done so, they kept their eyes to the floor and stepped warily around me, as if I could not be trusted to keep the sketches in my case and might whip them out at a moment's notice to confront them with the tormenting illustrations.

We made camp after about two hours' push through the jungle, by which time I was drained of my last ounce of strength and ready to fling myself to the ground and allow the oblivion of slumber to overtake me. But I have forced myself to eat and to write this entry: I believe Atlas himself would not have accomplished as much. My dreams of last night were a rich stew of incoherent fragments, peopled by an eclectic cast of characters drawn from all stages of my life, most of whom hardly knew each other but who happily and unselfconsciously shared the companionship of my sleeping images. Fortunately, little of these dreams survived my expergefaction and I need trouble this page with no further reference to them.

Morning of Wednesday 24th July 1861

No elixir or tincture concocted by Dr Stanhope and his medical colleagues will ever rival the efficacy of a good night's sleep; I arose this morning feeling replenished, restored and reinvigorated. I breakfasted on tea and porridge and, as the men are packing up our encampment and making preparations to depart, I have a few minutes to scribble these lines.

Using Mr Jennings's coordinates, Mr McGuire and I believe we have three or four days' march ahead of us to reach the vicinity where the Gorgon flower was found, although it would be hard to conceive of anything less like a march than our tortuous snail-like process through the rainforest. But we are coming to the end of our journey, and I sense my growing excitement – and impatience, for are not the final steps of a lengthy expedition to a much-desired object or location the longest and the hardest to endure?

It is time to lay down my pen and close my journal: the men are assembled, and Mr McGuire is looking pointedly in my direction …

Evening of Wednesday 24th July 1861

This morning, as I walked behind Mr McGuire, we speculated on what might have caused the fear displayed by our two guides on beholding the images of the Gorgon flower. The flower did not generate a sticky secretion poisonous to humans and animals as many other tropical plants and fungi did; its colouration and anatomical appearance were unusual in the extreme but not necessarily more so than, for example, *Nepenthes bicalcarata*, the pitcher plant, with its two erect fangs emerging below the lid of each pitcher, or *Amorphophallus paeoniifolius,* the elephant-foot yam, with its crinkled pendulous folds of brown plant-flesh. Even the huge circumference of the Gorgon flower was eclipsed by that of *Rafflesia arnoldii*, one of the class of parasitic corpse flowers, which attracts the insects it feeds on by exuding the stench of rotting corpses (although I should add that the Gorgon flower shares certain characteristics of the corpse flower: it too has no stems, leaves or roots and appears in many respects to be fungi rather than flower). Perhaps, we reasoned further, the Gorgon flower has a cultural or a quasi-religious significance to the tribes that inhabit these rainforests, which accounted for the queer behaviour of our two guides. If so, I cannot recall either Father or Mr Jennings ever commenting on this.

However, any further dialogue on this topic was curtailed by both of us being required to restrict our breathing to tackle the increasingly arduous passage through the jungle. I had not, of course, expected a leisurely stroll through a well-proportioned wood on a summer's day, but I had not been prepared for the sheer difficulty of beating a path through the rainforest. It was as if the lattices of branches, the curtains of vines and the veils of thick, rubbery leaves were all elements of a vast organism whose sole purpose was to slow us down. No two successive steps ever proceeded on the same level: fiendish skeins of roots; sudden drops into boggy pits; random rocky outcrops; massive protruding buttress roots – all necessitated continuous attention to where one took the next step.

Away from the relatively cooling effect of flowing water, the air was heavy but perfumed with the rich, exotic aromas of exhaling flora. Although my eyes rarely strayed from the ground before my feet, I saw flashes of iridescent colour out of the corner of my eye, accompanied by flurries of beating wings. The constant buzz of cicadas, interwoven with an insect choir and overlain with the swooning calls, the hoots and the high-pitched trills of birds, bombarded one's hearing, a constant backdrop to the chug of my laboured panting.

Late afternoon of Thursday 25th July 1861

Shortly after we established our camp this afternoon, the thunderous clouds parted to unleash a torrential downpour. The sky darkened; tree branches thrashed; rain hissed; the canvas walls of our tents became soaked, and their ceilings sagged alarmingly.

A tropical storm is usually like a casual acquaintance; on arrival, it stays for a few minutes only before departing. But this storm was like an old friend: it settled in for the day. The storm had advertised its arrival by a steadily darkening sky and a cool breeze, and Mr McGuire had consequently brought a halt to the day's trek much earlier in the day than was customary: as we had commenced walking shortly after dawn, this was not an unwelcome decision.

Confined to my tent, and days away from seeing the Gorgon flower again after over thirty years, I am conscious that I have never committed to this journal my impressions of my first encounter with it. I seem to remember the day clearly, but I must ensure my memories remain accurate – neither embroidered by an imaginative retelling nor viewed through the prism of the knowledge of my later years.

Thirteen years of age, I was home from school and in the state of excitement that preceded Father's return from one of his expeditions, a frequent occurrence when I was young. His carriage had been sighted turning into the estate and this gave Mother, my sister Lucinda and me, together with Mr Forbes-Haggard and some of the senior servants, time to assemble on the front steps. As he climbed down from his carriage, I rushed to embrace him but not before I had glimpsed his face. Parents are ageless to their young children and, up to that moment, I had never thought of Father as elderly, but I saw a weariness, an inner exhaustion exhibited in his features, that I thought had not been there when he departed six months ago. But this observation was jostled to one side as Father and Mr Forbes-Haggard began to supervise the unloading of the terrariums, those cases of glass and wood that housed Father's botanical specimens, which occupied two carriages of their own. The cases, adapted by Father from a design promoted by a Dr Nathaniel Bagshaw Ward, were completely sealed but allowed light and heat to penetrate, thereby furnishing the essential ingredients for the operation of a miniature water cycle, enabling the plants they contained to be transported successfully from one continent to another.

I was aware that an especially intense animation accompanied the removal of one particularly large case, cloaked in a sheet of gauze; while conversing with Mr Forbes-Haggard, Father gestured to it a number of times and it was clear that he was giving instructions as to the unpacking and transplanting of the plant that nestled, unseen, therein. As I joined them, he put an arm around my shoulder and said: 'Please join me in the conservatory after dinner tonight with Mother. I'm looking forward to showing you a truly remarkable plant. I have scoured the literature and corresponded with many fellow botanists, and I have no doubt that I am the first European to make its acquaintance and introduce it to these shores. Mark my words, it will put the *Rafflesia arnoldii* of Mr Stamford Raffles quite in the shade.'

Father's conservatory, built as an extension to his library, was a large two-storey affair, consisting of an iron frame, embellished with intricate fretwork, all painted in white, from which hung the specially made glass sheets which served as the walls and ceiling of the edifice: here he exhibited the rarest, most exotic or most unusual plants and flowers in his possession. After dinner, it was usual for guests to be invited to take a stroll in the conservatory with Father, who took great pleasure in introducing flowers that he thought would amaze, interest or instruct them – and sometimes, if possible, all three at the same time.

On this particular evening there was still light in the conservatory as we gathered at its entrance after dinner, waiting for Father, who had gone on ahead of us to liaise with Mr Forbes-Haggard and ensure that all was in order. When he bade us enter, he led us to a large fig tree that grew in the south-eastern corner, where Mr Forbes-Haggard and two of his men were standing. In a hollow at the base of the giant tree, between two of its buttress roots, a very odd flower lay flat on the ground, with six wide overlapping petals or leaves (I could not say which they were) that bulged in the middle but otherwise seemed to be embedded in the earth. The petal-leaves, which must have been nearly two feet long, were ruby red streaked with mustard yellow, made of a soft velvety material that rippled at the lightest touch. They framed a deep-set circular orifice; at its base was a slimy cream-like substance the colour of stagnant pond water, out of which, quite remarkably, three long black antennae or tentacles protruded. Almost three feet in length, and made of what seemed to be tight coils of hair tapering to very fine points, these appendages swayed from side to side in the warm air of the conservatory, as if the plant were a denizen of the deep seabed. All in all, the plant must have been almost five feet in diameter.

'Watch this,' Father said. One of Mr Forbes-Haggard's men handed him a small fieldmouse and Father placed it carefully on one of the huge petal-leaves. The fieldmouse scampered up and down the petal-leaf and then, suddenly, froze to the spot and stayed there, motionless. Father leant forward and, pinching the fieldmouse between his thumb and forefinger, plucked it from the petal-leaf. 'Look, no adhesive syrup is affixed to its paws,' he said, holding it up for us to see. 'I am at a loss to explain why it yields its independent motion to the plant. It seems stunned and quite unable to move. Now, watch again!' Father placed the fieldmouse back on the petal-leaf and stepped back. The fieldmouse continued its stationary stance at the spot where Father had set it back down. After about thirty seconds or so, one of the tentacles reached over and sinuously wound its tip around the body of the fieldmouse; once the immobile creature had been secured, the tentacle lifted it and placed it in the pale-green viscous fluid at the plant's centre. The tentacle tip then uncoiled itself from around the poor animal, leaving it floating in the slimy liquid, its diminutive body coated by the substance, until it slowly slipped below the surface, leaving a tiny circular ripple in its wake that, contracting to a single small bubble, then vanished, leaving a perfectly smooth disc behind. From the moment it had ceased its scurrying across the plant until the moment it had been apparently consumed by the plant itself, the fieldmouse had made not one twitch of its nose or one flick of its tail.

'Quite extraordinary,' Father said. 'I have barely begun to understand its digestive and reproductive systems. One thing is clear though: it does not use odour, either of the sweet- or putrid-smelling kind, to attract its prey as other carnivorous plants do. Nor does it trap its prey or lure it down a funnel from which it has no hope of escape. Instead, it appears to paralyse its victim through no agency that I can detect.'

Father carried on in this vein for a while but, to tell the truth, I had ceased to listen to his words. I stared at the plant before me, fascinated rather than appalled, as I reflected on the fate that had befallen the fieldmouse. So absorbed was I in my ruminations I was startled when Father, who had turned in my direction, exclaimed: 'Toby, for heaven's sake, stand back!' Tumbled out of my reverie, I realised that all three of the plant's tentacles were aligned and reaching towards me, stretched taut with the effort, the tip of the nearest tentacle only inches away from touching me.

I hastily stepped back, and the tentacles retracted and assumed their vague, directionless swaying. Father smiled, ruffled my hair: 'I have no intention of sacrificing you to the plant so early in my investigations. Now, I think it is your bedtime, Toby.'

I have been so engrossed in transcribing my memories that I did not notice the cessation of the storm. It is now night, and I can hear movement outside my tent as the men embark on the task of drying our equipment. Water is pooling on the far-right corner of my writing desk and, now that I have become conscious of my surroundings, I can hear the metronomic plinks of dripping water in my tent, the interval between the drops different in each case, resembling an orchestra where none of the instruments is in time with the others.

I have, I realise, been scribbling for too long. Now I am prescribing food, brandy and bed for myself – in that order.

Evening of Friday 26th July 1861

We started later than usual this morning as Mr McGuire wished to harness the early rays of the sun captured in our clearing to dry our tents, but we then made good time, as we hacked, slashed and chopped our way through the jungle.

How to convey the impression of walking through a rainforest? Here nature is present in unparalleled fecundity, a rich intensity that excites but also exhausts. Left to its own devices, nature flaunts its exuberance and revels in its flamboyance. Stare at a leaf or a patch of ground for more than a few seconds and you will see miniature forms of busy life: a spindly stick insect like a walking twig; a two-inch-long giant forest ant with black-bristled armoured body-plate, serrated mandibles and quivering antennae; caterpillars sprouting tufts of iridescent hair. Creatures ordinarily separated by geological aeons are spliced together in fantastical combinations – here, a trilobite beetle; there, a true weevil. We passed through vast chambers of green-tinted light, ornamented with white and pink mokara orchids, red and peach hibiscus, deep purple lotus and wild ginger; while swallowtail butterflies, their wings patterned with chequerboards of yellow and black, flittered around dappled patches of sunlight. I very much wished we could stop so that I could sketch a striking flower or insect but, alas, I had made the location and retrieval of a specimen of the Gorgon flower the absolute priority of our expedition; all else was self-indulgence.

As we trekked, Mr McGuire and I wondered why we had not recently encountered any victims of the terrible illness stalking the land: the last body, which we saw on Tuesday morning, lay face down in the river, inserted into the water from the waist up, the legs stretched up the muddy bank. Was there something in the nature of the sickness that compelled those it afflicted to seek out water? Was the river the quickest way of fleeing the mission stations and communities ravaged by the disease? If there was any likelihood of procuring some medical relief, it would reside in the coastal regions, we surmised. Whatever the reason, we had been spared the sight of any further corpses since departing the river for the rainforest.

It was only much later that day that one of the men noticed that our two local guides had disappeared; at what stage during the day's trek they had slipped away was unclear, but it was certain they no longer accompanied us. No matter: we can navigate our course well enough without them; besides, we are only a couple of days away from where the Gorgon flower grows.

As we prepared our camp, I sensed some agitation amongst the men; delegations of men approached to speak with Mr McGuire and there were earnest whispered conversations between him and them.

Late evening of Friday 26th July 1861

Mr McGuire has just been to see me in my tent. He told me that there is considerable unrest amongst certain of the men. A faction believes that, as the country we have for some time been travelling through is in the fierce grip of an implacable plague, we should turn back, make our way to HMS *Stockport* and stay there until this disease has released its hold on this place. I asked him how many men this faction contained; he looked evasive and muttered, 'A considerable number.'

'A majority, Mr McGuire?'

'Yes, sir, I fear that is the case.'

He grew even more uncomfortable, no doubt conscious that such fecklessness amongst the men reflected poorly on his leadership, although, in truth, I did not see it this way. If not in the confines of this journal, where can I be candid? I, too, had entertained such thoughts in the last few hours although *entertain* is not perhaps the most apposite term; rather, such ideas had pushed open the door of my mind and barged in. Yet I resolved to offer no hospitality to such doubts, showed them the door and bolted it after they had left. Mr McGuire needed to propose to his men that they implement the same approach, and I suggested this to him.

This must be the right approach. We are two – three, at most – days away from the Gorgon flower. Once we reach our destination, it will take but a few hours to transplant four or five specimens into my botanical cases, another four to five days to hike back to the river and, given we will be travelling downriver, a further two days to reach our ship. We could be back on board HMS *Stockport* in a little over a week. Although I was not impervious to the men's concerns, thousands of miles and

months of travel lay behind us: to baulk at a few more miles and
a couple more days made no sense to me. I offered to counsel the
men along these lines but, unaccountably, Mr McGuire thought
it would be better if he spoke with them.

Evening of Saturday 27th July 1861

I did not, in truth, write a full account of what transpired the
evening I first encountered the Gorgon flower. There is more
to relate, although my recollection of what happened later that
evening is indistinct, as if seen through a muslin veil or in a
mirror in a shuttered room. We all have an episode or two from
our very early years that we cannot be certain whether we really
experienced or merely dreamt. Perhaps I was mature enough for
my reminiscences of that night to be subject to such doubt but,
try as I may, I cannot disentangle my memories and say, 'This
happened!' and 'This did not!'

I remember it was a still, sultry summer evening and, after I
had left Father and the others in the conservatory and repaired
to my bed, I lay awake, hot, unable to sleep, my thoughts gently
bubbling as if my mind was a pan of simmering water. When it
was well past midnight and the household was quiet, I climbed
out of bed and, in my night shirt, wandered into the corridor
outside my room, where it was cooler. I padded along in my bare
feet by the moonlight washing through the window at the end of
the corridor. I could not have said at what stage I realised I was
heading in the direction of the conservatory, nor could I have
consciously supplied a reason for making that my destination, but
it seemed entirely natural that I should do so as I descended the
grand staircase, crossed the hall and opened the door to Father's

library. That I should have entered Father's sanctum so blithely, even at night when everyone was asleep, supports the proposition that my perambulation was a dream-occurrence, for I was strictly prohibited from setting foot in this room unless with Father's express permission and then usually only as a means of accessing the conservatory.

The library was steeped in shadows, but when I opened the door into the conservatory it was as if I was stepping into daylight, so bright was the moon. Flooding through the high walls of glass and iron, it created bright lozenges of silvery light across the stone flags and the rows of plants and trees. I remember observing the moon-shadows, created by the lattice work around the windowpanes, rippling across my feet and legs as I moved forward, as if I had become a moon tiger: surely that means I was awake, for is that the sort of detail one is likely to experience in a dream?

The air in the conservatory was warm and scented with the night-time breath of the flowers and plants. I had never been alone in the conservatory before, and I wandered down the pathways with my arms held out, letting my fingertips brush the passing petals, leaves and ferns. After a minute or so I came to the fig tree, which soared high above me, its highest branches flattened against the curving glass roof. There was a faint luminosity at the base of the tree's trunk; leaning forward I saw that it came from the orifice at the centre of the Gorgon flower. A glow emanated from the pale-green liquid pooled there, casting a soft light on the red and yellow markings of the surrounding petals.

The tentacles waved gently, their tips describing a strange corkscrew motion in the illuminated space above the flower. Whether I stood by the flower or only dreamt I did, I can distinctly recall a warm feeling of calm suffusing my body and I became conscious that I was standing before a fascinatingly intricate and distinct organism – one pulsing with a vitality that seemed to echo within me. As if in response to these feelings, the nearest tentacle seemed to stretch towards me in its peculiar corkscrewing fashion. As it drew level with my face, the integument of the tentacle drew back from its tip, unsheathing a pinkish protuberance coated in a glistening liquid; then, the tentacle delicately ran this nodule down my right cheek, resting it against my lips. A flood of pleasure surged through me in a burst of convulsive quivers, and I remember falling to my knees.

And that is as far as my memories or dreams of that night extend: the next thing I knew it was morning, I was lying in my bed with the sunlight squeezing through the gaps in my shutters, and I had nothing to show for my wanderings or dreams of the previous night, other than a novel stickiness staining the front of my night shirt.

Evening of Sunday 28th July 1861

Like rank noxious weeds, mistrust and suspicion have sprouted within the party and it will require a Herculean effort to uproot and destroy them. I sense a latent disaffection within the men; when I pass them on the path, there is a silence which I do not doubt is directed at me; none of them will hold my gaze or give me the reserved yet respectful nod which I have hitherto been greeted with. If I make myself unpopular by insisting on the continued performance of our expedition, so be it.

Fearful, dour and uncommunicative our party may have become, but we made solid progress today, as if the men, forced to go forward when their every inclination is to retreat, at least exhibited a determination to consummate the quest as expeditiously as possible. For this, I am grateful. We should reach the location where Mr Jennings beheld the Gorgon flower by nightfall tomorrow.

What phantasmagoric scenes, what profoundly unsettling encounters inhabit my dreams!

I cannot recall ever having nightmares of the intensity and strangeness I have experienced over the past week. Our forefathers subscribed to the view that dreams were sometimes messages delivered to us by the gods that ruled our lives, neglectful sovereigns though they frequently were. That belief has now been discarded in most quarters, displaced by the notion that dreams are the expressions of those fears or longings that we hide from ourselves and keep locked in the mind's vaults – unsuccessfully, it seems, for they find the key and escape and, barred from entering our conscious thoughts, instead infiltrate our sleep.

But what fears are these that I conceal from myself? What longings? It is axiomatic that if they exist they would appear as strangers to me; however, I find myself speculating whether they might not also be alien to me, that the landscape through which I journey is saturated with such terror and fright that by an undetectable process of osmosis these sensations have leached into my psyche and, at night, emerge like cockroaches to scuttle around the chambers of my sleeping mind. Although I have only to give thought to such a notion for the rationalist and scientist in me to dismiss it contemptuously, I cannot shake the suspicion that, while I may continue to be the actor, I am no longer the manager of my nightly dream-productions.

Late evening of Sunday 28th July 1861

Mr McGuire interrupted my writing an hour ago and asked me to accompany him. In a tent on the far side of the encampment were two of the men, one of them, pale and glassy-eyed, sitting hunched on the ground, the other standing over him with a lamp. Mr McGuire asked the sitting man to show me his hand. He got to his feet and unwrapped a cloth, stained with dried pus and blood, to uncover in his left palm a suppurating gouge the size of a sovereign, swimming with a mucilaginous yellow-brown exudation. I stared at the man's hand, stupefied. Neither of the other men spoke, and I myself wondered for a while what I would say, what I could say.

Under questioning I learnt that his name was Harris and that he had become cognisant of the infection a couple of days ago. It was painful and he was beginning to run a fever.

'Have you showed it to anyone else? Does anybody else know about it?' I asked.

'Don't think so, sir. Just Thomas here, and now you and Mr McGuire.'

I asked Harris whether he had been in contact with any part of the flesh of any of the dead bodies we had encountered; he vigorously denied it.

I assured him that Dr Stanhope would be able to treat him and encouraged him to be brave – and hopeful. 'Not a word to any of the other men, mind,' I enjoined Harris and Thomas, as I left the tent. 'You should leave at first light.'

Outside, Mr McGuire and I retreated to the edge of the clearing where the rainforest began and we could not be seen by any of the men in the camp. A vertiginous sensation fleetingly overwhelmed me and I seemed to see the encampment as if I were a denizen of the starry night, wings gently pushing against the air, gazing down at a thimbleful of lighted pinpricks surrounded by darkness.

This hideous malignancy had now afflicted a member of our party. But we had no understanding of whether the means of its propagation was airborne transmission by way of a noxious miasma or whether the infection was conveyed by physical contact with infected persons or their secretions. Either way, once contracted, the disease consumed flesh and tissue in an implacable and horrifying manner. Not for the first time, I had cause to acknowledge Mr McGuire's perspicacity; he expressed the view that it was likely Harris would expire of the infection before reaching HMS *Stockport*, which was at least five days' journeying away. The poor fellow's demise being almost inevitable, it was better that it took place with only Thomas for companionship, away from the remaining men, who would thereby be shielded from knowledge of the necrotic malady to which Harris had succumbed. We agreed that Mr McGuire would remove some of the laudanum stored in my chest, take Thomas to one side, and adjure him to secrete it on his person and administer it to Harris to ease the intensity of his suffering as his body was increasingly consumed by the deadly contamination.

Of course, perhaps Harris was not the only person of our party carrying the infection: the gangrenous condition could be insidiously worming its way into others even as we spoke. If that be so, then we – *I* – must be prepared. I sensed that Mr McGuire wished to discuss the possibility of us abandoning the quest and turning back but I forestalled him by reminding him that if we maintained a steady pace the following day, we should reach Mr Jennings's location for the Gorgon flower by dusk; in anticipation of a strenuous day's marching, I was repairing to my camp bed with immediate effect. With that, I wished Mr McGuire good night and headed back to my tent. I had intended to spend some time in the company of Spinoza and his *Ethics* but my migraine, that ever-constant companion, put paid to that.

Evening of Monday 29th July 1861

Like antic lords of misrule, my dreams caroused raucously through my sleep last night. With as much control over my volition as a shuttlecock batted between strokes of the racquet, I hurtled from my schooldays to my cabin on HMS *Stockport* to the Bornean rainforest in a frenzied loop, pursued by people I knew and people who were strangers, each of whose bodies exhibited varying degrees of bodily degradation (here, a man whose eaten-away torso exposed ribs like a miniature ivory rowing boat nestling in his chest; there, a woman whose head resembled a hard-boiled egg whose top had been bitten off). Each episode culminated either in me watching a column of fearsome orange flames twisting and writhing inside Father's conservatory like some infernal giant fire-plant or in encountering Father's unconscious supine form, his flesh a deep emerald, seized of a repellent transmogrification, vomiting a thick pale-green paste, a small black object wriggling and quivering in the viscous liquid cupped in his mouth, which became the tip of a tentacle reaching into the air ... after which I would awake, panting and sweat-doused, only to be plunged, once my palpitations had eased, back into the freakish carnival of my dreams.

It was still dark when I heard Mr McGuire collect the phials of laudanum I had left at the flap of my tent, and I assumed he then sent Harris and Thomas on their way. The remainder of the men were awake and folding up the tents before it was fully light. Before we set off, Mr McGuire explained to the assembled men that he had ordered Harris and Thomas to rejoin the boats by the river and to return to HMS *Stockport* with news of our location and the expected timing of our journey back. This explanation seemed to satisfy the men and, before long, we were making expeditious progress towards the western slopes of Mount Taliboko. As the topography began to rise, one began to sense the rainforest thinning a little and the air through which we walked ceasing to be as dense and humid, the infernal mosquitoes less infuriating. I also sensed, before long, a return of the sullen fractiousness and suspicion that had spread amongst the men yesterday. Muttered snatches of conversation passed up and down the file of trudging men like ripples through the exoskeleton of a millipede.

When we stopped to take water mid-morning, Mr McGuire took me aside to inform me that he did not know how it had happened but it was common knowledge amongst the men that Harris had contracted the infection and that was the reason he had been sent back. The men were of the view we should abandon the expedition, return to the boats and head back to the ship as swiftly as possible.

I was perspiring prodigiously as a result of the uphill character of the track we were following, and it took a moment for me to mop my face with my kerchief and gather my thoughts. My migraine had wandered off and spent the couple of hours after breakfast enjoying its own company, but it had now rejoined me. Unfolding Mr Jennings's map, I ascertained we were now no more than half a day away from the location of his meeting with the Gorgon flower. I asked Mr McGuire to gather the men and then, raising my voice so that all could hear, I spoke to them along the following lines.

I acknowledged that one of their number had an infected hand but that we could in no wise be certain that it was the same affliction so prevalent amongst the unfortunate souls we had encountered. Nevertheless, Mr McGuire and I had thought it expedient to permit this person to return to the ship, where he could receive medical treatment. No other member of the group was displaying a similar infection. We had travelled halfway round the globe to retrieve a botanical specimen which would not only be of unparalleled interest to the scientific community but would also be of peculiar fascination to the general public, and we were hours – *mere hours* – from our destination. I reminded them that, in signing up to the expedition, they had undertaken to do everything they could to ensure a successful conclusion; furthermore, their contracts of employment provided for the bulk of their remuneration to be payable only on the realisation of such a successful conclusion. Finally, I understood their fear of contagion: this sickness was an unforeseen obstacle, wholly unanticipated: in recognition of the additional weight it placed on their thoughts, an additional payment of twenty sovereigns would be made to each of them, or to their families should for whatever reason they not make the journey back – but only on the condition the Gorgon flower was located and conveyed back to London. I was therefore counting on their continued support.

I had not given any indication to Mr McGuire that I would, in effect, bribe the men; indeed, I did not know myself that I would do so when I commenced speaking. He appeared surprised as I finished my address and we both keenly observed the men to see how my words had been received. One or two of the men appeared reflective but the majority uttered growls of affirmation or muttered words of thanks or just nodded. *Faber est suae quisque fortunae!* The party had been held together, albeit by way of a further drawing on the funds financing the project. However, I was by no means certain that the attraction of additional monetary compensation would survive the contraction of the infection by another of the men.

We pushed on for the rest of the day, gaining ground one moment, dropping down the next, as we traversed a series of shallow gullies marking the lower reaches of Mount Taliboko, which loomed ever larger to the north-east. By six o'clock in the evening we had reached the boundary of the shaded patch on Mr Jennings's map, representing an area of no more than a square quarter-mile, which indicated the location where he had found the Gorgon flower. We made our camp in a clearing approximately thirty-five to forty feet in breadth at the base of the gully which occupied most of the territory demarcated by Mr Jennings. Feet blistered beyond easy repair, limbs forced to perform far more than their habitual usage, my head pounding as if it were a molten red hoof being hammered into shape by a blacksmith – yet, our destination being reached, I savoured the moment, reflected on the five-month journey which had brought me to this spot, and thought finally of Father.

Dusk does not advance slowly at this latitude; it thunders down the hill and storms through the door. It was too dark to search for the Gorgon flower. This will be a task best performed in the pellucid light of early morning while the men are assembling the Wardian terrariums for the transportation.

A troop of proboscis monkeys screams and chatters above the encampment; a short while ago one of them cannoned against the roof of the tent, nearly spilling the lamp and its contents across the desk. For a moment I glimpsed the impress of a body bulging against the canvas sheet and I saw in my mind's eye a short stooping homunculus with potbelly, fleshy pendulous nose, and tail hanging like an inverted question mark. I have taken some laudanum for I shiver and not with excitement. Before retiring to my camp bed, I shall peel off my socks and inspect the blisters, lesions and grazes which have transformed the flaccid white skin of my feet into a painful landscape of craters and swellings. But, so far as I am able to detect such things, no manifestations of gangrenous consumption.

Pen down! I have written enough for this evening.

Early afternoon of Tuesday 30th July 1861

All is not lost but nothing has yet been gained. It cannot be found. I have searched all day, meticulously, square foot by square foot, my eyes bombarded by an endless procession of orchids, ferns, pitchers, lianas. Three times Mr McGuire and I have cross-checked our maps against Mr Jennings's original, confirmed our coordinates, compared our observations with his detailed descriptions. We are both convinced we are at the right spot. But where is the Gorgon flower? According to Mr Jennings, there were dozens of specimens to be found in this valley barely fourteen months ago, far too many for the species to have died out. Can Mr Jennings be trusted? He was a man of impeccable reputation; he carried an aura of unflinching rectitude and unimpeachable integrity with him at all times. His sketches, maps and notes were thorough and precise. If they were no more than elaborate fictions and this expedition has been launched on the basis of a charade designed to elicit a pecuniary advantage, that would be a prospect wholly repugnant to my understanding of the explorer and scientist. The odd behaviour of our native guides to the illustrations we shewed them of the Gorgon flower bespoke familiarity with it, although the associations clearly bestowed discomfort and apprehension on them. The Gorgon flower *must* be here; patience and further investigation will induce a favourable outcome. For now, some laudanum and rest in my tent. My head continues to ache, as if a wild animal, trapped inside my skull, struggles to escape. If my clamorous dreams will subside, sleep, howsoever brief, will do much to restore me and I will assuredly locate that which I seek.

Evening of Wednesday 31st July 1861

A most peculiar dream, less lurid yet more troubling than those which are my normal lot: I must record it before it floats from my memory like a wisp of silk borne on a gentle eddy of air. I was in the sitting room with Charlotte, who was holding a babe in her arms. As she bent down her head to coo at the tiny face, I glimpsed white woollen swaddling over the top of which the baby's minuscule fingers were splayed, watchful dark brown eyes and a head like a golden peach with a handful of black fur dabbed on it. Charlotte gestured to me and as I took the babe from her and cradled it in both my arms, my dream-inhabiting other self instantaneously knew that the baby was mine and that my dreams had seen fit to bestow on us that which life had withheld. I stroked the baby's cheek with my right forefinger and my daughter (instinctively I knew the baby was a girl) gurgled appreciatively and, my finger on her lips, she began to suck vigorously on the tip of my finger. I looked up at Charlotte and beheld a countenance of such empathetic intelligence and unrestrained affection towards me that I took her right hand in my free left hand and said: 'Our tree must contain some goodness in it to bear such fruit.'

Charlotte smiled and placed her other hand on top of mine.

'She's not yours, you fool,' she said to me sweetly. 'Is she, Newton?' She turned and I saw a man standing behind her dressed in a blue frockcoat and white linen breeches, locks of blond hair tumbling over his ears, his hand resting on her shoulder; he had abruptly appeared, as if conjured into being from the air by a magician. 'Of course not, my darling,' he said jovially, bending down to place a kiss on top of Charlotte's head.

Mr McGuire and I searched again for two to three hours this afternoon but to no avail. The flower has vanished. Night has now closed its curtain on the day. I informed Lawton, our cook, that I did not wish to eat.

Mr McGuire came to my tent just now. He tells me that the men are restless: they were expecting to be on their way by now. Although enjoying respite from the arduous trekking of recent days, many of the men are complaining of febrile heads and aching limbs. I could sense Mr McGuire studying me carefully as he asked how I was. I assured him I was well, although nothing could be further from the truth. I sensed there was something he wished to discuss with me for he stood hesitantly just inside the flap of my tent, stroking his beard. But he simply nodded, bade me good night and left.

Huttert, Van der Vries, DeMoyeller – the key botanical texts – include examples of orchids and orchid-hybrids migrating considerable distances due to changes in their pollination strategies – say, a decline in insect numbers, or water run-off eroding the germination potency in soils. But the Gorgon flower, having no stamen or pistil, self-pollinates, so no explanation along these lines would account for a change in the loci of its flowering. Maybe an explanation lies instead in changes in the climatological or mineralogical environment. Or something else entirely. Conjecture is my only companion for the time being, certitude having jilted me. But I resolve to widen my arc of exploration tomorrow, perhaps go further up the gully and the slopes of Mount Taliboko. All the while the proboscis monkeys screech and jabber, as if they laugh at my feeble and deluded efforts to account for, and overcome, the wreckage of my plans.

Evening of Thursday 1st August 1861

My spirits are too low to wield my pen today. You will immediately gather from this that I have endured another day of fruitless searching.

Evening of Friday 2nd August 1861

That which I have most dreaded has occurred: the infection has proliferated amongst the men. I shall write of this morning's occurrences. Increasingly it is incumbent on me to be a faithful scribe, to keep a record of all that transpires, so that I may answer the questions that those bloated toads, those gatekeepers of the domain of respectable science, who swarm though the corridors and committee rooms of the Royal Society like carrion beetles on a carcass, will inevitably have for me on my return in triumph.

I crawled through dreams that clung to me like feculent sludge, following voices that crystallised into a commotion without my tent: angry voices, scuffles, Mr McGuire's peremptory bark. Once emerged from the cocoon of my tent, I discovered that four men were suffering from the rotting tissue that is the hallmark of this terrifying affliction. It is unclear whether they succumbed overnight or they had been harbouring their corrupted and spoiling flesh from public view for a while precisely to avoid being treated with the fear and suspicion that was now their fate. The four men had been corralled to one side; they crouched or lay beneath a tree; a more abject and sorrowful image it was difficult to imagine. How soon we cast out and shun, deem as lesser human beings, those marked by this dreadful disease! Mr McGuire and a phalanx of armed men were watching as another group of men were in the process of donning their attire. The naked form of each had been subject to a thorough examination to ensure they were not shielding manifestations of the deadly infection.

When I approached Mr McGuire, it was not the Mr McGuire I had known on our expedition to date: purposeful and resolute, yet deferential, respectful. He was transformed – equally authoritative and decisive in his judgements and actions, but I sensed that these were now bent not towards the success of our expedition but to mere survival. He continued to display to me the due deference naturally dictated by my rank in life and status in the expedition, but he shewed by a subtle alteration in his manner of discourse and disinclination to discuss his ratiocination with me that my views were not to be accorded an automatic priority; rather, they were to be weighed against what he judged to be the dictates of our predicament and, if they were to be found wanting, might well be disregarded.

After begging my pardon and delivering profuse apologies, he surprised me by asking that I demonstrate that I had not contracted the infection by baring my limbs and torso to him, in private if I preferred. My initial reaction was to reject this impertinent request and ask him to rely on my word. However, a moment's reflection disinterred my good sense: it was essential to align myself as much as I could with Mr McGuire's wishes and strategies, the better to persuade him to yield to my requirements where no compromise or alternative was possible. We repaired to my tent, where I was able to satisfy Mr McGuire that I was unblemished. He then told me that he had taken the decision to lead the expedition back to the ship; he intended to depart within the hour. He had the good grace to apologise but stressed that it was essential to quit the rainforest and return to HMS *Stockport* as expeditiously as possible to minimise the spread of the contagion amongst the men. Those already suffering would be quarantined from the rest of the party to the extent possible and, on the trudge back to the river, would be made to follow the main body at a distance of a hundred yards or so.

I realised instantaneously the utter futility of remonstration with him: the only sovereignty I had remaining was over my own personal fate.

'I shall not come with you. I must stay for a couple more days to give myself more time to locate the Gorgon flower. I will then proceed at pace and catch you up. Wait at the river for twenty-four hours. If I am not reunited with you by the end of that period, proceed downriver – but leave a boat for me.'

I paused before making an additional request, uncertain what its reception would be. 'I need just two men to help me transport the terrariums and, if required, help me on the boat downriver. Tell them I will pay them forty sovereigns if they stay, regardless of whether we discover the flower.'

Mr McGuire regarded me for a moment. I hoped he recognised the equivalent futility of seeking to undermine my unbreakable determination, and the look of calculation in his eyes signified his mind already flicking through the roster of men to alight on those he thought susceptible to my offer. He nodded and exited the tent, although he returned a few moments later and inclined his head at the stock of laudanum stored in my chest: 'Begging your pardon, sir, but I'll get a couple of the men to relieve you of those.'

Once he had left me I collapsed on the chair at my desk, drained of vitality. My migraine was a heavy iron helmet clamped tight to my head; even the slightest movement caused the pain to slosh around my skull, like bilge water in a listing boat. I closed my eyes and sought in vain for an inner equanimity to soothe my agitation, while I heard around me the sounds of the camp being dismantled and packed up. Fifteen minutes later Mr McGuire returned with two men: a youngish fellow with fair features whom he introduced as Tamworth and a much older man, called Liscombe, with skin the texture and colour of a leather purse handed down through generations and who possessed an unfortunate tic – his lower jaw slithered from side to side, causing the two remaining teeth in his head to jiggle maniacally. Neither would have been my first choice of the men in the party to help me, but I was not so insensitive to the precarious situation I found myself in as to spurn their assistance.

I do not judge Mr McGuire harshly. Indeed, I do not judge him at all. When questions are asked about him deserting the expedition in this manner, I shall defend his actions and will argue against the issue of any censure or reprimand arising from his behaviour.

Preferring not to witness the departure of the party, I bade Mr McGuire farewell and then set out to explore the upper reaches of the gully while the men were finishing off the loading of the expedition equipment. I mustered some scraps of renewed optimism, notwithstanding my sore limbs, but, alas, four hours later, had precisely nothing to show for my fossicking and foraging. A melancholy sight awaited me on my return to the abandoned campsite; in place of an animated encampment milling with men, there was my tent in an empty space that was occupied only by Tamworth and Liscombe listlessly playing cards, serenaded by the raucous cacophony of a chorus of monkeys.

Evening of Saturday 3rd August 1861

What did the old King cry? *Let me not be mad!* Never have I empathised so profoundly with that anguished sentiment. I did not come across the Gorgon flower in my explorations today, but I did come across Father, looking not a day older than he was when he died!

For the best part of three hours I scoured the upland slopes to the north and the east of the gully that Mr Jennings had marked in his map, until the light faded and shadows began to thicken and pool in the indentations and hollows of the path at my feet. I turned back and descended by the same route I had used earlier that afternoon. At this height, the canopy of the rainforest stretched away to the horizon like a bushy carpet, dusky green in hue except where the cloud-filtered sun rays painted golden-green stripes in the distance. I had paused to catch my breath, and was thinking that somewhere in that vast expanse Mr McGuire and his men were following the track back to the river, when I heard a voice to my left saying: 'It's hiding itself from you, don't you realise that?'

I whirled around and was astonished to see Father sitting on the trunk of a fallen tree by the track, regarding me with equal parts puzzled affection and weary resignation. But this was not Father as he had haunted my dreams as a young man – burnt beyond recognition by the conflagration that had consumed him. Nor was it the Father who had inhabited my most recent dreams – hideously transformed, his body wrought by horrifying forces, rendering him a simulacrum of a man hybridised with a plant form. He seemed normal to me: holding his pocket watch in his hands and possessed of the same number of years as when he had parted company with his life over twenty-eight years ago. Naturally, I assumed my throbbing head was causing me to hallucinate. However, there was a tangibility, a gritty particularity about Father (the purply veinous filigree on his nose, the dimples in his fleshy knuckles, the familiar sweet whiff of pipe tobacco attached to his tweed jacket) that distinguished him as a most superior hallucination and I marvelled at my brain for conjuring up such a vision. Was this madness? Or would it only be madness if I believed this image truly was Father? In any event, I resolved to ignore the apparition and continue on my way. Strangely, I felt guilty, as if I was turning my back on a living presence, as if Father indubitably sat a few feet away from me rather than lying beneath a flagstone in the Lady Chapel attached to the Hall.

'You'll never find it if you won't listen to me,' I heard Father say as I passed him.

I carried on striding down a shallow incline but glanced back before I dipped through a thicket of trees. He was sitting where I had passed him, still looking at me. I shook my head and pressed on.

Back at the clearing, Tamworth served me roasted bananas for dinner. Too weary to speak, I stared at this singular repast and then at Tamworth.

'Begging your pardon, sir, but Mr McGuire forgot to leave us any food.'

I groaned, picked up one of the rifles, thrust it into Tamworth's hands and, pointing at the troupe of monkeys performing their acrobatic show in the encircling trees, exclaimed: 'Breakfast.' I then took myself to my bed, grateful both that Mr McGuire had not taken this with him and that I had had the foresight to secrete some phials of the laudanum in my personal belongings before the remainder had been spirited away at Mr McGuire's command.

What did Father say? *It's hiding itself from you.* Since this apparition must have proceeded from my own brain, these words could only be a message from some part of me hidden to my conscious self. What does it know, that shadowy surreptitious other self that lies submerged below the wakeful, sentient *me* and which reveals itself in fleeting glimpses only in my dreams and hallucinations? What knowledge is it seeking to impart? Father told me that I would never find the Gorgon flower unless I listened to him. What did he – *what did I* – mean by that? Perhaps this perception of myself as divided between a conscious and an unconscious self is itself the first step along the path of delusion whose final destination is insanity.

Late morning of Sunday 4th August 1861

After my torrid dreams I set off with my hopes bolstered, but I endured another morning of fruitless searching. It is stifling in my tent as I sit here, my poor head thrumming as I write. I stew like a shank of lamb in the pot. Why I taunt myself by scribbling such images I do not know, for I will not be tasting lamb shank this month, or the next, or the one after that! Having awoken scoured by hunger, I anticipated relishing the slices of monkey meat Tamworth cooked for breakfast, but strips torn from my canvas tent would hardly have been less edible.

A strange experience last night. My sleep was broken once when I needed to leave my tent to relieve myself. As I stood a few feet away in the pitch dark, I became conscious of a multitude of tiny lights dancing in the air around me, like embers whirling above a fire. The earth seemed to fall away from my feet and for a fleeting moment I had a curious sensation that I had been catapulted into the heavens and that the stars had abandoned their fixed and lonely positions to congregate in swarms around me, as if they knew I was alone in the vast emptiness. A dark shape seemed to arise and expand before me, extinguishing the points of light one by one and then in waves, as if thick black curtains were being drawn around me, and in an instant the fireflies were gone, and I was surrounded by a darkness so intense I could almost feel it on my skin, as if I was lying in a shuttered black velvet-lined box. And in the night air, the truly black darkness blazed before me, towered over me, and I scrambled back to my tent, chilled, sucking in air.

Evening of Sunday 4th August 1861

Since I have nothing to report after this afternoon's search, I will impart a short note on the digestive system of the Gorgon flower.

On my first meeting with a specimen of the species, Father sacrificed a small fieldmouse to demonstrate the plant's carnivorous inclination. After that he experimented with mammalian creatures of increasing size and varying composition to delineate the scope and nature of its appetite: rat, hamster, puppy, kitten. When, with a full-sized hare or cat, the dimensions of the petrified creature were too large to be absorbed by the orifice containing the digestive fluid, one of the tentacles would wrap itself around a limb or part of the poor creature: over time some acid or enzyme secreted by this tentacle eroded the flesh, tissue and, finally, bone so as to sever the designated limb or chunk of flesh from the remainder of the unfortunate mammal. The severed item would then be scooped up by a second tentacle and plopped into the plant's 'mouth', followed later (how much later being determined by the size of the piece being digested) by another chunk of the dead or dying creature, and so on and so on until the last piece of the poor creature had been consumed by the Gorgon flower.

This feeding process fascinated Father. While the antennae or tendrils cut the unfortunate prey into digestible pieces and transported such pieces to the ventricle storing the digestive fluid, they played no role in capturing or restraining the animal in the first place. Instead, prey was rendered immobile by the operation of some invisible, undetectable force or substance. The limbs of a small mammal might lose all animation while it scampered across the plant's petals but a larger creature did not even need to come into contact with the organs of the Gorgon flower; as long as it occupied a sufficient proximity to the plant, it would succumb to the paralysing force emanating from it.

The search to understand the nature of this force and how it operated obsessed my father. One hypothesis was that the plant emitted a colourless and odourless gas which instantaneously affected the organs of any animal that breathed it in. If so, no instrument used by my father was ever able to detect it. An alternative theory supposed that the flower transmitted a sound at a frequency too high to be discerned by the human ear but which could not only be heard by other animals but served to mesmerise and render them inactive. It was not possible to prove this hypothesis either. Surprisingly, in light of what we know about the appetite of other carnivorous plants, the Gorgon flower eschewed insects and reptiles; these were permitted to crawl or scuttle unhindered over its surfaces.

Here on my desk is Father's monograph from the 1831 Proceedings of the Royal Society, open at the appendix, which records the rates of consumption of those mammals not consumed in a single motion:

Large Brown Rat	*two hours forty-seven minutes*
Rabbit	*six hours thirty-five minutes*
Fox	*nine hours eighteen minutes*
Average-size British Shorthair Cat	*seven hours two minutes*
Dog (King Charles Spaniel)	*ten hours twenty-two minutes*
Dog (Labrador Retriever)	*twelve hours forty-two minutes*
Lamb (Romney Breed)	*sixteen hours ten minutes*
Derbyshire Pony	*twenty-six hours fourteen minutes*

This is a selection; I will not copy the complete list. The appendix runs to four pages and most domestic mammals are itemised: Father was nothing if not thorough. These experiments were carried out when I was a boy at school; it was only later that I learnt of the considerable censure they had attracted in some quarters, the practice of feeding sentient creatures, many of them so domesticated as to have been elevated to the status of household pets, to a large tropical carnivorous plant not being universally popular. Father was not impervious to such criticism and the full appendix was omitted from Father's monograph when it was reprinted as a single volume by the Cambridge University Press in 1836.

After what passed for dinner, Liscombe sidled up to me while I was trying to hold down the greasy slivers of meat-mottled fat Tamworth had presented to me. He asked me what time we would be setting off after Mr McGuire and the rest of the men tomorrow. I replied that we would do so after I had located the plant we were here to find and we had successfully transplanted several specimens of the same to the Wardian terrariums. This induced much distracting jaw-wiggling and tooth-jiggling on Liscombe's part. Somewhat nervously, he told me that Mr McGuire's orders had been to have my remaining belongings packed up and ready to depart no later than midday. I stared at him and then ostentatiously looked around. 'I don't see Mr McGuire here. Do you?' At this, Liscombe looked around too, as if Mr McGuire might not have departed for the ship yesterday but concealed himself behind a strangler fig tree and might step out at any moment. 'We will leave when I am ready,' I muttered, taking my leave of him.

Upon retiring to my tent to write up this journal and submit myself to the nocturnal freak-show my slumbers no doubt have in store for me, I heard the low drone of Tamworth and Liscombe chuntering for quite some time, but they were too far away for me to hear what they were saying and, in any event, they were competing with the persistent, stentorian honking and inane chitter-chatter of the damned proboscis monkeys.

Early afternoon of Monday 5th August 1861

There is no way one can avoid the unavoidable fact: matters did not transpire as I would have wished today. I have always endeavoured to withhold no part of my experience or intellectual activity from these pages and to implement a policy of absolute frankness, even if such policy has come at a considerable cost to my dignity and sense of self-worth. I am aware that, after I have related the events which unfolded this morning, I will pay an even higher price for my unstinting honesty. Be that as it may, I cannot disavow my intention of bearing witness to what truly happened even if my own actions have deviated from the path of civilised conduct and moral rectitude I have ever strived to adhere to.

As I awoke, dawn had torn off a narrow strip of the gloom over our heads and through that aperture a pallid light was leaking. Feeling neither refreshed nor rested, although the ache in my head had abated a little, I nevertheless resolved to make use of the cooler temperature afforded by the early hour. Skipping breakfast, I left Tamworth and Liscombe slumbering on the ground by my tent under their mosquito net.

Wispy streaks of cloud hung close to the rainforested slopes above me like fluffs of wool caught on a brush as I headed up the north-western flank of Mount Taliboko, plodding through thick vegetation, enjoying the early-morning respite from the humidity. As rays of sunlight crested the slope, the drops of moisture adorning the leaves and twigs were transformed into crystal beads; the spider webs hanging between the branches glowed like the metal filaments through which Mr Swan had so recently passed electricity.

Father was waiting for me in a small clearing, sitting on a fallen tree just as he had the previous time I had encountered him, as if he had been waiting for me to return. I again received a most vivid sensation of his palpability, his physical immediacy, as he knocked his pipe against his trunk-seat to dislodge the tobacco ash.

'How do I find it, Father?' I asked. As with before, I believe I detected affection in his regard but this time adjoined by the merest hint of asperity.

'Tobias, my boy, why did you write in your journal yesterday about its feeding habits?'

I stuttered a nonsensical reply.

'No, no, no, it's because you do know, you do know. Come here, listen.' He motioned for me to approach, and as I knelt before him he leant forward so that his face was close enough for me to see the yellow tobacco stains in his moustache.

'It ate more, much more,' Father continued, 'but I couldn't include the details in my published work. But you know that, don't you, you've always known that.'

'What do you mean?' I asked.

He tutted. 'Well, I'm not going to speak of it aloud, Tobias, but you know me well enough, I hope, to be assured that we behaved with circumspection, propriety and generosity. Mothers who died in the agonies of childbirth. Labourers who perished as a result of unfortunate accidents in the factories where they worked. Never children though, not that. Forbes-Haggard was quite wrong about that. Perhaps if he knew the truth he wouldn't have taken the action he did.'

'And what,' I enquired, 'did he do?'

'You know what he did.' Father sat back, a little irritated. *Did I know?* I searched my memory but my obvious incomprehension must have annoyed Father even more. He stood up abruptly and exclaimed: 'He consigned it all to fire, all of it.' He glared down at me. 'You know what you must do to entice it, to give it a reason to reveal itself to you. Now off you go, get on with it.'

I searched for another three hours, befuddled, endlessly churning Father's words around in my head like scraps of paper in a tombola, clutching at their meaning as if grabbing at blossom petals set whirling by a gust around my head. By the time I got back to the clearing and our miniature camp, it was getting on for midday and the ache in my head was a petulant potentate demanding attention.

Something was askew with the encampment and I must have

stared at it for ten or more seconds like a loon before I realised what it was: my tent had been dismantled and packed up along with my other personal possessions. I could see my writing instruments together with the few books I still had with me, including this journal, stuffed together, jumble-wise, into the top of a canvas sack. Tamworth and Liscombe, who were finishing off tying buckles and fixing straps, desisted as I approached, their faces ashamed and nervous.

'Forgive us, sir, but Mr McGuire, before he left he gave us orders to pack up your things so as to be ready for our leaving. We must set off within the hour if we are to have any chance of catching him up.'

I had difficulty in identifying what was most enraging about the situation: that Mr McGuire had assumed I would have been reluctant to leave at the end of the forty-eight-hour period I had negotiated with him and prepared for this eventuality; the effrontery and cunning with which the two wretches had packed my possessions in my absence; the thought of their callused and grime-scored hands pawing my books, my medication, my personal items; the fact that if they refused I would have to re-erect my own tent, which I had never done before.

I had an equally arduous task in ascertaining what response might best achieve my desired end: flamboyant fulmination underscored with righteous indignation; cold fury tinged with menace; the offer of yet more money. While I considered my options we indulged in a futile, time-wasting tit for tat, rather like a tawdry music hall act: I asked them to unpack my belongings and set up my tent; they refused; I asked again; they refused again.

The course of action I finally adopted was not an option that I had previously considered and it surprised me as much as, I suspect, it surprised them. I picked up my rifle standing propped against my pack, slid the bolt propelling the bullet into the firing chamber, pointed it at Liscombe's head and asked him, one last time, to unpack my personal possessions. I did not intend to pull the trigger and I was not even conscious that I had, but the bullet nevertheless exited the rifle and entered his head through his right eye, so that in the few seconds he stared at me – while the thunder-bang, reverberating around the trees, unleashed a storm of shrieks and beating wings from the birds and gibbering screams from the monkeys – he did so from one good eye and one neat circular dark hole, which looked for all the world like the black button eye of a child's teddy bear. And then a drop of blood trickled down his cheek from the gap where his eye had been, he crumpled to the ground, and I saw the back of his head had been replaced by a bowl of lumpy grey-blue porridge, soggy with blood not milk. The blood oozed from the shattered cranium and soaked into the ground where the soil particles were instantaneously transformed into a pullulating mass of ants, millipedes and beetles that wriggled and foamed as they feasted on the red liquor so bountifully and unexpectedly vouchsafed to them.

Evening of Monday 5th August 1861

I wrote my first entry for the day sitting at my writing desk just inside the flap of my tent, gazing out at the verdant rainforest throbbing with life both seen and unseen. I have reoccupied this spot to pen this later report. You may entertain the thought, *well, he may be a murderer, but at least his fears regarding his inability to erect his tent were unfounded.* But by no means the least shameful of the confessions I must make today is that it was young Tamworth, not I, who was responsible for unpacking and assembling my canvas lodgings. He did so in a most jittery fashion with much clanking of poles and scrabbling with pegs, no doubt the result of performing his task with my rifle trained upon him, wondering whether he might be dispatched from this life at any moment with the cruelty and random savagery that had attended the death of his erstwhile colleague. The look on Tamworth's face in those seconds following the unfortunate discharge of my weapon when, as those penny-dreadful novelists would put it, *time itself seemed to stand still*, was not the least of the burdens I had imposed upon myself. In his eyes were shock, confusion, terror, but also more than a modicum of disappointment that I had shown myself to be other than what he had supposed me to be: a self-disciplined, respectable member of a superior class; reserved and even perhaps sometimes offhand, but steadfast, uncomplaining and committed to the ideals of responsible behaviour, moral probity, unostentatious courage and fair play. I had failed to abide by the standards of the class of which I was such an unillustrious representative, as well as the lights by which I had attempted to live.

Once my personal possessions had been unpacked and my tent fitted out as I had left it this morning, I lowered my rifle, put it to one side and told Tamworth that he could leave if he wanted to. 'I didn't mean to kill him,' I said, but I knew he did not believe me; he collected his own things and backed away apprehensively, alert to the possibility I might reach for the rifle and shoot him notwithstanding the distance I had put between myself and the weapon. Once he had gained the proximity of the rainforest, he turned on his heels and bolted, and the last glimpse I had of him was his bobbing blond hair flickering between the tree trunks; then, to quote my novelist friend again, *I was alone with only my thoughts for company.*

What thoughts they were indeed. My crime did not necessarily mandate my personal punishment: I could always claim that Tamworth and Liscombe, both sotted with rum, had squabbled over a game of cards; the squabble had curdled into a murderous rage on Tamworth's part and a violent tussle had resulted in him shooting Liscombe. It would be my word against his; need I say more. But I had no intention of disowning my misadventure. Liscombe may well have been a slack-jawed weasel, a leathery dried-out husk of a man – and my imagination signally failed to summon a Mrs Liscombe and Liscombe offspring mourning the loss of their tattooed paterfamilias – but he was still a man and, in all the circumstances, I had not been justified in depriving him of his life. I would not overstate my sympathy for Liscombe's personal plight, but my belief that I had violated the moral order, that I had lowered myself in the estimation of the great German philosopher Immanuel Kant, dead for half a century but still alive to me in that I looked constantly to his teachings for wisdom and moral guidance, was a grievous burden.

After Tamworth had fled I sat at my writing desk for the remainder of the afternoon: I was too weary to stir and my head pain, that ever-present companion, like someone beating continually on my brain tissue with a truncheon, had returned. Tamworth had covered Liscombe's cadaver with a canvas sheet and positioned the tent so that it was not in my line of sight, but I could not dismiss from my mind's eye the vision of the fleshy integument of his body shrinking to its bony core under the clacking mandibles of the innumerable beetles burrowing into his carcass. The mental agitation and inner turmoil of the day faded and I must have dozed, for when I came to with a start, the light in the clearing was clotting purple and grey and Father stood a few feet from me, staring down at me with a calculating look.

'Well, well, you are full of surprises are you not, Tobias? You are to be commended on your perspicacity and ingenuity in using the materials to hand. But you have rested long enough now: come, rouse yourself! There is much to be done. I can offer little in the way of practical assistance but I can be a supportive sentinel to your efforts.'

I put my head in my hands. 'What is it that I am to do, Father? Please tell me.'

Father explained what he thought my next steps should be. After a moment's hesitation, I put down my pen and complied with his wishes.

Morning of Tuesday 6th August 1861

It took me two and a half hours to execute Father's design yesterday evening and for the last hour I was working by the illumination of only my oil lamp; under its juddery oval light, objects jumped out at me from the shadows at its periphery, the ground at my feet seemed to yaw and pitch, and the evening air became a soup swimming with fireflies, mosquitoes and countless other flying insects that made up the microscopic traffic of the night. The deficit of natural light undoubtedly made my job harder and yet it was entirely appropriate to the task at hand: an unpleasant, nefarious business to be carried out in the darkness, alone, shunned by all right-thinking men.

I have vowed to withhold nothing from these pages; not for me the carefully bowdlerised account, the scrupulously manufactured prose calculated to flatter and dignify the diarist at the expense of the truth in all its raw ugliness. Here you will find me as I truly am, not as who you would wish me to be – or as I myself might wish me to be. And yet I quail at besmirching this journal with an admission of what I have done, let alone a description of how I did it; the ink with which I write the words will surely become the colour of blood – to match the red whorls imprinted on the pages by my bloodied fingertips. But the truth must be recorded: I can at least ensure that. I will be brief though; exhaustion threatens to render me insensible.

I wrapped my kerchief tightly around my mouth and nostrils and then removed the sheet covering Liscombe's body, placed it on the ground next to his supine form and then rolled his corpse onto it. Wielding his machete with all the strength I could muster, I proceeded to dismember his body, deploying the art of the butcher rather than that of the surgeon as I severed his head and each of his limbs from his torso. I could barely see the body below me through a continually crawling carapace of fat blowflies: each downswing of the blade triggered a mini-explosion of them like someone throwing a bowl of sultanas in my face. Liscombe's head I discarded but his limbs I stacked in one of the Wardian terrariums. Since he had been dead for some hours, his blood was well on the way to congealing and it oozed rather than flowed from the stumps. The torso was too large to fit into the terrarium in one piece, so I was forced to divide it into three. This proved the most challenging aspect as it involved separating the body trunk into upper and lower portions and cracking the rib cage apart. My clumsy hacking soon resulted in organs slithering loose from their fleshy sheathing and plopping one on top of the other on the sheet. Before long I was smeared with gore from head to toe and reduced to scooping up armfuls of body parts – the yellow concertinaed tubes of the intestines; the matt maroon of the kidneys; the grey gelatinous mass of the lungs – and dropping them into the terrarium until it was brimming and I could shut the lid.

Father was as good as his promise and stood observing my actions from the distance of a few feet. Once the terrarium was sealed I stood up and wiped my face, dizzy, breathing stertorously, close to collapse.

'Show me where, Father,' I gasped, and he motioned towards a large strangler fig tree a few feet away.

The terrarium was usually used to transport plants and a bed of soil but this one must have weighed not far short of a hundred pounds: I was worried the brass handles would snap off. I was about to ask Father to assist before recognising the idiocy of doing so. Bending down, I alternated between dragging and pushing my portable charnel house across the clearing, heaving and straining, until I was close enough to the tree Father had selected. Once I had retrieved the lamp and the shovel from my tent and re-fastened my kerchief, I prised off the lid and shovelled out about a third of the contents of the terrarium between two of the fig's buttressed roots. I repeated this exercise at the base of two other trees – a banyan tree and a sago palm tree – both adjacent to the clearing. I then wished Father good night, splashed water on my hands and face from my canteen, and retreated to my tent and my dreams.

Afternoon of Tuesday 6th August 1861

I dozed at my writing desk after busying myself in preparations for the day (unwrapping the strips of monkey gristle, checking the level of the drinking water in my canteen and flask, draping the netting over the table, preparing my nib) and after transcribing this morning's entry in my journal.

Now I am awake I can see the strangler fig from where I sit.

Its tube-like limbs wrap themselves around its imprisoned tree in a filigree of merging and crisscrossing strands like solidified rivulets of liquid which, as they descend the trunk, swirl into thicker streams that become tentacle-like roots, snaking across the ground before plunging into the earth. These roots sometimes form thick buttresses with deep hollows between them.

In one of these hollows nestles a Gorgon flower.

It was not there before I dozed and I had been insensate for no more than a couple of hours: how had it grown so rapidly during my period of unconsciousness?

The last time I set eyes on the flower, I was a boy; since then, I have only seen it reproduced in watercolours and oil in botanical texts. But here it is, scarcely a few feet in front of me – the magnificence of its girth, the richness of its botanical plumage, the savage beauty without which one could not comprehend its perfect fusion of form and purpose.

Petals, large as elephant ears, streaked deep yellow and the glossy red of ruby lips, that have the texture of softly brushed velvet. At the centre of the petals nestles a deep-set cup of phosphorescent lime-green mucilage, out of which thrust three tentacles, as tall, straight and motionless as spears. Even from thirty feet or so away, the vibrant yellow and red of its petals vibrates against the greens – dark, mint, lime, olive – and browns of the rainforest. I can hardly believe it is there; I keep throwing glances in its direction like a coquettish lover, eager to pleasure the eye with that which delights it, but too shy to display one's affections too overtly.

I have not approached it yet; indeed, have not strayed further than the tent and its immediate vicinity. At last, that which I have sought! And now I am like a child holding a parcel containing a fabulous gift, quivering with excitement at the thought of unwrapping the precious object within; how exquisite to experience the anticipation of pleasure before the pleasure itself. But I must not be giddy, must not lose myself at the botanical banquet in store for me. To strive to expand the domain of what is known and understood is noble and sweet, and every time we succeed we light one more candle that mitigates a little further the ignorance and superstition which encircles us. But when we achieve that which we have so long, and so ardently, desired, we are often minutely diminished by the satisfaction of our wishes, the realisation of our dreams. It cannot be helped; it is a condition of being human.

Evening of Wednesday 7th August 1861

A sensation of joy pulses through my weary limbs, the same happiness I remembered feeling as a child as the brightly lacquered box of the natural world opened its lid to reveal the beautiful ingenuity, the unconscious intelligence flowing through the intricate clockwork of its beating heart.

What have I observed so far? Six or seven hours ago, a large mature male proboscis monkey approached the Gorgon flower, his right hand clutching by their tails half-a-dozen or so pygmy squirrels (*Exilisciurus exilis*) which swung from side to side as the monkey waddled like an inebriated sailor. He stopped in front of the plant and dropped the small creatures onto its petals, then retreated a few paces. The pygmy squirrels scuttled hither and thither across the petals, which rippled under the patter of their paws.

The tentacles of the plant were ramrod straight, their only movement a barely perceptible sway occasioned by the breeze, seemingly indifferent to the tiny mammals who continued their boisterous play, exhibiting no inclination to escape from the petals. Then with a rapidity that could have been shielded behind an eye-blink, one of the tentacles flicked the squirrels off the petals and onto the ground, where they tumbled head over heels until, righting themselves, they darted into the undergrowth. The tip of the tentacle that had so forcefully ejected the erstwhile visitors now wrapped itself around the wrist of the monkey standing before it and gave a tug-shake to the arm as if to say: *Now look here! Pay attention!* One of the other tentacles pointed to something over and above the monkey's shoulder and I turned to trace its line of indication. The tip was pointing towards the upper half of a large ironbark tree and nothing initially presented itself to me that could have incited the Gorgon flower's attention until I saw a male infant monkey, eight to twelve months old, its nose not yet fully extended, slumbering on a branch, its limbs dangling languidly.

The old monkey, also looking at where the tip was pointing, honked and jabbered in a way that bespoke remonstration, and the tentacle around his wrist tightened its grip; he snarled and shrieked and tried to loosen the fibrous manacle with his other hand but to no avail. This state of affairs continued for another minute or so until the monkey fell silent and appeared to deflate in size, settling on his haunches in a submissive pose. The tentacle released him and the old monkey ambled off to sit at the base of the ironbark, where he glanced up from time to time at the young monkey still drowsing on the branch high above, oblivious to what I surmised was the determination of his fate.

What else have I observed? Apart from the old proboscis monkey, no living creature, whether insect that crawls or flitters, or reptile that skitters, or bird that flits like an explosion of colour from tree to tree, or monkey or other mammal of whatever size, has gone near the Gorgon flower since my observations commenced this morning. It resides in splendid isolation, the vivid colours of its petals lending it a regal aspect, a monarch of all it surveys. When it is flooded in the sunlight shafting through the canopy, those colours burn, the vivid scarlet nubs glisten at the end of the tentacles, and the air around it seems to glimmer. It reminds me of a visit to a Tuscan chapel with solid brick windowless walls where, at noon each day, a solitary sunbeam admitted by a single slit in the wall penetrated the gloomy interior to illuminate a golden chalice housing a precious relic; the reliquary seemed to vibrate with a force that emanated from within it, indubitably the effect of its positioning rather than any manifestation of its miraculous properties. But with the Gorgon flower the sunlight is not responsible for its appearance of singular power; it merely embellishes it.

It is clear to me that the Gorgon flower carves a space around itself; it alone determines who enters that area; it alone initiates the interactions it desires with the flora and fauna in its proximity. No surprise that I recall Tuscany. There I encountered the finest and most beautiful art yet created by man – to wit, Bellini, Titian, Michelangelo, Giotto: I find an echo of their brilliance here in my encounter with the most magnificent plant yet created by evolution. If it is a plant. For the more I observe *you*, the less certain I am that I know what *you* are.

Afternoon of Thursday 8th August 1861

I ingested one of my two remaining phials of laudanum before lying on my camp bed last night. Savage, restless dreams plagued my slumber – but I tire of recording them. This morning, I do not know which discomfort is most pressing – the ache in my head or the weariness that etiolates my body, that drains me of the vitality to attempt any task other than to sit and write. A sharp pain in my right foot also makes an insistent call on my attention; when I stand and place my weight on it, I can do so only with the utmost difficulty. I cannot recall twisting my foot in my crepuscular activities of Monday evening. Nor do I recall an inadvertent lacerating of my foot by a downswing of my machete; the leather of my boot discloses no aperture, although when I painfully extract my foot, the stocking is stained with blood and discharge and the underlying flesh is pulpy to the touch.

I have taken stock of my resources. A canteen two-thirds full of water. A stream comes off the mountain a couple of miles to the north, although making my way there in my current condition will be a challenge. A few strips of barely edible monkey hide. One phial of laudanum. The box with Dr Stanhope's medicines and medical equipment, Mr McGuire took with him. I have no oil for heating or light other than the tiny amount that slops in the base of the oil lamp when I tilt it: if it were whiskey, I would say barely two fingers. Rifle, machete, watch, compass, map, the clothes I wear. Liscombe's personal belongings, such as they are, lie in and around his sack but I shall not scavenge these. But I have my journal and my writing instruments. Sadly, my books (*The Gallic Wars*, Alexander Pope's translation of *The Iliad*, Montaigne's *Essays* and Spinoza's *Ethics*) went with Mr McGuire and his men, leaving only the volume containing the 1831 Proceedings of the Royal Society, which includes Father's monograph on the Gorgon flower. Which flower, may I be permitted to say, I have rediscovered.

I should walk over to the Gorgon flower, admire its form from its close vicinity, compare its lineaments with those enumerated by Father, sketch it and even touch it. But I will do these things tomorrow. Today, I will rest and watch the brightness of its colours smoulder and fade to grey in the incipient gloaming.

Evening of Friday 9th August 1861

My right foot roars with pain as if it roasts on a griddle. Remarkably, I have been insensate for much of the day in spite of the growing agony. The Gorgon flower sits at the base of the strangler fig, its yellow and red markings seeming to pulse in the amber luminescence of the afternoon sun. I can see quite clearly the remains of a proboscis monkey – its looping tail, brick-red posterior and legs – draped across the petals, and my eyes automatically flick to the branch on which I had seen the youth so indolently sunning himself the day before yesterday. He is not there. The monkeys congregating on the monumental ironbark sit motionless and quiet, festooning its branches like monstrous misshapen fruit. At this distance and with the sun behind them, they are robbed of their individuality. I cannot say with certainty whether the young monkey is amongst them or not.

Morning of Saturday 10th August 1861

I have been awake half the night but did not light my lamp in the small hours, intending to preserve what little oil I have left. Would that I had been so careful with my last phial of laudanum, but I devoured that around three o'clock this morning after my nocturnal visit to the Gorgon flower, hoping to obtain some release from the torment in my foot. I then drowsed in and out of consciousness, the agony in my foot dwindling to a dull throb. But deep, nourishing sleep evaded me. Now that there is light enough to write, I shall recount what occurred last night.

A woman's voice, familiar to me and yet incongruous in this setting, calling my name awoke me just after midnight. I poked my head through the flap of my tent into a world soaked with a moonlight so intense that the clearing, grass, leaves, branches and trees shimmered as if coated with frost. I heard my name called again and then I saw my wife, Charlotte, standing in front of the Gorgon flower, wearing a long dress blanched of colour and holding out her arms in my direction.

Barely able to trust my own sight, I hobbled over to her, using my rifle as a makeshift crutch. 'How did you get here?' I asked.

'Dr Stanhope brought me,' she said, taking my hands in hers. Her lustrous eyes, the exquisite curve of her cheekbones, her flaxen locks tumbling onto her shoulders: one would have said she had stepped from a Botticelli painting, if one did not know better.

'Stanhope? Is he here?' I looked around.

'No, no, I left him by the river. My darling, it is such sweetness to me to see you. Come, let us sit.' She sat down on something behind her and, my hands still in hers, I followed suit, only realising after I had done so that we had perched on the petals of the Gorgon flower. I made to stand but as I rose her hands tugged me gently back so that I resumed my seat next to her. The petals, softly accommodating, yielded to our weight. I opened my mouth to explain but, releasing one of my hands, she placed a finger on my lips.

'Shush, shush, Tobias, my sweet one. I am so sorry, so very sorry for all the hurt I've caused you these past years. Verily, you didn't deserve any of it. I am ashamed of the way I have behaved.

But all that is in the past. That is what I've come here to say. And to congratulate you, of course, and to bring you your prize.' She smiled enticingly at me. 'Can you guess what it is?'

Close up, I comprehended her dress was a diaphanous gauze through which I saw, up top, the two round red garnet tips and, below, the priceless ruby jewel of her womanly treasure. She leant forward and kissed me on the lips and then, her lips brushing my ear, she whispered such blandishments to me! Though I have withheld nothing from this journal, I shall never share those sweet endearments, not even if the earth should shatter and heaven's vault crack. For years I had endured a drought, wandering lost and abandoned, deprived of the sweet liquid that rejuvenates and consoles, forced to shell out shillings for potions foul and malodorous in order to quench my raging thirst. As I held Charlotte in my arms, only the moonlight touching her ivory skin, I was drenched in that elixir that delivers comfort and peace. Our union was all the sweeter for it came wrapped in the memories of our enchanted years together when we made the best of our youth and denied ourselves none of those pleasures that wither and shrivel with the passage of time. As we reached the pinnacle of our bodily congress, our limbs straining with the joy of our effort, we each uttered the exclamations of fulfilment and I fell forward onto the petals and immediately fell into a deep stupor.

When I came to consciousness, I know not after what period of insensibility, I lay naked, stretched across the flower. Charlotte had disappeared and the juice of my manhood stained the petals beneath me in drops and dribbles. To my surprise and disgust, one of the Gorgon flower's tentacles seemed to be absorbing these traces through a minutely pulsing motion of its tip. I tried to raise myself but my limbs weighed as heavy as the sacks of meal in the ship's hold; it was all I could do to roll onto my back.

After a while, I levered myself up from the flower, groaning aloud as I pressed my weight onto my right foot; I looked around wildly for Charlotte but nowhere could she be seen. Just the endless matted tangle of the rainforest, silvered by the moonlight.

Evening of Saturday 10th August 1861

Foolish man, you may well be thinking, for it was only as I cast my eyes around to discover my wife that it occurred to me that she might have been only a vision. I had known instantly the chimera of my father had been generated by my diseased mind, not least as he had been dead these past twenty-eight years; no such intuitive knowledge arose in Charlotte's case. But was it really feasible that she had travelled all the way from London to this particular spot where I lay mouldering and benighted? And if she had done so, why had she now vanished and let the pathetic calls of a pathetic man ring out unheeded? My reluctance to abandon the faint possibility of her physical presence you may not unreasonably interpret as the nonsensical reasoning of my disintegrating mind but, really, the evidence of my burgeoning insanity lay in every direction around me, for what does it say about the soundness of my brain if she was simply an illusion?

As I finally embraced the certainty that I had been deluded, my emotions betrayed, my body duped, I felt anger and disgust at myself. But was I solely responsible? When I think about my dreamscapes these last few weeks and the apparition of my father and now my wife, a niggle worms into my brain, like a tick burrowing into the hide of a dog, that some external influence, some nefarious force *or thing* (I know not how to refer to it) might have been bearing down on my sensibility, subtly infiltrating my psyche. If I am anything I am an offspring of the Age of Reason, Enlightenment and Science, and yet I have found myself entertaining such thoughts oftentimes during the previous two weeks. But whether these thoughts are the valuable insights of a beleaguered rationality or clinching proof of a helter-skelter slide into lunacy, I do not think I have any way of determining.

Afternoon of Sunday 11th August 1861

Now that the laudanum has gone, I must face, without weapon or shield of any description, the assault on my senses mounted by the rotting of my foot. My stocking is now wet and stained from the tip of my toe to well above my ankle, and my foot releases a foetid odour which mingles with the underlying gamey aroma of my body to fill my nostrils. Removing my stocking would no doubt be beneficial, but I want the courage to do so. I am in a topsy-turvy state: the sun holds me in its beneficent arms but my flesh is slicked with sweat and I shiver from the chills that periodically race through me, like greyhounds pursuing a rabbit. I close my eyes and when I re-open them I do not know if a minute or an hour has elapsed.

My fortunes have taken a decided downturn for the worse, but I am determined to assess my options and plot my course with as much lucidity as I can muster and commit my thoughts to my journal for as long as I am able. A lingering and agonising death could await me but I am fortunate in that I have my rifle and a supply of ammunition and I can thwart this dread prospect at a time of my choosing. Although if I take this course I must do so competently and decisively; matters will be advanced not one whit if, intending to deposit a bullet in my brain, I miss and shatter my arm or hand instead, thereby disabling me from any further attempts to self-extinguish by means of deploying that weapon.

Something similar happened to young Viscount Samuel Partington shortly after he matriculated from Cambridge all those years ago. Ruined by gambling debts, spurned by an impertinent hussy (although, in truth, Partington would not have been much of a catch) he resolved to bring matters to an end prematurely. After he had hosted a rousing and suitably debauched evening at The Athenaeum (where he consumed a glass of claret, and sometimes more than one, from each of the bottles he had ordered, one for each year he had graced the world with his presence), he repaired to a single room with his howdah pistol. The report of the shot, when it came, was followed by the Viscount's screaming; when we rushed to the room we found that he had inadvertently shot himself in his leg, shattering his femur. Result: amputation of his leg just short of the hip and a not-insignificant increase in his arrears arising from the costs of the dinner.

Rest now.

Evening of Sunday 11th August 1861

Amputation: there is a thought. Could I summon the strength to sever my foot from my leg with a swing of the machete? I have, after all, garnered some recent experience in dismemberment. But it would be a brave or foolish man who attempted self-amputation without spirits to dull the senses and cauterise the stump, and not the least of the injuries done to me by Tamworth and Liscombe is that, between them, they finished off the paltry measure of brandy left by Mr McGuire. My foolishness rather than my bravery might equip me, but it is, in truth, an unappetising prospect. If I survived the severance of my foot, I would have to crutch up and make my way back to the river, trying to source sustenance as I did so. Would I be able to drag behind me a terrarium with a specimen of the Gorgon flower inside? A well-nigh impossible feat in the condition to which I have succumbed; if I was to have even the remotest chance of survival, I would have to leave the Gorgon flower behind. Besides, if the infection throngs and festers in my blood, necrosis could irrupt elsewhere in my body. I have regretted not investigating more assiduously whether the corpses of the poor souls we encountered on the way manifested single or multiple instances of necrotic contamination.

Supposing I lopped off my foot and freed myself from the deadly contagion, and supposing also I both abandoned the Gorgon flower and then survived long enough to reach HMS *Stockport*, what ignominy would I face if I returned home with nothing to show for the cost, time and physical effort of the expedition except a missing foot? No doubt there would be superficial welcome and relief at my appearance, but behind the closed doors of every chamber that mattered, from the wardroom onboard HMS *Stockport* to the committee rooms of the Royal Society at Somerset House, I would be branded a failure, a nincompoop who squandered the valuable resources of his family and his patrons on a misguided and ultimately futile attempt to follow in his father's footsteps.

There would be less shame attached to my name if I failed to return; a subtle alchemy invariably operates to mutate death in the exercise of one's duty or profession into a noble and heroic act. There would also be the unpleasantness regarding Liscombe to deal with; I don't believe I intended to kill him and I certainly regret doing so, but it appears as if his body parts have played a part in luring the Gorgon flower to reveal itself and an external observer could perhaps infer an element of design on my part in taking the actions I did.

Delineating the possible courses of action available to me has been a salutary exercise. The least unattractive of the routes that lie ahead of me is death by my own hand at the point of time at which the pain becomes unbearable. Put like that, it doesn't sound so bad. How long do I have? Possibly a day or two, but it could be less. I know little of this mysterious plague other than that it consumes flesh quickly and remorselessly.

Morning of Monday 12th August 1861

It is doubtful that these words will ever be read by another living soul: what, then, is the point in continuing to craft these sentences, to consider laboriously, nay, *to agonise over*, which word to use? When not writing, my mind escapes from the tyrannical regime of consequential, logical thought and wanders freely over the landscape of my life, and my memories come running to me like eager puppies wanting to be picked up and cherished. Easy it would be to put down my pen, scoop them in my arms and hug them to my bosom! But writing forces us to articulate what would otherwise be inchoate, formless and unsaid. When we write we carve ourselves, one letter at a time, into the insensible, material world, conferring permanence on our transient thoughts, hopes and fears. We communicate something of ourselves by breathing life into words that, once born, exist separately from us. No other creature is capable of doing this. Every time a person reads the words of another, a unique bond arises between them; every sentence becomes an open door to the writer's consciousness, emotions or, *if you will*, spirit, and whether one person, millions of people or no one at all passes through that door, those written words have a place and a purpose in the universe.

Afternoon of Monday 12th August 1861

The Gorgon flower has moved. It no longer dwells in the hollow formed by the buttress roots of the strangler fig. It now grows in the open of the clearing, no tree overshadowing it, a spot equidistant between the tent and the position it had previously occupied. I write *the same flower* but reason dictates that to be nonsensical; a flower has no independent locomotion; a more rational explanation is that the flower at the base of the strangler fig has died and a new specimen has grown in the clearing (although I saw no sign of the withering of the first or the sprouting of the second). But nonsensical though it be, *I know that it is the same Gorgon flower*: the dimensions and shape of the petals, the markings that adorn them, the height of the tentacles – in each respect the new flower is identical to the old one.

I am not sure when the strangler fig ceased to harbour the Gorgon flower; I speculated that it might have been some time last night, although, if that was the case, I am sure I would have noticed before now that the Gorgon flower had moved closer to me. Which makes me think the flower shifted its position barely a moment ago, perhaps when I closed my eyes for a moment's repose.

Evening of Monday 12th August 1861

Although I have given little advance thought in earlier years
to the circumstances of my death, I did assume I would not be
alone. Question: am I alone if I die in the presence of the Gorgon
flower? Father always thought it possessed sentience and it is now
clear to me, if I ever doubted, that it does, although the nature of
that sentience is mysterious to me. I dream of it, night after night:
but does it dream of me? It captured my imagination in boyhood
and has never relinquished it; it has haunted my memories and
populated my dreams; it constituted the great ambition of my life,
sunbathing me in the invigorating radiance of its beams, beside
which the love of my wife, my family and friends, my monarch
and my country emitted only the pale flicker of a candle flame.

In a plot device I am sure my novelist companion would
refrain from using, I have rediscovered the majestic Gorgon flower
but will not live to enjoy the renown that should be my reward.
Although I suspect the truth of the matter is that the Gorgon
flower revealed itself to me, allowed itself to be discovered, just as
it had allowed itself to be discovered by Mr Jennings and, all those
years ago, by Father. Now I think I understand why Father did not
name the Gorgon flower after himself, unlike those insufferable
bores Sir Stamford Raffles and Dr Joseph Arnold, who gave the
appellation *Rafflesia arnoldii* to the flower they discovered.

I can face with equanimity forgoing the professional respect
and popular acclamation I should have enjoyed on reintroducing
the Gorgon flower to the scientific community and the wider
public. I never wanted to don those gaudy robes. My deep regret
is that I will be unable to continue Father's scientific investigations
into a flower whose properties and potency he and I have barely
begun to comprehend. I would say it pains me but I shall not,

in the brief time remaining to me, deploy that word cheaply, for the agony creeping up my right leg, like a dozen fox-traps grinding my flesh and bones to a gristly paste under their sharp teeth, dictates a strict schooling in the real meaning of pain.

Morning of Tuesday 13th August 1861

Last night I dreamt I rose easily from my cot and ventured outside my tent. As I looked above me, an intense darkness filled my vision, banishing the moon and the stars, a darkness so heavy and complete I felt it pressing down on my eyes, my face and my limbs. And then it was as if sight had been vouchsafed to me but not the sight of those who walk, pad, slither or crawl under the sun: rather, the sight of the blind, clicking bat navigating labyrinthine rock tunnels, or that of the deep cave-dwelling troglobite, or the jellied tube-like eel in the freezing pitch-black waters of the ocean bed. I sensed a form take shape before me, and I felt the pulsing of a living being a breath away from me.

I yelled in terror and flung my arm across my face. I did not know then when consciousness ended and unconsciousness began, only that time passed. After a period – I know not how long – I lowered my arm. I could see that circular reflector of the sun's rays, serene, impassive, in the night sky above me and I gazed at it while, one by one, my senses were restored to me.

Afternoon of Tuesday 13th August 1861

My heartbeat skips and patters like a prancing pony, light on its feet. My canteen of water is nearly exhausted. Although I sit still at my writing desk, my swollen leg extended before me, I slip in and out of slumber as easily as the monkeys swing in and out of the patches of light beneath the trees. It seems my novelist confidant is determined to compose the final pages of my life; his major theme is sorrow, his minor theme regret and his style sentimental in the extreme.

It is a conventional trope of much mediocre art that the imminence of death dissolves those whalebone corsets that, for much of our lives, cinch the untidy passions of our emotional life into figures of sober rectitude. Yet surely I can be forgiven a modicum of mediocrity on my death seat? I was niggardly in my love and my affections. My true self I withheld from Charlotte; is it any revelation that she sought sincerity and tenderness in the company of other men? My assumption that she would have eschewed my interests in the magical realms of art and science seems to me callow and unimaginative. My marriage became a forced march across a blasted heath when it could have been a companionable stroll through the chalk downs and limestone bluffs of our intellectual and emotional life together.

And what would a philosopher versed in epistemology say about my keening after a person who didn't even exist: the son or daughter I never had.

My hand aches. I can write no more for now.

Evening of Tuesday 13th August 1861

As I look back on my life, I would not jettison those endless boyhood hours of joy at St Agnes Beach, Cornwall. I watched as the water level in the rock pools rose and dull lifeless mounds inflated into bright red cushion stars, stringy inverted mop-heads became the wavy fronds of dahlia anemones, and dull green smears took on the vivid blues and purples of rainbow wrack: a miniature kingdom populated by crabs, sea scorpions and shrimps, a world entire of itself.

The intellectual excitement of reading my friend Charles Lyell's *Principles of Geology* and comprehending for the first time the innumerable aeons the earth has existed before us.

My thrill at discovering the plates in *The Temple of Flora* by Robert John Thornton, that sadly neglected masterwork of Gothic melancholy and botanical illustration.

Above all things, my growing interest in the Gorgon flower, the memory of my encountering it as a boy, before its destruction in the fire that also took Father away from me, prompting me to immerse myself in Father's writings and research after his death and culminating in my letting it be known that I would be most eager to hear reports of its rediscovery in the wild. And so on.

I treasure all these memories. All of them. But, as these images flash past my galloping mind, I have a curious sensation that if I had done one small thing and not maybe another, well, my life could have been quite different, although I do not know how or in what way.

Even stranger, I find myself mourning a life I never lived, the person I did not become.

The lamp flickers. It must be nearing the end of its …

Morning of Wednesday 14th August 1861

It is here, in front of my writing table, barely three feet from where I sit.

Dreadful night. Periods of unconsciousness I would not deign to call sleep. Waves of agony repeatedly crashing over me and an endless sea of torment stretching ahead. I am at the limit of what I can endure. An eternity to lift myself onto my chair by leaning on my rifle but I want to sit not lie.

The Gorgon flower towers over me.

I sense its presence. It blocks my vision. So close. Its tendrils revolve in the space between us; they could touch me but they hold off. Does it mean me harm? It can't inflict greater pain on me than that which I already bear, but I check my rifle, hold it on my lap, while I scratch out these words. The question I should have faced days ago. What are its intentions towards me?

In my dreams it has horribly mangled Father but has always been kind to me, I think. Does it mean to consume me? Stupid me. I should put down my pen and prepare my rifle but I can't just yet. Keep a scientific record to the end but little science recorded in recent days.

Here comes its tendril, wet and red at the tip coming towards me. It touches my cheek. Cool soft wet. Strokes me so gently. I close my eyes. Write what I see. So long as I can write I am myself alive; I have not succumbed to the darkness.

That darkness towering over me in my dreams at night all this time. I see it for what it is – the profound eternal darkness that lies in wait for all of us. The darkness from which we come and the darkness to which we will return made visible. The perpetual darkness against which my life is nothing but the explosion of a firework. How I would have so wished to see perpetual light at the end and not darkness!

To be touched is a comfort now at the end I think. There is love in that touch but I am wary I hold my rifle ready to thrust the barrel in my mouth why would I do that if there is love but I don't trust the love it shows

No more writing I will finally lay down my pen for I need both hands on my rifle

If these words are ever read know this I am sorry God does not exist but if by some miracle He did I would not exist to him

14th August 1861 Anno Domini
Tobias Henry Edmundson

Afterword
Dr Percival James Louis Stanhope
18th November 1862

I am Percival James Louis Stanhope, Doctor of Medicine, born in Norfolk on 18th May 1826, late of the University of London, now Chief Medical Officer of St Mary's Hospital, London, and a Fellow of Jesus College, Cambridge. At the time of the events related in the accompanying journal, I was a physician on board HMS *Stockport*, under the command of Captain William Denton, on a voyage of botanical exploration which set sail from Portsmouth on 2nd March 1861, arrived on the southern coast of Borneo on 17th July 1861 and returned to England on 15th March 1862. The expedition had been financed by the Edmundson Family Trust with a generous grant from the Royal Society and was led by Lord Tobias Henry Edmundson, the author of the said journal (whom I shall hereinafter refer to as Tobias, for this is how he wished for me to address him in the normal course), although overall control of the ship and the voyage lay with Captain Denton.

The journal came into my possession in distressing circumstances which I shall go on to relate later in this paper. The journal itself is a most disquieting read as it charts the mental disturbances which increasingly afflicted Tobias, as well as his obsession with the Gorgon flower, a plant which his father, the late Lord John Gordon Edmundson, had discovered in Borneo between 1828 and 1830, and a single specimen of which he brought to England in 1830. The flower was quite a cause célèbre at the time, partly due to its size and striking appearance but mostly arising from its carnivorous appetite. Unfortunately, the plant was killed, and Lord Edmundson tragically lost his life, in a fire which destroyed a considerable portion of Hamilton Hall, the family's ancestral seat in Derbyshire, in 1833, when Tobias was only sixteen years of age. One can only speculate on the effects on the young Tobias of losing his father at such an early age. He followed in his father's footsteps by adopting an interest in science in general and botany in particular, and manifested a determination, on coming of age, to rediscover the Gorgon flower, a preoccupation which came to dominate his life and contributed significantly to his death.

Although the exact cause of Tobias's death is open to some conjecture, there is evidence that he had suffered from the flesh-attacking infection which devastated the population of the missionary communities of southern Borneo in 1861. This dreadful, highly contagious disease, subsequently popularly referred to as The Devil's Kiss, arose mysteriously in early 1861, seemingly originating deep in the rainforests of south Borneo. It spared the indigenous inhabitants of the region, only affecting those white Europeans who had made it their business to settle in that part of Borneo, mostly missionaries from the Kingdom of the Netherlands but also some traders and civil administrators. It soon spread to the coast, where it raced up and down the missionary communities embedded within the fishing villages which faced the Java Sea, before equally mysteriously disappearing approximately six months later. It infected all but a handful of the party of men who, against my strong advice, disembarked from HMS *Stockport* and followed the course of the Jimbala River upstream to locate the spot where the Gorgon flower had been seen by Mr Daniel Jennings, an English scientist and explorer, in early 1860.

This frightful affliction was a source of singular fascination to me. Like the final plague that killed only the firstborn son – inflicted by Yahweh on the Pharaoh and Egyptians in the time of Moses – this infection was selective, ravaging the white man but sparing his indigenous neighbour. I had never before encountered a disease that appeared to affect one set of people and not another, and indeed such a phenomenon would be repugnant to medical science as we understand it. We do know that populations can build up a tolerance over time to certain diseases so that the virulence of the malady amongst such people becomes blunted. When that disease is introduced to communities who have no previous exposure to it, its toxicity is quadrupled and it lays waste to all in its path. A single soldier of Hernán Cortés, the conqueror of Mexico, introduced smallpox to that country, and the disease then spread like a roaring wildfire through the Aztec population. Had the local tribes in south Borneo developed a resistance to whatever toxic miasma or substance was responsible for the horrendous infection, a resistance entirely lacking in Western visitors to the country? The problem with this explanation was that, following my conversations with local tribespeople, this was not an infection that had been seen before in this part of the world: it was novel to the region and seemed to be selective in who it infected from its genesis. For those who wish to know more about this disease I would humbly refer you to the article I submitted to *The British Journal of Tropical Medicine* 1862 (Volume II, Book IV, pages 117–135), where I set out my thoughts on the pathology of this affliction as well as a description of certain of its quite horrifying features (the first to appear in a European medical journal, I believe).

But back to Tobias. When I read the journal, it was clear to me that Tobias appeared to be in the grip of a strong compulsion regarding the Gorgon flower which led to nightmares, delusions and, towards the end of his life, hallucinations, each of which affected his behaviour profoundly. Intrigued, shocked and then saddened in equal measure by Tobias's account, I resolved to show the journal, on a confidential basis, to Dr John Langdon Down, a physician who specialised in the treatment of patients with mental disabilities. I had met Dr Down when we were students together at the Royal London Hospital and, when I approached him, he was Medical Superintendent of the Earlswood Asylum in Surrey. At Earlswood, he advocated a treatment of the insane in his custody that relied on kindness, the stimulation of physical activity, and a sensible diet in place of a regime that relied on strict discipline, physical confinement and 'starving cures'. He took a keen interest in mental infirmity of various descriptions and, although a busy man, he agreed to read the journal.

After he had done so, Dr Down contacted me to report that he had found the journal a fascinating case study depicting a steady descent into psychosis on the part of Lord Edmundson. He speculated whether the flesh-consuming disease might have been responsible for a miasma which, present in voluminous quantities in the stagnant, humid air of the rainforest, insidiously attacked the mental functions of those who breathed it in. It was likely that this toxic gas did not affect persons equally; some men might be oblivious to it. This made sense: when, five days after parting from Tobias, Mr McGuire and the remaining group of sailors made it back to HMS *Stockport*, I detected no diminution in the power of Mr McGuire's reasoning or the force of his character. It was possible, Dr Down reasoned, that Tobias had a latent weakness of the mind, manifested in the migraines which plagued him for most of his life, and this made him susceptible to this noxious miasma; once his mind had been affected it was only a matter of time before Tobias began to display its dreadful physical symptoms.

Dr Down asked if he could share the journal with a Professor Herbert Culverstone of Edinburgh University, another physician who studied mental infirmity in all its various manifestations. I knew Professor Culverstone by reputation only – that he was considered one of the leading authorities of the age in the diagnosis and treatment of mania, dementia and melancholia. I hesitated before giving my permission, however. The journal is a personal document and Tobias does not come well out of a perusal of its pages. Indeed, it is arguable that there is sufficient evidence contained within it to charge Tobias with the offence of murder, although given his state of mind at the time it is more likely that a court would find him guilty of manslaughter. If the facts of Tobias's delusions and accompanying behaviour leaked into the public domain, they would have a profoundly deleterious effect on his reputation. The image of him as a brave, intrepid explorer, felled by a virulent tropical disease, as portrayed in his obituary in *The Times,* would be instantly and indelibly stained.

Dr Down assured me that Professor Culverstone understood my concerns and would treat the journal and its contents with the utmost confidentiality. The Professor, he informed me, treated many members of the aristocracy and other high-ranking members of society for their mental infirmities and was used to cloaking his relationship with his clients with an impenetrable veil of secrecy. I therefore allowed Dr Down to share the journal with Professor Culverstone and was subsequently pleased that I had done so for, after the Professor had read the journal and wrote to me with his observations, we embarked on a fruitful and enlightening correspondence on the topic of Tobias's mental illness.

I shall refer to a number of Professor Culverstone's theories later in this paper, but suffice to say at this stage that he was of the opinion that Tobias had, from an early age, established an unhealthy fixation on the Gorgon flower, and that he then wove a narrative around it which incorporated his burgeoning sexuality, his lurid dreams, the death of his father and the estrangement from his wife into a personal myth based on the Arthurian quest for the missing Holy Grail. His father introduced him to the flower at an impressionable age and Tobias established an emotional connection with it, but this was cruelly foreshortened by the fire which took the lives of the two most meaningful presences in Tobias's young life. Thereafter, Tobias was duty *bound upon a wheel of fire* to rediscover the Gorgon flower both to reinstall its physical presence at the heart of his life and to prove himself worthy of his father's memory. At a conscious level, Tobias refused to ascribe mystical or extraordinary powers to the Gorgon flower, as these would be wholly repugnant to his belief system as a man of science. Unconsciously, he appeared to believe the Gorgon flower possessed sentience, the ability to infiltrate his mind and control his dreams, and the power of independent locomotion; furthermore, that it could be summoned by the 'sacrifice' of recently slaughtered human flesh because, one surmises, it had acquired a taste for it as result of being fed the same by Tobias's father thirty years previously.

Professor Culverstone was of the view that there would be much interest in the journal amongst the leading physicians of the mind, particularly on the Continent, where the study of the brain and its maladies was much more advanced than it was in this country. He proposed taking responsibility for the publication of the journal in book form – but a strictly limited publication, no more than twenty copies, each one numbered and designated for a particular recipient. As an appreciation of the journal would be enhanced by an understanding of the circumstances in which I took custody of it, and the context I could give in relation to certain matters contained therein, Professor Culverstone proposed that I write an Afterword (as he was of the view that my contribution should *follow* rather than *precede* Tobias's account).

At first, I was reluctant to comply with this request, not least as the condition in which I had found Tobias had, up to that point, been divulged to one or two persons only and I was anxious that the details, horrifying and strange in equal measure, not be widely known. However, I took considerable reassurance from Professor Culverstone's representations as to the extremely restricted circulation of the proposed volume and the academic standing and professional distinction of the intended recipients. I finally acceded to the Professor's request and *this*, Esteemed Reader, explains the treatise currently in your hands.

~

A brief explanation as to how I found myself on board HMS *Stockport* may be in order. In November 1860 I secured a position as Chief Medical Officer at St Mary's Hospital in Paddington, London. I was to take up my new post at the start of April 1862, which was when the incumbent occupant of the role, Sir Frederick Clifford, was due to retire. I was at that time Lord North's personal physician, and his Lordship was so good as to allow me to relinquish my position at the end of December 1860 so that I could undertake a period of travel on the Continent before I assumed my new position. I was making plans to embark on a tour of France, Germany and Italy when, one evening in January 1861, dining at my club with an old friend, I was introduced to Lord Edmundson.

Tobias was at that stage in discussions with the Royal Society to mount an expedition to Borneo to bring back specimens of the Gorgon flower, which, first being discovered by his father thirty years prior, had not been seen, or at least recognised, by a Western traveller until spotted by Mr Jennings the previous year. The intention was to set sail for Borneo on HMS *Stockport* under the command of Captain Denton by no later than mid-March 1861. Tobias let it slip that they were considering applications for the role of ship physician, but I do not believe for one moment he was soliciting my interest in the position: the soon-to-be Chief Medical Officer of a major London hospital would not ordinarily be a candidate for the position of ship's physician. Such jobs are usually taken by young doctors, fresh out of medical school, anxious to secure their first appointment, or, alternatively, doctors whose careers have foundered or practices run aground. I must confess that Tobias's description of the flower, his account of his father's research into its singular nature and his narrative of encountering the flower as a boy captivated me and appealed to my imagination and it was this, rather than the excellent brandy Tobias plied me with, that compelled me to declare my interest in being considered for the role aboard HMS *Stockport*. Tobias delightedly appointed me on the spot although he let it be known that he would not hold me to the appointment if the following morning, once the effects of the brandy had worn off, I had second thoughts.

Upon awaking I did have cause to consider whether I had been rash but, after cogitating on the matter during my morning constitutional, I returned to my residence determined to go ahead with my decision. I had a period of thirteen months to kick my heels, and the prospect of a voyage to Malaya and Borneo in a quest for a rare and mysterious flower appealed to that thirst for adventure I had possessed as a young man but never had an opportunity to satisfy before. I was thirty-five years old, in good health and unmarried; it was not unreasonable to suppose that this would be the last opportunity I had to indulge myself in an exploit of this nature: a tour of the Continent could surely wait, I reasoned, until my hair was a little greyer, my reflexes a little slower and my limbs a little more unsteady.

So it was that on a cold morning in early March, 1861, I stood on the fore-deck of HMS *Stockport* watching, in the pale grey light of dawn, Portsmouth and the coast of Hampshire recede to a green-brown smudge on the horizon. I could not have possibly known what I would see and experience in the months to come – the terrible infection, the deaths it caused amongst the crew of the ship and the missionaries in Borneo, the fate that awaited Tobias himself. If I had, I would have appealed to Captain Denton to turn the ship around and sail back to harbour and, if he refused, I would have flung myself into the water and taken my chances on swimming to shore.

~

I thought I would share my observations on the character of Lord Edmundson as I perceived it. In an early section of the journal, Tobias makes some very gracious remarks regarding my character and, although I hardly recognise myself in his exceedingly kind assessment, I took considerable pleasure from his observation that my friendship had been a *benediction* to him and I have pleasure in confirming that his friendship was equally a benediction to me.

I was his shipmate for over four months and interacted with him on a daily basis, and throughout this period he remained excellent company: witty, jovial, learned and kind. He was a handsome man, tall, strong-limbed and graceful in his movements. Immensely well read, he could easily be mistaken for a quadruped for he had a foot in a number of different camps:

he was interested in botany and science, well versed in the latest discoveries and theories in the fields of palaeontology, geology and evolution; he was fascinated by philosophy, particularly the writings of Spinoza and Kant; he was a skilled linguist, read fluently in Latin and Greek, and was a passionate devotee of poetry and the novel – he could quote whole chunks of Blake, Coleridge and Keats. Incidentally, he prided himself on being no mean prose stylist, although, to my taste, he might be said to have very occasionally strived a little too hard for effect. As a man honoured to be considered his friend, I would say that on occasions he did not wear his learning lightly, but his lively and agile mind made him a valued conversationalist and doughty debating partner. He could occasionally be over-dismissive of the views of others and insensitive to, and largely oblivious of, the often unseen and unsung efforts of any person whose rank in life was below his. But what man alive does not have his faults? These minor blemishes can be seen as the attributes, I do not use the word *prejudices*, of many who enjoy an exalted position in society. Of his personal life, such as his recent estrangement from his wife, much discussed by the rumourmongers and tittle-tattlers who dissect the comings and goings of our social superiors like the haruspices who pored over the entrails of sacrificed animals in Ancient Rome, I will make no comment for Tobias never discussed such matters with me.

I have been asked for my opinion of Lord Edmundson's health and, in particular, his mental state. I did treat Tobias while we were both passengers on board HMS *Stockport* but the normal duties of confidentiality to one's patient can hardly be said to arise given that Tobias himself disclosed that he sought treatment from me for his migraines and, furthermore, he wrote openly in his journal about his mental state and his fears for his sanity. I am gratified that the medication I prescribed provided some relief from his headaches. Nothing is more satisfying to a physician than learning that his efforts to ameliorate the suffering of his patient have, to some extent, been successful. Of the bizarre and outlandish notions that came to increasingly prey on his mind, I saw no indication; he spoke to me of the Gorgon flower and his growing sense of anticipation and excitement as we sailed closer to our destination but I detected no lack of balance, no obsession, in his disquisitions on the subject.

Nevertheless, there is one decision he made for which I must censure him. I refer, of course, to his decision to proceed with the journey upriver with Mr McGuire and his men, even though we had been told a virulent flesh-infection was running amok in the locality and I myself, together with Captain Denton, had seen the horrifying effects of the disease. He should have deferred his departure for a couple of months. And yet I am not myself without some responsibility for the action he took. I was the doctor and it was incumbent on me to explain with sufficient force and clarity, with patience and understanding, the dangers he faced in not delaying his journey up the Jimbala River. Fearful that I might become an instrument of contamination, I shut myself away and failed in my duty, although I have speculated that even if I had the oratorical accomplishments of a Cicero I would not have prevailed against the wishes of Tobias, so determined was he to proceed. In any event, it was Tobias, and the other men who perished, who paid the price for any ineffectiveness on my part in this regard.

~

Tobias, Mr McGuire and the other men left HMS *Stockport* on Friday 19th July 1861. We did not see any of them again and received no news until Mr McGuire and a small bedraggled group of men reappeared on the flat-bottomed boats on the evening of Sunday 11th August 1861, twenty-four days after they had first set off. Besides Tobias and Mr McGuire, some thirty men had embarked on the boats upriver; only eight men accompanied Mr McGuire on his return to the ship, and two of those were infected and died within days of reaching HMS *Stockport*. The balance of the men in the party who on 2nd August had left Tobias on the lower slopes of Mount Taliboko expired on the trek back to where the boats had been left by the river. Fever and weakness preceded the awful gangrenous ravages to the body; once these sprouted on the flesh, death followed in a matter of two or three days. By then the afflicted were too weak to walk; they were left in the jungle dosed with laudanum, clutching whatever extra doses could be spared, slipping in and out of consciousness. They died in the rainforest, sometimes paired with another of the infected, often alone, thousands of miles from home. They are surely joined by Harris, Thomas and Tamworth, none of whom were ever seen again – in the case of Harris and Thomas, after leaving the expeditionary party; and, in the case of Tamworth, after fleeing Tobias following his slaying of Liscombe (although, of course, I only learnt of this horrific act when I read Tobias's journal later). It was a desperately tragic and harrowing business. I can confirm, though, that Captain Denton and I ensured that the families of all those who died received the payments due to them from the sponsors of the expedition.

The severity of the devastation inflicted by The Devil's Kiss (if I may use that popular designation) came as no surprise to me. In the days that followed the mooring of the ship and the disembarkation of the party, first one, then another and then a steady succession of bloated corpses floated past us in the river, heading towards the estuary and the sea. I knew not how the disease spread but I had never witnessed such a ferocious and unforgiving contamination before. That was when I realised that the disease appeared to spare the indigenous peoples of the region, for the bodies that floated past were all pale – graphic evidence of the extent of the devastation wreaked amongst the missionary community that ministered to the local population dwelling in the rainforest.

Once I was satisfied that no contagion had attached to me after my visit to the Mission Officer's hut, I took steps to quarantine the ship from the surrounding territory. The crew were forbidden to go ashore; all communications between those on the ship and those who lived at the river's edge took the form of sign language and the shouting of those few words understood by both sides; supplies of fruit and fresh water were deposited on the bank near where the ship had moored and only picked up by a crew member at night. Mr McGuire and the men who returned were quartered in a part of the lower deck sealed off from the rest of the ship, other than the two men who were suffering from the infection. Their final hours were spent stupefied with laudanum, lying on blankets and shaded by a small square of sail in a dinghy which had been lowered from the ship. When their merciful release came, both their bodies and the dinghy were burnt after a short service of commemoration led by Captain Denton.

After a period of ten days, with neither Mr McGuire nor any of his men showing any signs of infection, I deemed it safe for them to rejoin the ship's community. Notwithstanding the tragedy that had overtaken the expedition, it was a salutary day when I was able to shake Mr McGuire's hand and welcome him back. We then had to address the question of what action to take in relation to Lord Edmundson. Mr McGuire had related how, on reaching the area that Mr Jennings had outlined, the Gorgon flower was nowhere to be seen and, after three or four days of fruitless searching and facing an outbreak of the infection amongst the men of the expeditionary party, he had made the eminently reasonable decision to return to the ship. He further explained how Tobias had asked for two more days to carry on searching for the Gorgon flower and had asked Mr McGuire to spare him a couple of men to assist him in the event he did successfully locate the flower. Against his better judgement, Mr McGuire had acceded to both requests. On reaching the river, Mr McGuire was to wait a day to give Tobias time to catch up. If, after twenty-four hours, he had not caught them up, Mr McGuire would head downriver on the boats, leaving one behind for Tobias. In fact, Mr McGuire had waited for a day and a half for Tobias and then, with more of his men succumbing to the infection hour by hour, decided he could afford to wait no longer.

Later, Mr McGuire confided to me that he feared that, even with the addition of a couple of days of extra searching, Lord Edmundson would be reluctant to return to HMS *Stockport* without the Gorgon flower. He believed that Tobias had elevated discovering the Gorgon flower above all other considerations, even his own safety and that of the others in the party. For the two or three days before Mr McGuire's departure, Tobias had let slip he was suffering from headaches and fatigue (although Mr McGuire was keen to emphasise that these were not complaints on the part of Tobias; he was generally of a stoic disposition, hardly ever referred to the condition of his health and rarely gave any sign that he ever felt sorry for himself). Many of the other men had also complained of headaches and weariness at that time and Mr McGuire had put this down to the after-effects of the preceding strenuous days trekking through the jungle. In retrospect, he realised that these symptoms might instead betoken the initial stages of the infection. It was not unreasonable to assume that Tobias had succumbed to the dire disease and that he had lost his life as a result and that a similar fate had befallen Tamworth and Liscombe. Nevertheless, we could not know this for sure.

As we entered the second month following the expedition's departure date, the number of dead bodies floating downriver began to dwindle and then, one day, stopped altogether. Two weeks later a party of Dutch missionaries, who had been carrying on their proselytising activities upriver, passed by in a state of profound shock and abject misery: they told us that they believed they were a handful of the very few missionaries from the inland region who had survived the rampaging infection. They had strictly quarantined themselves for six weeks in a longhouse in a settlement they had established about fifty miles further north. They had had to ignore all communications, visits and entreaties for succour from other missionary communities and local tribespeople, who had turned up at the gate of their stockade. They too had observed that the local Dayak tribes seemed unaffected by the disease. They had successfully held the sickness at bay, but it had been a hard discipline for those whose Christian ministrations to the indigenous peoples served to demonstrate the superiority of their faith. But they had seen no signs of the infection for three or four weeks now: the terrible affliction had apparently disappeared, and the customs and practices of normal life were gradually, tentatively, re-establishing themselves in this savagely beautiful but remote part of the world. Although they had survived the infection they had not, perhaps, survived their sense that God had abandoned them to this horror; worse, in fact: He had allowed this terrible contagion to affect only those whose sole purpose was to spread the news of His gospel. They asked me why I thought this might be the case, but I of course had no answer for them.

Captain Denton, Mr McGuire and I debated earnestly the course of action we should adopt. So long as there was a faint chance that Tobias might still be alive, we felt it incumbent upon ourselves to return to where Mr McGuire had parted from him. We were also cognisant of the purpose of the expedition, although if the Gorgon flower had eluded discovery by Tobias and the first party there was no guarantee that the efforts of a second party would yield a different result. We could not ignore the weather in our deliberations, either: the wet season, when torrential rain would drench the rainforest for four or five hours a day, would start in just over a month's time, so it would be prudent if the purpose of the second expedition had been accomplished by then. After much dialogue we eventually came to a decision. Mr McGuire and I would head a group of no more than ten other men that would take two of the boats upriver and then retrace the footsteps of the first party. We aimed to be a smaller, nimbler version of the first expedition, which had been weighed down by the voluminous equipment that had been packed for it: Tobias's travelling chest, books and scientific instruments, and a writing desk, canopy and rugs for his tent; half-a-dozen terrariums; and enough equipment, food, spirits and water for a party of thirty-odd men for two months. This time, we restricted ourselves to two tents (Mr McGuire and I would sleep with the men) and only enough provisions to last a month. We assumed the terrariums transported by the first party would be where they had been left behind, but we brought one with us just in case they had disappeared or been damaged. The preparations did not take long and at dawn on Monday 7th October 1861, almost two months after Mr McGuire and the first party had reached the safety of

HMS *Stockport*, the boats were lowered again into the water and a second expeditionary party set off up the Jimbala River.

~

We pushed ourselves hard and made excellent progress. By the end of our third full day on the Jimbala River we had reached the spot where we were to proceed on foot through the rainforest. There was an exceedingly remote possibility that Lord Edmundson could still be alive and this, together with a desire to minimise our exposure to a rainforest which had so recently harboured a deadly flesh-ravaging disease, engendered a determination to insist on nothing less than the maximum effort our aching limbs and weary sinews could yield. The path hacked through the forest by the first party could be discerned in some places and we stuck to this where possible, but for long stretches the track was either overgrown or had disappeared. It had taken the first party just over six days to cover the ground from the river to the clearing where they established their camp – at the base of the gully on the lower slopes of Mount Taliboko, marked on Mr Jennings's map. We covered the same distance in just short of five days; it was close to four o'clock in the afternoon of Friday 15th October, the eighth day since we had left HMS *Stockport*, when we reached the outskirts of the clearing and Mr McGuire, lowering the kerchief from across his mouth, pronounced: 'We are here.'

Over the past couple of hours, thunderhead clouds had been stacking up in the sky, obscuring the sun and rendering the rainforest beneath the canopy a Stygian gloom. It was lighter in the clearing, but not by much. The air was heavy and still, the clearing silent except for the hoots coming from a troop of proboscis monkeys inhabiting the trees to the east. I could see a number of objects near the tree line on the far side of the clearing.

There was a dirty beige-coloured mound and, right next to it, a bush or plant of a type I had not encountered before, broad at the base and about four feet high, consisting of branches, tendrils and vines crisscrossing and winding around each other. A few feet away was a large flower close to the ground with bright yellow and red colouring that stood out in the dimness and tall tendrils projecting in the air. With a jolt I recognised the flower from the illustrations Tobias had shown me. Presumably it had flowered since Mr McGuire had departed: Mr Jennings had been correct all along. We had found it – but what about Tobias? Had he seen it as well?

As I came closer to the objects, I realised that the first was the remains of a tent, still pegged to the ground but with its canvas walls collapsed, torn in places and streaked with damp and dirt. The object in front of it was more mysterious: I had never seen a plant like it before. The branches and tendrils seemed to create a sort of lattice around a hollow interior – I caught a glimpse through gaps in the vegetation of something beneath, but they were not big enough for me to ascertain what was lurking beneath this cocoon of sorts. And then, as I stepped closer, and stood right in front of this plant-mound, I registered rather than distinctly saw the flicker of a movement through a slit in the encircling vines and branches. I turned to look more closely at where I sensed the movement had been. A human eye stared at me through the gap and as, I am not ashamed to admit, I screamed and staggered back, it unmistakably blinked not once but twice.

'Good God,' I cried, 'there's somebody in there!'

We fell to cleaving the entwining greenery with our knives and machetes. This proved exceptionally difficult as the stems were thick and fibrous: it was like trying to cut a ship-pulling hawser with a pocket-knife. We hacked and sawed and gritted our teeth as we did so and, agonisingly slowly, we were able to peel away the layers of tendrils and branches to reveal the outline of Tobias sitting at his portable writing desk. He was motionless, barely breathing, his flesh cold to the touch and a deathly grey with a viridescent tinge. His face was expressionless, his blinking eyes the only indication that he was conscious, albeit in a trance or stupor that rendered him insensible to our words of encouragement and exclamations of relief and delight that babbled out of us as we worked. As more and more of the vines that had enfolded him were cut away to reveal those that were wrapped directly around his body, I could see that these had, in a number of places, pierced his clothing, then his skin, burying themselves in his flesh. I cut away his tunic and breeches as much as I was able and, examining his body with greater scrutiny, I could see that these tendrils appeared to enter his body in some places and emerge from it in others. There was no blood attendant on these apertures and his skin was so translucent that I could see, in certain places, the ridged outline of the tendrils as they burrowed beneath his skin.

I ordered the men assisting me to desist from trying to disentangle him any further from his plant-like carapace as I feared that we were more likely to injure his body than liberate it if we continued. He sat at his desk, pinioned by the remaining tendrils, drained of life but somehow still subsisting, his rifle resting on his knees: a peculiar and profoundly disturbing vision. Parting his parched and cracked lips, I poured a few drops of water into his mouth from my canteen. I then listened to his heart: it was extremely slow and faint, the patter of tiny feet across a floor; the same with his pulse. His lips twitched and his mouth opened almost imperceptibly; was he trying to speak? I placed my ear next to his mouth so that his lips brushed my ear. He exhaled the faintest stir of air and I heard a murmur which some part of my brain interpreted as the word *release*.

I hastened over to my bag where I had packed a few of my medical instruments, extracted a surgical knife and doused the blade with spirits. Breathing deeply for a few seconds, I attempted to calm my frantic sensibilities and then, summoning all the exactitude I could muster, I applied myself to severing the tendrils at the point where they plunged into his body, taking care not to tug them or to tear his skin in doing so. It was an arduous and painstaking process but gradually, limb by limb, I was able to emancipate him from the plants that had infiltrated into, and fused with, his body. I noticed that his right foot and lower leg were swollen; when I slit his stocking and breeches, I saw that his foot, although free from contamination now, manifested signs of a previous infection. It was much eroded and there were gouges in the parts that remained; his toes had been worn down to fleshy nubs. But the skin covering the foot was newly grown like the slightly crinkly, shiny skin that grows over burns and cuts.

Once it was possible to do so, Mr McGuire and I picked Tobias up and laid him on a blanket on the ground, his naked body emaciated and pale green in hue, stippled and pocked by the insertions the tendrils had made, their green stubs, beaded with drops of a clear liquid, poking through the holes in some places. We placed another blanket on top of him and I knelt down, held his hand and placed my ear next to his mouth as he appeared to be trying to speak again. But all I heard were inarticulate, unconnected noises. After a short while, I thought the word he was whispering repeatedly was *home*, but that wasn't quite right and then I thought what he was murmuring was *not home*, but I don't know to what extent my imagination was conferring a meaning on the sounds he was making. Then his eyes closed and he started to shake. He began convulsing, which, after twenty seconds or so, escalated into a violent spasm which again lasted another twenty seconds or so before he abruptly stopped. His body then lay at peace and, although I couldn't be exact regarding the timing, he ceased breathing about a couple of hours later without regaining consciousness or murmuring any more sounds.

~

Once we had cleared away the debris of severed vines and tendrils which lay draped over his writing table and his canvas chair, I saw Tobias's journal lying open on the table. I flicked back through the last three or four entries. Tobias had contracted the flesh-consuming infection and, able to walk only with great difficulty, his water and food exhausted and operating under the influence of certain mental delusions, he had nevertheless been able to marshal his thoughts and write with a coherence and fluidity I doubt I could have matched even in possession of all my faculties. He had penned his last entry on 14th August 1861; his prose on that date for the first time seemed disordered and, on the cusp of death, he appeared to have given way completely to his fantasies regarding the Gorgon flower. Yet we had just found Tobias alive – barely clinging to life, but alive nonetheless – almost two months later. How on earth was that possible? I was at a loss to explain it. The position in which we found him suggested that he had not moved in all that time; how did he survive without access to water and food? Equally incomprehensibly, why had he not expired from the ravages of the infection? Not only had he survived weeks longer than anybody else who had fallen prey to this lethal condition, but the infection appeared to have been repelled, to have fled the body we had discovered.

I was to give these questions substantial thought over the following days and months. There was a possible, but unlikely, explanation lurking in the recesses of my mind – one that was so repellent to our current state of medical and scientific knowledge that I incarcerated it in a mental dungeon, denied it fresh air and sustenance and tried to ignore it, until, one day, it overpowered its gaoler, seized the keys and, unlocking the door, emerged, blinking, into the sunlight. Tobias had somehow been kept alive by the intervention of the tendrils and vines, the plants they emanated from, the rainforest itself. Plant sap had been introduced intravenously into Tobias and, somehow, the water and nutrients it contained had kept him alive. Furthermore, some chemical substance in the sap had blocked the spread of the infection and even rehabilitated or partially reversed the necrosis it had caused. When we had severed Tobias from the tendrils that had been keeping him alive, it was inevitable his death would shortly follow. If this bizarre and outlandish exposition approximates the truth, it is exceedingly difficult to contemplate the quality of life Tobias must have experienced for the past two months: I hope he did not suffer too much and was insensate most of the time.

I am only too aware how ridiculous and nonsensical these speculations must sound, particularly to the erudite and august readers of this volume. I do not say that I subscribe to them myself. I have never read or heard of anything similar occurring elsewhere, although I have searched subsequently. It is possible the natural world has powers and qualities we do not yet comprehend; the elapse of time will unlock the key to understanding them and it would be well for us, as doctors and scientists, to keep an open mind. One can see why prehistoric man believed fire to be a gift of the gods; electricity must seem like witchcraft to those uninitiated into its properties. An open mind, however, is not an excuse to jettison our rationality, our hard-won intuitive experience of the world.

Had Tobias died in a similar fashion in a civilised part of the world, I could have subjected the corpse to an autopsy, and speculation would have taken flight from a stoutly built citadel rather than a construction of paper and air. However, Tobias died in the heart of Borneo, thousands of miles from his home; even if I could have stayed the effects of death on Tobias's body, I would have recoiled from subjecting his corpse to the indignity of ferrying it back to the ship notwithstanding I could have carried out a rudimentary postmortem there. We buried Tobias in an unmarked grave, a few feet away from where we found him. Knowing that he abjured a belief in the Divinity, and aware of his boundless admiration for Mr Charles Darwin, I read out over the mound of freshly turned earth that marked his final resting place the final paragraph from *The Origin of Species*. The last sentence of that paragraph was a particular favourite of Tobias's; indeed, he quotes from it in his journal:

> There is grandeur in this view of life, with its several powers, having been originally breathed into a few forms or into one; and that, whilst this planet has gone cycling on according to the fixed law of gravity, from so simple a beginning endless forms most beautiful and most wonderful have been, and are being, evolved.

It is fitting, perhaps, that a level of uncertainty attends the cause of Tobias's death, for a similar uncertainty hangs over the causes and extent of his mental instability. If Professor Culverstone's theories are correct, then Tobias's fate was sealed by two events: his introduction to the Gorgon flower by his father, and his father's subsequent death in the fire which also destroyed the Gorgon flower. In his journal, his father's hallucination (in Shakespeare's age, he would have been treated as a ghost) referred to Mr Forbes-Haggard, his father's Head Gardener, as having started the fire himself in outrage, so it seems, at Tobias's father feeding human corpses to the Gorgon flower. Tobias's father, at one point, claims that Mr Forbes-Haggard's suspicions that the bodies of children were fed to the flower were not true. It is extremely difficult to read this section without a profound sense of unease. The notion of the former Lord Edmundson procuring human corpses as food for the Gorgon flower, let alone that this human fodder might have included the bodies of children, is arrant nonsense, pure and simple. What possessed Tobias to put these words into the mouth of his father, a man Tobias respected and revered all his life?

I put this question to Professor Culverstone, whose response, as ever, provided a rich intellectual feast to linger over. A part of Tobias, he opined, felt supplanted by his father's fascination with, and absorption in, the Gorgon flower. From being the adored centre of his father's universe, he was relegated to a part-player occupying a minor role. This generated a sense of resentment, not towards the object that had replaced him in his father's affections, but towards his father himself. This sense of grievance towards his father crystallised into a feeling of barely suppressed bitterness when his father, together with the Gorgon flower he cherished, was immolated. Tobias could never acknowledge this sense of betrayal, even hatred, towards his father: he thrust it deep down into a part of his mind where it festered unacknowledged for the most part and from where it occasionally surfaced in dreams and hallucinations. This explains the apparition of his father who, in his third and final manifestation, hinted both at how the monstrous appetites of the flower had been satiated and how the distribution of Liscombe's body parts might entice the Gorgon flower to appear.

Reflecting on Professor Culverstone's words, I am struck by the thought that of all the strange and exotic living organisms that sprout bright-coloured, wafer-frilled and spore-shaped from the soil, or of all the gelatinous, phosphorescent and bristle-toothed marine bodies dwelling in the deep oceans, or of all the legions of microscopic fleas, mites and spiders that Dr Hooke discovered churning and swarming in their countless multitudes beyond the reach of the human eye and which he so painstakingly illustrated in his *Micrographia*, nothing, absolutely nothing, is quite as strange and exotic as the human mind.

~

And what of the Gorgon flower? While I concede my select and cerebral readers may have weightier and more sophisticated matters to engage their time and interest, I would feel remiss in not relating what befell the specimen we encountered, so integral has the flower of which it is a representative been to the narrative that has filled these pages.

The terrarium we had brought with us was put to good use. We transplanted into it the Gorgon flower that grew near where we had found Tobias, and transported the specimen back to the ship, where it was stored above deck for the journey. Amongst Tobias's papers, in his cabin, were some notes regarding the conditions and nourishment which he considered best suited to ensure the flower survived, and indeed flourished, on the long sea passage across the oceans back to England. And flourish it did! By the time we were docking in Portsmouth, four and a half months after we had left Borneo, the glossy petals and endlessly waving tentacles of the Gorgon flower were straining against the glass walls of its temporary home.

I didn't know whether Mr McGuire was joking when he remarked, as we said our farewells on the dock, that he had never sailed into harbour in a ship so denuded of rats. In fact, I did meet Mr McGuire again. A month after we arrived home, he, Captain Denton and I were invited to the ceremony to welcome the Gorgon flower into the Royal Botanic Gardens, Kew, a function presided over by Sir Benjamin Collins Brodie, Baronet, President of the Royal Society. It was a splendid occasion and in the speeches over lunch the contributions of both the last and the penultimate Lord Edmundson were duly celebrated. The Gorgon flower can be found in the north-eastern corner of the eastern wing of the Palm House, growing in the lee of a fig tree. A plaque commemorating the role of Tobias and his father in discovering and rediscovering the flower was affixed to the nearby supporting pillar. A huge fanfare attended the induction of the flower into the gardens at Kew – a special report adorned the front page of *The Times*; a special edition of *The Illustrated London News* was printed; cartoons appeared in *Punch* – and this has generated widespread public interest. At the weekend, the queue of prospective Gorgon flower visitors snaked around the perimeter of the Palm House. I have taken to visiting the flower on a regular basis on Wednesday afternoons, when I am able to complete my medical duties by lunchtime, and when the crowds are less in evidence. I had resisted the charms of the Gorgon flower for some time, but now find myself intoxicated by its rippling, velvety mustard- and red-coloured petals, its sinuous, air-stroking tentacles and the oleaginous mucilage that pools in its green beating heart. I don't like to watch the sessions where small mammals are fed to the flower (this occurs twice on weekdays, three times at the weekend) but I do like to sit by myself watching the Wednesday afternoon visitors and the interest they take in the flower. I fancy I detect a particular animation on the part of the Gorgon flower's tentacles in the company of children, when they seem to stretch in their direction, as if in yearning for the young faces transfigured with awe and wonder. This, I am sure, is just my imagination playing tricks on me.

And as I bring my paper to a close I must share a disturbing report from last week's *Times*; I crave the indulgence of my audience if I relay this snippet of news. The Gorgon flower is gone: it has been stolen! There is a concavity in the soil at the base of the tree where it previously grew. The flower was *in situ* when the doors to the Palm House were closed after the last of its visitors had departed in the late afternoon of last Tuesday but had disappeared when the doors were opened the following morning. There is no evidence of forced ingress; the glass walls of the Palm House are intact; the authorities are quite baffled as to how it has been taken. One ought to hope that they secure its return swiftly.

I have, I am sure, overstayed my welcome – if welcome I ever had.

I remain, yours,

Percival James Louis Stanhope

Jacksi Packsi

1.

When I was young and I'd had a really bad day, like the day Melissa Tessevo put chewing gum in my hair at school, or the day the vacuum cleaner dismembered Bungo Bear, or the day Mother told me my teeth were going to be in braces for years and years, Nana would take a dab of Tiger Balm from her tiny red-gold pot and, as I sat next to her on the sofa, rub it into my right palm, running her finger round and round. This action was always accompanied by the stirring introduction to the third movement of Sibelius's Fifth Symphony, playing on the record player by the north-facing window in the sitting room. You'll know the piece: a glorious tune supposedly inspired by a gaggle of swans, wings beating majestically, that the composer witnessed take to the air. (Of course, back then, I didn't know who the piece was by – I was at the Konzerthaus Berlin some years later listening to a programme by Sibelius when I heard it again; I'd blinked furiously to thwart my eyes from sprouting tears.) As Nana's finger traced ever smaller circles on my palm and I breathed in the aroma of camphor and menthol, she would intone the same words over and over: *jacksi packsi, jacksi packsi, jacksi packsi.* The anointing of my hand with a chrism that to me smelt of winter, the chords that seemed to swell in my chest like an inflating balloon, the soothing effect of Nana's incantation: while these did not undo the originating event, they enabled me to look beyond it, to *put it into perspective* as people would say nowadays, and, in so doing, restore me to equanimity.

The sitting room was my favourite room in Nana's apartment; it was by turns my study, playroom, conservatory, art gallery and sanctum. A bookcase took up the entire height and breadth of one wall: a mosaic of black, dark blue, tan and white leather spines. The two bottom shelves nearest the window housed my well-thumbed favourites (including *The Midnight Folk*, *The Wind in the Willows*, *Anne of Green Gables*, the Narnia books; as I grew older, Jane Austen, *Jane Eyre* and *Precious Bane*). Nana assured me that these books were mine; she gave them a home only so I would not need to transport them to and fro. The sitting room occupied the corner of the apartment: windows on two sides looked down onto the university gardens where birch, elm and willow trees shaded gravel paths that skirted a tidy lawn. In the centre of the lawn stood a magnificent cedar, its lower branches sweeping the ground; as a child, I thought it looked like an oak tree flattened by a giant's fist. During the summer, students lay on the grass reading or chatting or stood throwing frisbees at each other, their voices and laughter floating in the air, merging with the distant drone of traffic and the chitter of birds to form a hazy aural backdrop; when winter came, the gardens emptied and sounds carried with a crisp precision: the dry, papery rustle of bare branches agitated by the wind; the scratch of crunching gravel as pedestrians trod the path; the muted sizzle of a downpour of rain. The apartment was owned by the university; Nana had occupied the rooms all the time she taught there. When she retired from teaching, she retained her professorship and this entitled her to continue to reside in what had been, for most of her professional life, her home.

Between the ages of eight, when Nana retired, and fourteen, I considered it, for long stretches, my home too. My mother was an internationally revered concert pianist (her stage name was Catherine Butatick: you may have heard of her) and she often toured while I was young – for example, when I was nine she spent two months in the US; when I was ten, six weeks visiting Asia. My father invariably accompanied my mother, in part because he was her manager and in part because the alternative would involve looking after me for weeks on end and that wasn't going to happen. Photographs aplenty show my mother in a satin evening gown, tall and elegant, standing next to my father in black tie. I am in none of them. Looking back, I wonder whether it wasn't rather selfish of my parents to impose on Nana, who would have been in her late fifties and sixties at the time she took care of me, a lively girl-cum-early-teenager. If there was ever any feeling that she was being taken for granted, then I never detected any trace: all I remember was the unreserved joy with which she would enclose me in a hug when my parents dropped me off on the way to the airport.

Each evening of a stay at Nana's followed a set ritual. First, I got to choose dinner. Nana never really cooked: *that paddle-steamer passed me by*, she would say. Eggs boiled or fried and served with toast occupied the entire sphere of her competency, although her pantry was always stocked with treats: Battenberg slices, panettone and sakotis tree cake, sourced from Angelino's, her delicatessen of choice. Dinner was ordered by phone and delivered to the door in sealed foil containers courtesy of Ghibertine's (Italian), L'Ancienne Cuisine (French) or Oszkars (Hungarian): anything originating east of a line drawn from

Riga in the north to Sofia in the south was too exotic for Nana's culinary tastes. Once the order had been placed, Nana would exclaim: *my granddaughter has come to visit me!* And, without anything more being said, extra servings of ice-cream, lemon mousse or túrógombóc would accompany our dishes. After dinner, we played cards, and Nana would play to win with adamantine determination. A battle of wills to rival Sherlock Holmes and Moriarty or Inspector Javert and Jean Valjean ensued, and if I triumphed, more often than not this was attributable to the decisiveness and nimble thinking of youth rather than any grandmotherly indulgence on Nana's part. Once my yawns surpassed the twenty-second mark (Nana actually deployed a stopwatch for this purpose), it was time for bed.

Every night, before brushing my teeth, Nana and I would wave good night to the Man Who Watched.

The front of the apartment, where our bedrooms were situated, overlooked the street that led to the university's main entrance; directly opposite our bedroom windows, across the road, was a row of three shops. There was a cigar lounge whose wood-panelled interior could be seen during the day; stencilled lettering on the glass advertised that loose tobacco and snuff could be purchased inside. Next to it was a shop that sold umbrellas; at night the umbrellas hanging in the window looked like rows of sleeping bats. On the corner was a university bookshop, with window displays of pyramids of books. There was a streetlight on the pavement in front of the bookshop and beneath this, day and night, staring always at the windows of Nana's apartment across the road, stood the Man Who Watched.

I have a memory of the first time I saw him although, as I would have been only eight at the time, I very likely imagined the encounter. It was between eight and nine in the evening and, it being autumn, night had fallen. The shops were shut up and dark, closed for the day. The man stood in the disc of buttery yellow light thrown by the streetlamp. He looked to be in his forties or fifties, short dark hair with a prominent parting on his left, angular nose, expressionless face, wearing a long dark overcoat and shiny black shoes. As Nana and I stood at my bedroom window, the man caught my eye. I raised my hand in greeting and the man stared back, unmoving, and I thought that it was too dark for him to see me. Then, just as I was about to turn away, he raised his hand and, his eyes still holding mine, nodded ever so slightly. Nana drew the curtains, the man disappeared from my view and I climbed into bed.

Nana told me the Man Who Watched made his first appearance just before she retired from teaching. Of course, it wasn't the *same* man all those years; according to Nana, he changed approximately every two years. Also, a different man undertook the evening and night shift; the man we were observing had only been standing there since nine o'clock that morning. The man stood there during the day, and then another stood at night, a silent, ever-watchful sentinel, occasionally taking a few steps either side of the streetlamp but never straying further – at least while Nana was home. Christmas Day, Easter Day, All Saints' Day, my birthday, Nana's birthday, *his* birthday: he was there; in winter when the sky was the colour of porcelain and the water in the gutters crusted with thick, cloudy ice like bacon rind; in spring when the blossoms frothed and trees wore their pastel-coloured frocks; in summer when the sun turned pale flesh the colour of strawberry jam.

He became such a familiar presence in my life that his vigil took on the aspects of the unremarkable and the quotidian, and my curiosity waned. It was not that Nana didn't acknowledge his presence (indeed, she would sometimes draw my attention to him so that, if I noticed him myself, I would not become alarmed), it was just that she did so in a low-key, unconcerned manner as if there was nothing out of the ordinary about him – as if everybody had a Man Who Watched (incidentally, the name I used shortly after he first appeared and which stuck thereafter).

He followed Nana at a discreet distance when she went out shopping (she treated herself to a new pair of shoes every two months, and a new book every week). When she had lunch with friends, he would stand across the street from the restaurant or, if it was raining and there was availability, take a table inside and, so Nana noticed, order only soup. When I stayed with Nana, there would be a weekly visit to the Science Museum (my choice: I loved the gigantic dinosaur skeletons, the trilobite fossils and the rows of shiny beetles as big as my fist) and a weekly visit to the Museum of Art (Nana's choice: she was inducting me into the history of art and grouped visits around particular periods; I remember it took us weeks to do the Romantic movement). From time to time, as I drank hot chocolate in the café beneath the skeleton of the titanosaurus suspended from the high vaulted roof, or stood mesmerised in front of a Jacques-Louis David, I sometimes became aware that the Man Who Watched was hovering a few feet away, silently observing us.

Later on, Nana told me that when the Man Who Watched first appeared, she had been alarmed and had contacted the police. When the police arrived, the man disappeared. When they left, he reappeared. This went on for a fortnight until the police became exasperated and asked Nana some searching questions about her eyesight and what would now be called her mental health. At no time, Nana said, did she feel threatened by the Man Who Watched; he was impassive, stolid, uncommunicative but never hostile or aggressive; there was no whisper of malevolence, quite the opposite, in fact – he exhibited a quiet, calm watchfulness.

Three weeks after the Man Who Watched first arrived, Nana went down to the street and, confronting him beneath the streetlight, asked him why he was watching her. The man looked at her and said nothing. But Nana told me that his eyes spoke to her and they said: *Please don't ask me that because I cannot tell you. Rest assured I mean you no harm. I am here to protect you.* After returning his stare for a while, Nana went back upstairs to her flat. The next day she made a flask of tea and carried it downstairs and tried to give it to the man but he refused to take it from her. This time his eyes said: *Please don't offer me this because I cannot take it. Please don't think me ungrateful, however, for I am not.* After that, Nana never spoke to the Man Who Watched or tried to give him anything. The most she did was give him a little wave from time to time from her window. After a few months, the man waved back – reluctantly, and with some hesitation, at first. Whenever I visited Nana and looked down at him, he'd not only wave, he'd even give me a slight nod.

2.

But who is he? Why does he watch you? Nana fobbed me off when I was young, made light of it, told me it was a service extended to certain special elderly persons: a confidential service, so I could never tell my father or mother about it. They only found out about the Man Who Watched when I was fourteen, when what happened happened. I think Nana had worked out who he was and why he was watching her long before I was fourteen, but she never shared that knowledge with me. After what happened, she couldn't tell me

161

and I had to work it out for myself. What I discovered later was so strange and frankly unbelievable that there were times when I didn't believe it, that I thought I had conjured, from my imagination, an elaborate, richly detailed façade like a baroque altarpiece bursting with gilt-encrusted cherubs, angels and saints.

To explain who the Man Who Watched was, I need to tell you about Nana's research. I don't understand most of it, never have, never will – but, over the years, I got to understand a little, enough not to be tripped up by my own ignorance but to work around it and not to give in to despair because of it. It's not easy to comprehend what Nana was studying, so be warned. If you want to skip ahead you will get no objection from me.

Nana was a mathematician. Not just any mathematician but one of the most brilliant of her generation (as they say). Internationally respected and admired, when she was only thirty-six she won the Fields Medal, probably the most prestigious award any mathematician can receive. She was the first woman to do so and only one of two women to have ever won it. Applied mathematics was her field: the application of mathematics in the service of science, technology and engineering. Nana applied her mathematics to physics, in particular quantum mechanics, which is the study of atoms and subatomic particles, what they are and how they operate. This is a fiendishly complex topic which has exercised the minds of great physicists, including Albert Einstein, over the past one hundred years or so: I am not going to say much more about this area (and your relief is nothing compared with mine) except to explain that it was through working on the equations that model the quantum behaviour of subatomic particles that Nana found the mathematical basis for, first, alternative dimensions and, secondly, parallel universes.

Whoa, hang on, I hear you saying, *alternative dimensions, parallel universes, are you kidding me?* But I'm not, believe me, and I can quote in my defence a phalanx of immensely eminent, world-renowned physicists. You see, subatomic particles, the very basic foundation of all matter, behave in a very odd manner, acting as both a wave and a particle, both existing and not existing, being seen and not seen, at the very same time. Not only that, a subatomic particle can become 'entangled' with another one – they briefly become the same particle – even though they are feet apart! We're talking zeptoseconds here, a trillionth of a billionth of a second, but still. The upshot of all this is a realisation that the elementary building blocks of everything we see behave in an utterly incomprehensible manner.

Physicists have deployed the concepts of alternative dimensions and parallel universes to try to make sense of these mysteries, in what have been called thought-experiments. Mathematics has also assisted in providing a conceptual framework for the better understanding of quantum phenomena. But what Nana did was to extend the mathematical models that had been devised to map the behaviour of subatomic particles to these very weird, theoretical notions of additional dimensions and realities. She demonstrated that the mathematics worked, that by building on these hypothetical constructs not only did the maths go some way to explicating some of the more bizarre behaviour of subatomic particles, but that it also proved the existence of alternative dimensions and parallel universes – or multiverses, as they are called. As far as I was concerned, the most brain-shattering thing about all this was that this was discovered by Nana, who really didn't like losing three successive games of Go Fish and who sang Cher's 'Gypsys, Tramps & Thieves' in the bath at night. My Nana, who knew how to restore my spirits with the ritual intonation of *jacksi packsi*.

As you can appreciate, the mathematics we are talking about here was so mind-numbingly complex that only a handful of people would be capable of understanding it. And I mean *literally* a handful. When I was around seven, Nana organised a seminar. To be eligible to attend, one needed to solve a particular mathematical problem included in a letter sent only to a small number of the most brilliant mathematicians working in that field. Only seven recipients of that letter successfully solved the equation and sent the correct answers back to Nana: in return, they received an invitation to the seminar. It was to those seven mathematicians that Nana presented her mathematical proofs. Other than Nana and those seven mathematicians, no one knew about the existence of this seminar at the time, let alone the details of what was discussed.

Imagine, if you can, the aggregate intellectual firepower of the seven mathematicians (eight including Nana) assembled to hear Nana explain her equations and their implications for our understanding of reality and to discuss the question of whether, with the existence of alternative worlds and dimensions having been demonstrated, the mathematics would enable you to access them. Imagine the seven men (yes, they were all men: Nana's achievement was all the more remarkable given that academic high-end mathematics was pretty much an exclusively male enterprise) sitting before Nana, in a university seminar room surrounded by blackboards covered with scribbled equations indecipherable to you or me, thrilled to hear, first-hand, the limits of mathematical knowledge being dismantled and reassembled in an entirely new place.

Because now we get to the crux of the matter. Six of those seven mathematicians disappeared from the face of the earth in the twelve months following Nana's seminar. Simply vanished, as if plucked out of existence by an invisible hand. Of all the persons in attendance at the seminar, only Nana and Professor Louis Simovanner were present and accounted for in the world on the date of its first anniversary. Of course it was many years later before the connection between the disappearances and Nana's seminar was established. But this connection explains the Man Who Watched, who took up his post a few weeks after that anniversary. He was there to protect Nana, to stop what had happened to the other attendees at the seminar also happening to her.

3.

I only pieced all this together as an adult. When I was a child, the Man Who Watched barely impinged on my consciousness; if, from time to time, I became aware of him, it was of a constant reassuring presence like a character from a favourite book you read twice a year. When I recall those years of my childhood, what stands out to me now is how my happy remembrances, my positive experiences, are all associated with my stays with Nana. It's like one of those avant-garde films from the late sixties or the seventies that are shot in black and white but then switch to Technicolor for certain scenes: in an otherwise monochrome existence, my weeks with Nana glowed in my memory with joyous colours.

Because of the unyielding demands of the international classical music concert circuit, my mother and father were often away for my birthday in April. To celebrate my birthday, Nana took me to the ballet at the Opera House one year, to a famous musical the next, to the Moscow Circus the following year.

When I turned fourteen, we went to see *A Midsummer Night's Dream*. After the performance, we visited Caravaccio's for supper, a glamorous bistro with dark mahogany panelling, deep red upholstery, enormous mirrors and, either side of the entrance, gas lamps which flared blue and purple. I wore a blue mulberry-silk dress Nana had bought me for my birthday; it made me look taller and when I saw my reflection in a mirror as we made our way to the table, I didn't recognise the slim, pale young woman towering over Nana. The young waiter who brought the menus told me how beautiful I was; I blushed and, once he had departed, giggled uncontrollably. Nana looked at me sternly and told me that an intelligent woman had to *learn how to receive a compliment*. It was a lovely evening and, over the years, its lustre hasn't faded.

Christmas and New Year's was also a busy time for international concert pianists. When I was very young, my parents would come back from wherever my mother was performing over the festive period (I guess whichever place paid them the most) and at least spend Christmas Day with me, but by the time I was eight, they stayed put on the grounds that shuttling backwards and forwards was incredibly tiring. Needless to say, this was a win-win outcome for me as I got to spend the whole Christmas period with Nana, undisturbed by interregnums at my parents'.

A highlight of the Christmas festivities were the annual drinks Nana threw in her apartment for her friends, colleagues and students. The bar staff were drawn from Nana's favourite undergraduates, who served mulled wine and mince pies as a prelude to Nana's infamous Christmas cocktail (recipe by request only). I was always allowed to stay up until most of the guests had departed: seventy or eighty bodies crowded into the apartment generated a lot of noise, so this was evidence of Nana's pragmatism as much as a temporary abandonment of her duties *in loco parentis*.

The younger the guest, the more likely I was to be treated as if my age was the most important thing about me. Nana's graduates were friendly but often a little patronising, greeting me with questions along the lines of what I was hoping to get for Christmas. Nana's fellow professors, however, had perfected the art of appearing to treat me as an intellectual equal. At the last Christmas drinks I attended, I remember Professor Simovanner turning to me, after I had joined a group listening to him hold forth, and asking me, in all seriousness, what I thought of the government's policy of reforming the structure of university finance; what's more, he seemed interested in my reply, leaning forward to listen over the noise of the party, and although I feared my reply lacked both detail and originality, he gave the impression that my contribution to the debate was both considered and valuable.

In case you're inclined to read between the lines, let me fill that space right up: Professor Simovanner was my favourite of all Nana's colleagues. The only member of Nana's department who hadn't been tutored by her as an undergraduate and then graduate, he had applied for the post of Assistant Professor to Nana about six months before she hosted her fateful seminar. He was therefore the most senior academic in the mathematics department besides Nana, although a good thirty years younger than her, and stepped up to the position of Professor when she retired. *My darling boy*, she referred to him, a term of affection, albeit adjusted for gender, that she otherwise bestowed on only me. He had the wind-tanned, mildly crinkled looks of a professional golfer; in Nana's words he had *a mind faster than a food blender*.

But I was telling you about Christmases with Nana. Christmas Day followed the same pattern. We would walk to the cathedral for morning service, trailed by the Man Who Watched, who, sadly for him, was also the Man Who Had To Work On

Christmas Day. Against the soaring grey pillars of the nave and the intricately carved choir screen, the ministers, in their brightly jewelled vestments, busied themselves in self-important ceremony, all of which Nana revered. She particularly adored carols, which she played on her record player all year round. As regards God, she kept an open mind, telling me she had never yet found *a God-shaped gap* in her equations but that it was still possible, albeit unlikely.

Back in the apartment, Nana would heat up the Christmas lunch delivered that morning from the Grand Ambassador Hotel and set it out on the big table in the dining room while I spoke with Mother and Father on the phone from Geneva or Madrid or Reykjavik or wherever they were. Afterwards, if it wasn't raining, we went for a walk that took us down to the river, where we watched the sheet-like flow of water transformed by the weir, in an instant, into a cascade of dirty-white foam. There were few people about and we enjoyed the silence – the roads and gardens were deserted except for the two of us and, following ten yards or so behind us, like a recalcitrant child, the Man Who Watched. Even the robins and chaffinches seemed subdued, motionless for the most part, dotting the bare branches like musical notes on a stave. I pitied the birds; imagine not knowing it was Christmas Day, not waking up in the morning eager with anticipation; imagine inhabiting an existence where every day was the same. When the light began to leach from the sky and gather in tangerine and pink bands that glowed through the fretwork of bare branches, we turned round and retraced our steps home, to the magical sitting room and my favourite part of the day, the giving and receiving of the presents lying in wait for us at the foot of the tree.

You might think Nana's approach to gifts would be influenced by being an eminent mathematician, that she might buy me a personalised abacus handcrafted from wood collected from a Peruvian beach, or my very first electronic calculator with multicoloured buttons but nevertheless still possessed of the computational capacity of a small planet. Or a microscope, an astrolabe, a set of books by Richard Feynman, a case of fossilised ammonites, a sliver of the meteorite which struck Bechlyavod in Siberia in 1955. You'd be right: over the years, she bought me all of these things. But she also bought me a Build Your Own Theatre Kit, a make-up bag (with make-up inside), roller skates, a succession of Italian leather shoes, an album by Diana Ross and Marvin Gaye, and a computer game playable on the television. And much more besides.

What did I give Nana in return? When I was young, although I bought what I thought she'd like, what I really bought was what I thought I'd like if I were her. Slippers fashioned in the shape of two kneeling puppies; a tote bag from the Museum of Art made of a patchwork of images taken from the paintings in its collection; a paperweight like a cube of Arctic ice enclosing a mastodon tooth (my favourite). Nana gave no indication of being anything other than utterly delighted with these gifts. When I reached the heady age of eleven, possessed of the beginnings of a maturity that I neither deserved nor knew what to do with, these gifts seemed amateurish and self-indulgent. In their place, I endeavoured to buy what I believed Nana might purchase for herself, which involved me noting any expression of affection or admiration she made towards potential presents in the run-up to Christmas. This strategy generated a collection of gifts which were possibly more closely aligned with Nana's tastes and interests, although I was conscious that they were also imbued with an element of worthiness and that, in consequence, something had been lost from my gifts of earlier years. A two-volume guide to English church music. A cashmere cardigan in cobalt blue. A boxed set of albums of Thomas Tallis pieces. A trio of bonsai trees in a clay dish of burnt sienna. You see what I mean?

Of course, looking back, none of these items, howsoever thoughtfully selected and carefully wrapped, came close to being the greatest gift I gave to Nana. She had been an only child; there were complications with her birth and my great-grandmother was unable to have further children. In turn, my father was Nana's only child, the fruit of an affair between a twenty-seven-year-old Nana and a visiting academic from New York, who, after a twelve-month sabbatical to Nana's university, returned to his wife, leaving Nana to face the first major emotional crisis of her life alone. It was imperative to banish the vivid images she retained of him: if it did not fall to Nana to have her lover in person, she was certain that the only memories of him she could endure were those provoked by the features and mannerisms of her son. In fact, once born, her son displayed little trace of his paternal origins and Nana found the conscious discardment of all recollections of her former lover partook more of an act of mental filing than an epic emotional struggle. Nana never married in later life. Being an only child myself, there was a certain streamlined angularity to our family tree through recent generations.

My fiercest critic would, I think, acquit me of the charge of vanity and, hopefully, of sentimentality. When I grew older I wondered whether my centrality to Nana's life owed as much to an absence of other candidates for her affection as to any inherent lovability on my part. But there is little point, or satisfaction, in thinking along these lines and I berated myself for doing so. It is also possible that my ignorance of her work and standing in the international community of mathematicians, my indifference to the renown that steadily accreted around her name, may have been one of the qualities that endeared me to her.

Although it is an accepted wisdom that mathematics is a young person's game and that mathematicians do their best work when young, a survey of eminent practitioners throws up numerous examples of mathematicians still conducting brilliant and productive work in their forties and fifties. Nana would undoubtedly be included amongst this number: it was widely accepted that Nana did her most original and coruscating work in her fifties, particularly in the three to four years preceding her retirement. The longevity of her creativity, a prodigious work ethic tied to a most unacademic absence of ego, her femininity, even her stature – she was a little over five foot in height – all marked her out as *sui generis* amongst mathematicians. In a field populated by earnest, anxious, sometimes haughty young men, Nana embodied qualities which, if not the exact antithesis, were certainly distinctive.

I later asked many people what Nana was like as a mathematician – mostly those who had been graduate students or junior researchers when I was a child and were now established figures in mathematics and physics departments at universities all over the world. I came across fierce admiration, trenchant loyalty and undimmed affection as well as a fair amount of hard-to-disguise exasperation at the difficulty in explaining in lay terms the intricacy of her intelligence. *Most great mathematicians are like lions*, I recall one female mathematician explaining to me over coffee in her university canteen (she told me that Nana had been her friend, mentor and boss, in that order), *mighty beasts, they can conceive of nothing higher than themselves in the intellectual food chain, tearing apart ill-thought-out theorems with their terrifying teeth.* But Nana was different, she said, *she soared like a bird high above the intellectual savannah, indifferent to the frothing meat-show playing out far below her. She really did inhabit a different element, looked at things from a different perspective.* Another person I spoke to commented on *her immense humility in the face of the great mystery at the heart of quantum mechanics, a humility that energised rather than immobilised her.* One of Nana's favourite sayings was *just because something is unbelievably strange doesn't mean it can't be true,* an approach she no doubt put into practice in working on the mathematics of quantum mechanics.

But when she retired at sixty, when I was eight, she not only took leave of the rigours of academic teaching, assessment and administration, she also took leave of the pursuit of mathematics itself and ceased working on her theorems and equations. Although she would occasionally retreat to her study for a couple of hours in the morning, I saw little sign of ongoing intellectual activity when I stayed with Nana.

The mention of a study conjures up book-lined shelves, angle-poise lamps, a desk cluttered with papers, mounds of folders tottering on intermittently dusted surfaces; a cave-like refuge for the mind. But Nana's study was a light, open space, with nothing but an empty desk, a chair on rollers and a single bookcase containing a few papers. Blackboards were fixed to a couple of the walls, frequently covered with equations and formulae, a language incomprehensible to all but a tiny elite, although, after Nana had retired, they were nearly always blank. No pictures or other personal items detracted from what was a rigorously impersonal space, except for a large black-and-white print next to the bookcase: a photograph showing a small boy, wearing an overcoat, knee-length socks and a cap, a satchel over one shoulder, holding up his hands in the universal gesture of surrender while in the background a German soldier, holding a machine gun, looks in the direction of the camera. The boy is no more than seven or eight years old. He is frightened and on the verge of tears. Later, I realised this image was cropped from a famous photograph (I'm sure you would also recognise it) depicting a scene from the Warsaw Ghetto uprising in 1943: a group of Jewish men, women and children being forced out of a bunker where they have been hiding by a group of Nazi soldiers, overseen by SS-Rottenführer Josef Blösche, the soldier holding the machine gun. The man who headed up the SS in Warsaw and the man who took the photograph are known. Not so the boy. He remains nameless. Various candidates have come forward claiming to be the child but his identity has never been conclusively determined; most of the survivors of the uprising either were summarily executed or perished in Treblinka or Majdanek. This was the only image that Nana had allowed before her when she had tirelessly formulated, tested and re-tested her equations, when she had tried to construct the mathematics that would explain how the veil between this universe and others could be pierced.

A person's age, gender, race, sexuality or religious beliefs (if any) were not a matter of complete indifference to Nana, but they formed no part of Nana's assessment of that person's worth. To confuse an attribute with the essence of an individual would have been a category error in Nana's eyes, an error that undermined your ability to truly understand that individual and interact successfully with her or him. Nana's working hypothesis was that most people were fundamentally good; if not, there was usually a reason for it and even if there wasn't, it didn't absolve you from your obligation to be good in your dealings with them. *It's better to be kind than right*, Nana said, an odd thing for a mathematician to say, but I knew that Nana wouldn't want to uncover a parallel universe where that didn't hold true.

4.

I was fourteen when they came for Nana. She disappeared in the second or third week of January: it's difficult to know exactly, disappearing being more of a process than a specific event. We'd spent the most wonderful Christmas and New Year together and then I returned to my parents and to school. I heard on the twenty-second of January, a bitterly cold day. Second period, I was called out of my English lesson (we had been studying *Great Expectations*) to find my mother and father waiting for me in the corridor outside my classroom. They stood there awkwardly, side by side, my father twisting his gloves in his hands with such force his knuckles flashed white. For the first time in a long, long time I was pleased to see them for I knew instinctively that Nana had gone. I let them both hold me and I held them back.

The next day the police came to visit us. Detective Inspector Peters, a polite, very tall man in his thirties, was accompanied by Detective Constable Hardcastle, a youngish woman who, letting DI Peters do most of the talking, looked around at the lounge room where the meeting took place. I remember DI Peters folding his immensely long legs into the narrow space between his chair and the coffee table, while I sat between my parents on the sofa opposite, each of them holding one of my hands. He explained that Nana hadn't been seen since I had departed from her apartment on the sixth. That in itself wasn't unusual; Nana might not leave her apartment for periods of two or three days, particularly when it was cold. Lydia, her cleaner, had called on the telephone a couple of times to ask Nana whether she should bring anything in with her when she next visited, but on both occasions the phone rang out. When Lydia did turn up she found the door to Nana's apartment ajar. Within a minute she had determined two things: Nana was not in her apartment and there was a dead body lying on the hallway floor.

At that stage, the doctors hadn't ascertained whether the man had died from natural causes or had been killed; they were still investigating. There were no wounds or other visible signs of trauma to the body, although there had been some damage to his internal organs. The police did not know who he was; he hadn't come up on any of their databases. The only photograph they had of him was the one taken shortly after his body had been discovered, so they were sorry but they were going to show me the picture of a deceased person and ask me whether I knew or had seen the man before. *Was that alright?* Before either my mother or father could say anything I nodded and said *yes*.

The man's eyes were closed in the photograph but I thought they had been brown in colour, although I couldn't be certain given the distance from the window of my bedroom in Nana's flat to where he had usually stood by the streetlamp. He had nodded and raised his hand, as usual, in acknowledgement of my goodbye wave, the day I had taken leave of Nana. *I don't think I have ever seen him before*, I recall saying, and my instant decision to lie surprised me. I thought I had uttered the words with conviction, so I was taken aback when DC Hardcastle whipped her head around from her perusal of the montage of family photos on the wall opposite to look at me steadily for a few seconds before turning to her colleague. Other than shouting it through a megaphone she couldn't have made it clearer to everybody else that she thought I was lying.

After they had gone, my parents continued to hold my hands. My mother kissed the top of my head. *It's all about helping Nana now, wherever she is*, she said, and I began to cry. When she asked if we should ask the police to come back, I nodded my head miserably.

And that was the start. As I heard myself tell DI Peters and DC Hardcastle about the Man Who Watched, as I described, in terms barely befitting a fourteen-year-old, his constant, steadfast vigilance, I realised that what was entirely commonplace to me must appear a strange and sinister surveillance to others. Allowance was made for my age – I was eight when the Man Who Watched first appeared – and not one of the many people my parents and I subsequently spoke to ever gave the slightest suggestion that they thought it odd that I hadn't mentioned the Man Who Watched to my parents, or to anybody else for that matter. After DI Peters and DC Hardcastle, we spoke with a succession of other police officers of increasing seniority, sometimes at home, sometimes at the large police headquarters in the city centre. Our final meeting was in an anonymous office in a government building with an elderly gentleman who didn't appear to be a policeman at all; he was never introduced to us as such. Of all the people we spoke to he was the only one who had heard of my mother, shyly asking for her autograph at the end of our session with him.

The interviews yielded the same questions and elicited the same responses. *Did Nana ever appear threatened by the Man Who Watched?* Never. *Did she ever appear afraid?* No. *Did she ever speak to the Man Who Watched, give him anything?* Never. *Did she ever give you an explanation for his presence?* Not really. *How many of the Men Who Watched did you see through the years? Can you describe them? Did they ever look foreign to you?* An older and wiser interviewee might have thought of qualifying her answers along the lines of: *not so far as I am aware, never in my presence, not while I was staying with her,* but the absolutist nature of my replies conveyed the certainty of my views at that time. Now that a decade and a half in real time but aeons of lived experience have elapsed, I sometimes interrogate the certitude of my fourteen-year-old self. Nana's attitude to the Man Who Watched led me to assume that the Man Who Watched's purpose was protective and his intentions benign. I didn't doubt that then and I know it to be the truth now, but I have also wondered to what extent Nana suppressed any indication of the fear she must surely have lived under so as not to frighten me. I have also asked myself at what stage did she become aware that, other than Professor Simovanner and herself, each and every one of the attendees at the seminar she had arranged had, one by one, vanished within twelve months of her retirement?

I was shown endless headshots of middle-aged men, so many that my eyes ached and the photographs blurred, but, other than the photograph of the protector who had died, I didn't see a Man Who Watched amongst any of them. I was asked to describe the Man Who Watched in his various incarnations and shown sketches based on my remembrances. Some of these drawings approximated the faces I recalled but I have no idea what was done with these pictures, of what value they were. The police never did identify the Man Who Watched – any of them.

Although I frequently expressed my belief in the benevolence of the Man Who Watched, my views were treated with some scepticism by the police. In so far as I could intuit their thinking, they believed that Nana had shielded me from the potentially threatening and possibly unsavoury nature of these silent watchers. Besides, I was a fourteen-year-old girl: what could I know about these things? But they had no answer to the question why Nana, after initially asking the police to investigate, had lived under the diligent gaze of these sentinels for a little over six years without ever reporting them to the authorities or challenging them.

I know now that the Man Who Watched dedicated his waking hours to guarding Nana against the same fate that had befallen the missing mathematicians. And even at fourteen, when my awareness of those missing mathematicians was hazy, I understood that he had died or been killed (uncertainty lingered over which was correct) in the unsuccessful execution of his duties. To devote your life to protecting someone and to fail in your task and then to perish in doing so – there was something about this that my teenage self struggled to identify, to name; it pressed on my chest when I tried to organise my thoughts about it. I said the words *selflessness* and *heroic sacrifice* to myself; they sounded appropriate but had no connection to the suffocating feeling I felt; the words lay inert on my tongue. I remembered the eyes of the Man Who Watched, standing on the corner, looking up at the window as Nana and I looked down at him. It was never kindness I saw in those eyes and I now understand why; but, looking back, I believed I recognised decency, a sense of purpose and determination. Did I also detect a resigned awareness that, when the time came, his efforts might not be enough to save Nana, or was that just my imagination, retrospectively conjuring up something that wasn't there?

As I grew older I increasingly divided my life into two phases – *With Nana* and *Post-Nana*. I often asked myself what my life would have been like had Nana not disappeared. But I was incapable of answering that question meaningfully. I had only one life, the life I led, and in that life my grandmother vanished when I was fourteen, never to be seen again. To imagine a life in which Nana had stayed with me was like imagining a life in which I had brothers and sisters, the ability to play a musical instrument, my own dog, a hare-lip. An intellectual exercise only with no ability to deform or enhance my heart. There may have been a parallel universe somewhere in which Nana continued to live in her apartment, continued to grapple with her equations while staring at the terrified face of the little Polish boy who may or may not have survived the concentration camps, continued to softly chant *jacksi packsi, jacksi packsi* while Sibelius swelled in the background and she rubbed ointment into my palm to soothe me every time I had my heart broken or my hopes crushed (oh so many pots of Tiger Balm!), but that was not a universe inhabited by me, the *me* writing this, and to imagine such an alternative universe really was, for *me*, the epitome of an arid cognitive process.

In the universe I inhabited, my mother retired from the life of a concert pianist, cashed in her frequent flyer miles and, father in tow, settled down to look after me. The first thing she did was spend a continuous period of longer than a month at home and, after that, I'm pleased to say things got easier for all of us.

5.

I first met Hilary Dutton not long after I turned twenty-eight. She already had quite the reputation as an investigative journalist, working in the upper middlebrow to highbrow reaches of the media. She had done a piece recently on an object that had hit the earth from space, landing in a remote part of the Australian outback, which I had read with interest. Too small to be an asteroid but too large to comfortably be a meteorite, the object had been shrouded in mystery. Witnessed by a handful of locals (they had described seeing something *hurtling through the sky* followed by an *enormous blinding white flash* like a giant magnesium flare), the mulga scrub had been scorched to skeletal shadows for acres around the estimated impact site. What was even more striking was the response of the authorities; they denied anything unusual had happened, dismissing what people had seen as lightning magnified by atmospheric disturbance and the blackened vegetation as the result of a bushfire. This approach was at odds with the presence of a unit of white-suited scientists, ferried by a fleet of Sikorsky helicopters, who materialised at the location within twenty-four hours of the collision and who cordoned off the area and appeared to spirit away the detritus from whatever had hit the earth. Hilary Dutton explored all this in one of the weekend broadsheets, in an article that was intelligently questioning of the official line while avoiding sensationalism. So I was a little surprised, but then at the same time not, when she called to ask if she could meet me to discuss my grandmother's disappearance as she was writing a book about it.

I had just obtained tenure at the university where I had carried out a couple of years of postdoctoral research; I had my hands full with lecturing, supervising a number of doctoral theses and finishing off my book on the Köningswittle Circle, which was effectively my PhD thesis repackaged (for which read, *spiced up*) for publication by the university press. Spicing up the Köningswittle Circle, a movement of Scandinavian philosophers, physicists and scientists who were active in the 1920s and 1930s, was, frankly, proving a challenge and I had missed two deadlines for handing over the completed manuscript. I was at my desk in my one-bedroom flat in the university area, revising my chapter on the 1924 meeting in Geneva between Bertrand Russell and Caspar Schand (perhaps the most well-known of the circle), when she called.

Hilary told me she had been given my phone number by a mutual friend. She knew I had never spoken publicly about my grandmother before, refusing to answer queries or requests for interviews. She understood and indeed respected this but she, nevertheless, would like to meet me. She had, she went on rather breathlessly, perhaps fearing I would put the phone down on her, been investigating on and off for a couple of years not only Nana's disappearance but also the disappearances of a group of mathematicians which had occurred over a twelve-month period six years previously. She was in possession of other information that I would find interesting too – in short, a genuine two-way flow of intelligence to our mutual benefit.

Nice try, I said, putting the phone down on her after thanking her (Nana would not have approved of me being rude).

Two months passed before I heard from her again. During this period, I finally finished my manuscript and submitted it. I had been so focused on my work that I had forgotten all about her call, so that when one afternoon, after meeting some friends for lunch, I got back to my flat and found a thick grey envelope with her name on the reverse propped against my door, for a few seconds I wondered why she had contacted me.

The envelope contained a five-page précis of the book she was working on, selected chapters in draft and a letter. In the letter, she apologised for sending me so much material and made the point that she was entrusting me with work that no one else had seen yet (not even her publisher); this was proof of her desire to collaborate with me, to share the information we had. *I'm going first*, she was saying, *look at what I have discovered*. I sat down on the sofa and stared at the letter in my hand. Feeling the weight of the package of papers on my knees, I wondered whether I had lost more than I had gained by deciding that uncovering the truth about Nana had to be a solitary endeavour on my part, uncontaminated by the half-hearted, ill-informed efforts of others. So I made some coffee, took the papers to my desk and began to read.

At that time I was familiar, in a rather vague way, with the narrative of the disappearances, but Hilary Dutton had fleshed out her account with surrounding context and descriptive detail that were novel to me. Around twenty-one years ago, six of the most eminent mathematicians in the world had disappeared within a twelve-month period. An incredible, unbelievable coincidence? Surely not. Shortly after the last of these mathematicians had vanished, Nana retired from academic life. Six years after retiring, Nana herself disappeared. In not one of these cases did the missing person ever reappear, nor was his (or her) dead body ever recovered.

The first mathematician to vanish into thin air was Professor Ben Cantor, while he was returning home from the seminar (this wasn't known at the time: Hilary only established this later). Eyewitnesses saw him getting into a taxi at the railway station in Oxford, where he was the Emeritus Cornel Slope Professor of Mathematics. He never arrived at the university and the taxi he got into was never traced. A couple of months later, Dr Ajai Narasimhan, who taught at MIT, disappeared while taking a weekend break in New York with his wife. They had just finished a meal at their favourite bistro in Brooklyn and his wife had gone to the ladies' room while he settled the bill. When she returned to the table her husband had gone: she never saw him again. No one had seen him leave the restaurant after he had paid, and his coat and scarf had been left in the cloakroom.

So it went on. Luciano Altemezzer, who held a professorship (but didn't do much teaching) at UCLA, didn't return from a ramble in Malibu State Creek Park, although his dog did a couple of days later in a distressed state. Daniel Zhang, the Frederick Herschmeyer Professor of Mathematics at Princeton, was last seen leaving a juice bar on campus late one Friday afternoon. He didn't turn up for a graduate class the following Monday morning. In his cottage in downtown Princeton, the weekend papers were found spread out over the sofa and a cold, barely touched cup of coffee sat on a side table. At thirty-three, he was the youngest to vanish. Anton Oligoski, Professor of Mathematics at the Institut des Hautes Études Scientifiques in France, was in Moscow when he went missing. He had flown there to receive a prize from the Mathematical Society of Moscow and had hired a car at the airport to drive to his brother's apartment in the Arbat. He never arrived. A couple of days later, his hire car was found abandoned by the side of the road on the other side of the Garden Ring. Finally, almost twelve months after the first disappearance, Timothy Wellenburg, Professor at Stanford, vanished from a rented villa in Bali where he had been enjoying a short break after attending a conference in Singapore. He had been seen by his female companion leaving through the patio doors of his bedroom to take the short path down to the sands – a two-minute journey, if that – but he appeared to have never made it to the beach. Like the others, he seemed to dissolve into thin air: one moment there, the next gone; suddenly, without any evidence of forced abduction. Flies have been plucked out of the air by the sticky-tape tongue of a frog with more disturbance than the spiriting away of these six men.

Six separate disappearances in different parts of the world, six separate police investigations: no one established a connection or discerned a pattern at the time. And then, six years after the last of the six mathematicians had gone missing, Nana vanished. Except, in her case, there had been evidence of a commotion, or at least a body left behind: the Man Who Watched.

As I read Hilary Dutton's account, a gaggle of questions, like a bunch of noisy, jabbering party guests, crashed squabbling and shouting through the door of my mind. Why would anyone want these six mathematicians to vanish? Why had there been a delay of six years between their disappearance and that of Nana? Who had sent the Man Who Watched to guard Nana?

Hilary had prepared a list of topics she wanted to discuss with me and, at the bottom of the page, she had scrawled in block capitals:

I REALLY NEED TO TALK TO YOU. PLEASE CALL ME.

So I did.

6.

If you were to ask me when I put aside my reservations regarding Hilary Dutton, I would say that it was when she pulled her pencil case out of her bag across the table from me at Riordano's, the new Italian coffee bar opposite the main entrance to the university. It was the shape of an alligator's head with the zippered jaws parting to disclose the writing instruments inside. It's not that I'm a pushover for twee pencil cases: I have seen hundreds in my time, lined up in neat rows before the undergraduates I lecture. There was something about this particular pencil case though. That and Hilary's pale grey-green eyes, which snagged and held my gaze like bait on a hook. I had intended to be reserved and purely transactional in our meeting, expecting her to exhibit the professional but slightly weary air of the experienced journalist. Instead she seemed nervous and was younger than I had anticipated. She was sitting at the table when I came in and jumped up as I approached; she looked a little surprised, as if she had expected me not to show. When she resumed her seat she knocked over her coffee and was then flustered, berating herself under her breath as she mopped up the spill. *I'm not normally like this*, she said, *but you're a bit of a hero back at the Dutton homestead.*

A hero? I laughed. *Are you sure?*

You taught my sister in Philosophy of Science a couple of years ago.

You probably don't remember her, although she got both the brains and the looks in the family. I got the rest. I'd hear all about you; that's partly why I started looking at this matter.

What do you want to tell me? I asked.

She told me that six months ago she'd finally, after many requests, been given access to Nana's papers by the police who had investigated her disappearance. Amongst them she had found a note in the handwriting of Mrs Harris, the mathematics department's administrative assistant, with a list of names and what seemed like each person's lunch order. Ghibertine's phone number was scribbled across the bottom of the page. It was not clear why, of all things, Nana had retained this piece of paper. What struck Hilary was that seven of the names on the list corresponded to the seven mathematicians who had disappeared. The eighth name was Professor Simovanner's. This pointed to the existence of a meeting at which all the missing mathematicians had been present – but the police had failed to recognise the significance of this. Slowly, painstakingly, Hilary had pieced together further details: that the meeting had been private, by invitation only; that it was somewhat secretive – none of the attendees had advertised their attendance; and that no minutes had ever been found. But enough evidence eventually came to light to point to a seminar organised and hosted by Nana, following which all but one of the attendees had mysteriously disappeared. Leaving only Professor Simovanner and the question: why had he been spared the fate that had befallen the others?

As three of the disappearances had occurred in the United States, the FBI had carried out an investigation some years ago but had failed to establish any conclusive answers. Hilary shared her findings regarding the seminar with them; in response, they sent a couple of officers to question Professor Simovanner. They told Hilary that he said he had always been horrified, baffled and concerned by the disappearances, but he did not believe there was any connection between them and the seminar organised by my grandmother. When asked what had been discussed at the seminar, he told them she had presented her recent work on the algebraic formulation of the coordinates for the existence of parallel universes suggested by the radical uncertainty at the subatomic particle level revealed by quantum mechanical theory. This only elicited bewilderment and glassy-eyed stares from the officers, so the FBI arranged for Professor Stanley Edwards of NYU, an eminent academic who had also attained some public celebrity as a populariser of mathematical wisdom, to meet Professor Simovanner in the hope that he might be able to translate his utterances into a language that they might comprehend. After the meeting, Professor Edwards prepared a statement, parts of which Hilary Dutton read out to me: *I listened carefully to Professor Simovanner's explanation but I didn't understand a word of it. I think those guys were chasing unicorns – either that or blowing smoke up their collective asses. Look, this isn't sour grapes on my part that I wasn't invited to the seminar or anything like that. Professor Simovanner himself admitted that the breakthrough touted by Professor Millicent* [that's Nana] *proved anything but. He abandoned Professor Millicent's line of research pretty much straightaway after she retired and he took over the professorship.*

Hilary told me that she had herself tried to speak with Professor Simovanner, and he had politely but firmly refused. However, he did write to her; in one of several letters he stated that he wanted to be left alone to continue to reflect on *the huge loss to the international community of academic mathematicians represented by the disappearances and, in particular, the loss of the best mentor, colleague and friend I had ever known.* However, in the last letter he wrote to her (he didn't respond to any further letters she sent him) he confirmed that he had reluctantly discontinued Nana's work after her death. This was not because he thought it was a dead end, as Professor Edwards had suggested, but because continuing the research was, in his words, *quite frankly beyond me, I couldn't see what Professor Millicent saw, although I have no doubt that if I had been brilliant enough I would have done so.*

Do you have any memory of this seminar? Hilary asked me.

Only the very vaguest of memories, I said. *I was only eight at the time. But I remember Nana taking me to a university seminar room and introducing me to a group of professors sitting around. The only thing I recall clearly is that Professor Simovanner was there: he was a favourite of mine at that age.*

Did your grandmother keep in touch with Professor Simovanner after she retired?

I nodded. *He visited often. They continued to have a mentor—protégé relationship.*

Did you get any sense that your grandmother was unhappy or angry at Professor Simovanner? I wondered if she might have resented him discontinuing her work.

I didn't — but bear in mind I would have been too young to notice these emotions if Nana did display them.

Hilary leant back and ordered more coffee for us. I asked her, in the light of her discovery of the seminar, what she thought had happened.

She pondered for a moment and then said her initial working hypothesis was that the mathematics behind Nana's breakthrough was so valuable, was of such significance, that it had attracted the attention of a government organisation or corporate body — some entity — that had kidnapped or murdered the mathematicians, either to appropriate this knowledge to itself and deny it to others or to stop dead in its tracks any further cultivation of it. The resources possessed by this entity were sufficiently sophisticated and extensive to enable it to abduct seven persons in plain view without anybody seeing anything, without a single piece of evidence that might yield a clue as to their fate. But if this was correct, she couldn't understand why Professor Simovanner was still alive and kicking.

Then she wondered whether each of the group had engineered his or her own disappearance, whether they were working surreptitiously together in some secret location. One day in the future they would emerge blinking from their hidden lair and stun the world by announcing a mathematical breakthrough of such magnitude, of such unimaginable consequence, that ... that ... well, what? This particular line of speculation she had abandoned, embarrassed she had allowed it to wander unhindered, if only for a short while, around her brain.

She then focused on Louis Simovanner. He had to have been behind it; perhaps a latent psychopathic predisposition had been ignited by professional jealousy, or by an academic feud of some nature, and he had remorselessly, cold-bloodedly killed his fellow mathematicians one by one. Everybody who met him declared him the loveliest and gentlest man imaginable; this only added duplicity and dissimulation to the charge sheet she was mentally preparing against him. And then the axis of her brain tilted and she had to concede the sheer impossibility of Professor Simovanner orchestrating the disappearance of his academic colleagues around the globe while he verifiably and uncontestably remained in this country. Furthermore, her long-standing belief, mind-stamped in indelible dye, that life did not follow the contours of an airport thriller also weighed against Professor Simovanner being a psychotic criminal mastermind.

But she still believed he was connected in some way she hadn't yet figured. And she had more information about him that she wanted to share.

After the discovery of the seminar, I spent quite a bit of time investigating his past; there are some things that just don't make sense. She pushed a stapled document across the table. It was Professor Simovanner's curriculum vitae, his references and the report of the academic panel that assessed him and awarded him the post of Assistant Professor to Nana. *This is from his application for a post in your grandmother's department over twenty years ago.*

I put on my reading glasses and picked up the papers. *What am I looking for?* I asked.

As you probably know, academic mathematicians who reach the rank of Professor usually attain their PhDs from one of a select number of prestigious universities with eminent mathematics departments. Not so Professor Simovanner. He carried out his postgraduate research, leading to his doctorate, at a university in the US I'd never heard of. He obtained his first degree at another US university I'd not come across before. Both second-tier rural colleges. Nothing wrong with that, you might think. These places had a Louis Simovanner in their records: a reasonably strong but far from outstanding student. Same as the high school he attended in Tullesville, Maryland. So far so good. But here's the odd thing. Absolutely no photos of him have survived from his school or university days: no class photos, no yearbook, no graduation pictures. Nothing. I went to these places and searched their archives. The only evidence that he ever attended these institutions exists only in enrolment records, graduation lists and academic citations. Not only that. I tracked down some of his classmates and fellow graduates and they had real difficulty remembering him. One or two claimed they did but I'm not convinced that they weren't trying to please me. Of course, we're talking over twenty-five years ago; memories get shredded after all that time. But even at the place Professor Simovanner taught at before applying for the job with your grandmother, although the records indicate that he was on the teaching staff, I couldn't find anyone who could say they genuinely recalled him, could put a face to his name, remembers speaking to him. Nor could I track down his referees. It's all very weird. I don't know why the FBI haven't carried out the same investigations. I intend to share these findings with them but I want to speak to Professor Simovanner myself first. Hilary paused and took the papers from my hand. *One other thing: listen to this from your grandmother's assessment of him.*

She read out loud: *I've met a number of mathematicians that I've admired and respected, a somewhat smaller number that I've liked as well, and a smaller number where, in addition, I've been jealous of their intellect. Mr Louis Simovanner is the first I've admired, respected, liked, been jealous of and been humbled by.*

Wow! I said. *That's some recommendation.*

It certainly is, Hilary said as she returned the papers to her bag, signalling that our meeting was coming to its conclusion. *He was very helpful at first, but he refuses to meet me now. That said, I heard recently that he's unwell and has given up teaching. He lives in a cottage on the coast. I've decided to pay him a visit.*

Her bag packed, she looked at me.

Before I go I wanted to ask you, if you don't mind, what was it like losing your grandmother in this way, having all this in your past?

I babbled something about growing up with a sense of mystery and purpose in my life but what I said didn't sound authentic, didn't convey what I truly felt, either to me or – I suspect – to Hilary. After we had parted, I walked for a while, enjoying the cool air, experiencing that odd sensation of both exhilaration and exhaustion one can often have after a lengthy conversation, particularly a caffeine-fuelled one. I followed the street that ran along the front of the university, soon arriving at the corner opposite Nana's old apartment building. The cigar lounge and umbrella shop were both gone, replaced by an optician and an estate agent. The bookshop was still there, however, and I went in, greeted by that faintly woody, nutty aroma of new books. I had passed hours between the aisles of this shop as a child, using the pocket money from Nana and the spending money given to me by my parents. Nana believed, when it came to my choosing books, that a child should follow her own tastes and inclinations, be the sole curator of her reading experience and not be subject to the recommendations or prohibitions of a literary mentor, however well meaning. Nana's lips were therefore sealed as, after endless agonising about which titles to purchase, I approached the counter with my final selection. Her self-denying ordnance did not extend to visual expressions or to hand gestures, however. As I held each book before her, she would give it anything from a thumbs-up (strong approval), to a slight twitch of her mouth and shrug (try it if you like), to a display of gurning with rolling eyes, parted lips and lolling tongue (why are you wasting your money on it). I remember her eyes bulged as she attempted to strangle herself in response to Walter Scott's *Ivanhoe* or *She* by H. Rider Haggard. All these years on, I still wondered, as I paid at the till, what silent performance each title would provoke from her. I'd settle for a shrug for the new biography of Dostoevsky but hoped I might receive a more enthusiastic endorsement for the Gormenghast novels in a single volume.

I left the bookshop with my purchases and stood beneath the streetlamp in the spot that had, for so many years, been occupied by the Man Who Watched. I gazed up at the windows of Nana's old apartment and imagined her standing at the window to my bedroom, just behind me, her hand on my shoulder. I realised that she had now been gone from my life for as long as she been with me and that, as I grew older, the proportion of my life that I had shared with her would go on shrinking. I don't know how long I stood there but I realised that in my imagination another person had appeared in the window, standing on my other side and resting a hand on my other shoulder. It was Professor Simovanner. At that moment a cold sensation, more than a shiver, rippled up my spine and, quicker than a neutrino shower, surged through my arms and legs. I closed my eyes. I saw before me the outline, as if in an artist's sketch, of saints writhing in their martyrdom, of angels heralding the glory of the divine, of cherubs bestowing their benediction, all hanging off the pillars and cornices of an altarpiece ascending in tiers of marble and gold to a canopy pierced by solid shafts of heavenly radiance; our feeble attempt to visualise something greater than the greatest things we know.

Nana and I used to play a game: *what is the strangest thing you can imagine?* And we would compete to come up with the most outlandish, most bizarre, most extraordinary idea: a university for lobsters, talking rocks, musical weather, occupying another person's body and life for a two-week holiday. The ridiculous, fantastic idea that had just sprung into my mind, like a cat pouncing on a bird, would not have been out of place amongst such ideas and yet I realised – with the same certainty that Nana had loved me, and that if we let our imaginations die we will surely perish – that this ridiculous, fantastic idea must be the truth.

7.

The sea was a shimmering smudge at the end of a vast expanse of mudflat. The tide had leached away as quickly as it had flooded the bay in the morning, leaving shallow pools of standing water reflecting a sky of milky blue like jigsaw pieces scattered across a brown tablecloth. In the distance, black dots wavered in the hot air; impossible to say from the coastal path I was following whether these were gulls, terns, wading birds or oystercatchers dabbling in the goo, or human scavengers digging for bait. The olive-brown bubbles of bladderwrack and greasy bright green smears of gutweed skirted the path in a thick fringe, like the spewed-up contents of the stomach of a giant sea beast. Further on, dead jellyfish splattered the mudflats like discarded cellophane wrappers. I'd been walking for about forty-five minutes but didn't seem to be any closer to my destination, a tiny white object at the furthest tip of the headland that curled around the bay ahead of me. I stopped and took a drink of water from my bottle. The morning's heat, blended with the rotten-egg odour which wafted from the mud-beach, had thickened into a sense of something oppressive.

I had taken the road as far as I could along this uninhabited part of the coast and left my car in an otherwise empty car park. The occupant of the dwelling ahead of me, I thought, would have to use this path every time he needed supplies or required company, unless he had found a track through the saltmarshes on the other side of the headland, which was unlikely from what I'd seen on the map I had studied yesterday in preparation for my visit. It was difficult to imagine a more isolated place for someone to build a house and live.

It took me another thirty minutes or so to get there. By that time every part of me was coated in a layer of sweat and I had gulped down the remainder of my water. The cottage was small, single-storey, perhaps no more than three or four rooms. It was bordered on two sides by a modest vegetable garden. It looked as if cucumbers, peas, pole-beans and tomatoes had been grown recently although the beds were now thick with weeds and threatened by sedges and rushes, invaders from the marshes which stretched away just the other side of the wire fence. From a distance the white walls of the cottage had glistened in the sunlight; up close, the walls of the cottage were cracked and stained grey with damp.

I knocked on the door at the end of the short, shingled path which led from the gate. When there was no response, I knocked again and then tried the door. It opened into a small kitchen with blue fittings and a stove in the corner. *Hello*, I called, and a voice answered from further inside, *My darling girl, come in*.

The next room was a sitting room, just big enough for a fireplace, a sofa, a couple of armchairs and a table by the window which also doubled up as a desk. The window was open and I breathed in the warm salty air coming off the marshes – more noticeable in the room than outside in the garden. There was a small telescope in a stand on the table; he had obviously tracked my path along the coastal track. Above the mantelpiece hung a portrait. Although I knew I'd seen it before it took me a few seconds to recognise it as Yolanda Sonnabend's portrait of Nana, shortly after she had been elected to the Royal Society. It had been painted before I was born and showed a Nana I had never seen in person: in her early thirties, sitting at her desk, gazing calmly at the viewer, intelligence without arrogance blazing in her eyes.

He was sitting on the sofa opposite the door and slowly got to his feet. The last time I had seen him was at Nana's memorial service (at which he had given the eulogy), roughly twelve months after she had vanished, when it had been officially acknowledged that she would be unlikely to ever return. That was fourteen years ago but I was shocked at the extent to which he had aged: stooped, unsteady on his feet, his face shrunk to its underlying bones, with the beaky nose and hairy goblin ears of an old man. From the CV Hilary had shown me I calculated he was fifty-nine, yet he didn't look a day under eighty. He caught the shock on my face as he started to shuffle towards me.

Yes, yes, I know, the years have not been good to me. Coming here has been punishing for my body. It doesn't affect you going the other way, it seems. I hear your grandmother is still in excellent health.

He stopped suddenly, pursed his lips and glanced at me uncertainly. *You do know?* he asked. *That's why you're here, I assume.*

Yes, I know, I said. *But I'd like the details.*

He came and stood in front of me. It was odd but his eyes seemed immune to the accelerated ageing which had afflicted the rest of him; they had a vitality that I knew I would have to steel myself against. He took my right hand in both of his. *It's so good to see you. I thought I wouldn't see you again. The doctors tell me I have little time left.*

Will you return before you die?

He appeared not to understand, but then he smiled and shook his head. *No, no, no, my child. I can never go back. When you pass, that's it, you can't go back: one way only. Of course, I knew that. We all knew that. Now, can I get us some tea?*

No, thank you. I can't stay here long.

A cool drink, perhaps? I have some mint cordial.

I agreed to that and sat down on the sofa while he pottered in the kitchen. I had come to accuse, to protest, but already I sensed my anger trickling away in the face of his infirmity and incipient mortality. He returned with a couple of glasses, handed me one and lowered himself into an armchair.

You know it was all about the mathematics, he said.

Of course: that much I had gathered.

Your grandmother's genius took us all by surprise. Once it was clear the way she was going, there were those who wanted to extract her straightaway. More moderate voices prevailed, however, and I was sent here to try to divert her, slow her down. He laughed at some memory. *Which I singularly failed to do. Which, now knowing your grandmother, was always going to be a futile task. And then there was the seminar — I failed to put her off that as well. You see, once the maths is established, the science, the technology, becomes eminently attainable. We don't know when it would have been accomplished — next year, next decade, next century — but it would only have been a matter of time. Once you develop the ability to slip between universes, to leave here —* a brief roll of his eyes around the room, an expansive gesture with his hands to indicate that he didn't mean this particular dwelling — *then a great danger arises for you, for us, for others. Our experience tells us that we must act decisively and stop the process at the stage that the mathematics have been realised.*

Experience tells you. You've done this before?

A number of times. Not here of course. But there are fewer limits … elsewhere.

He paused and looked out of the window.

It's such a relief to be able to talk about this, he said. *You can't imagine — or perhaps you can.*

I sat forward. *So what did you do? They're not dead, are they?*

He seemed horrified. *Of course they're not dead. We opened a singularity and brought them to us. They are all well and content. There is not one of them that would trade where they are now for the ability to return here.*

But they had family, friends, people they loved that they were taken away from.

He thought for a moment. *It is no disrespect or dishonour to those who depart or those left behind to say that the loss and pain fades with time. There are considerable compensations in joining us for those who live in their minds. I have been told that not even your grandmother would return, if given the opportunity.*

He saw the expression on my face and, wincing, he leant forward and took my hand in both of his again. *Please, please, that's not intended to hurt you. I meant to give you comfort.*

It does give me comfort, I said. *It's just that I missed her so much, when I was young. So very much. Could she return if she wanted to?*

Regrettably, that's not possible. It is impossible both ways. In the same way I cannot return, neither can your grandmother.

But you had a choice.

Of course. I accept that.

I thought to myself: I will not cry, I will not cry.

Why was there a delay in taking my grandmother? I asked. *Presumably you know about the men who watched her?*

He closed his eyes as if in thought, but after thirty seconds had elapsed I thought he had fallen asleep. Perhaps he had – but he then opened his eyes and continued. *After your grandmother's seminar, I told her who I was, where I came from and what we were going to do. I remember, she didn't show any surprise at all. As if a part of her had suspected me all along. Of course, she wanted to know what it was like where I came from, how we effected the passing. She asked for a further twelve months here, and we agreed – on condition that she destroy her seminar notes and any other papers pointing to the fact it had taken place; and that she abandon her research, retire from active work and her professorship, and recommend me as her successor. All of which she did, of course.*

He shook his head and seemed, for the first time, embarrassed. *There was a problem with our technology at that time. The ability to take people from this universe wouldn't work if an interloper from our*

197

universe was in the vicinity of the person to be taken. A hundred-metre radius: I won't bore you with the physics. There is a faction where I come from which strongly believes we have no right to take people, no matter how advanced their mathematics. For a while your grandmother became quite the cause célèbre. This faction exploited this fault. They organised themselves and arranged for a series of volunteers to come and stay close to your grandmother on a round-the-clock basis to block us taking her.

I stared at him while I tried to make sense of this. *Let me get this right. A Man Who Watched, every day and every night, changing every two years. That's eight men who came here knowing they could never return, with the sole intention of preventing you from abducting Nana. If these people who didn't know Nana were prepared to sacrifice so much in order to protect her, doesn't that tell you that what you were doing was morally wrong?*

He didn't reply for a while and again I thought I had lost him, until he appeared to remember where he was and what he had been saying. *The official line was that the media sentimentalised the situation. They made a great deal of your grandmother's relationship with you. Ought we to break the bond between a lonely young girl and her doting grandmother? For a while, everywhere you looked there were pictures of the two of you. Eight volunteers? Hundreds came forward – they were even holding lotteries to choose your protectors. Entirely illegally. As soon as the fault in the technology was addressed, the authorities moved quickly to end the charade and take your grandmother.*

Killing her protector in doing so.

Yes, they did – we did. They would say they had no choice. I dare say I said the same at the time.

When people say that they had no choice, they usually did have one. It's sobering to see that people utter the same falsehoods where you come from.

A dry, entirely mirthless laugh, like something had lodged in his throat. *That's not surprising. We are, after all, the same as you – just different.*

Hilary Dutton, the journalist, knows about the seminar. She's on to you. She's planning to visit.

She'd better be quick then. But she won't understand or believe a word of it. But you, it's different. I see your grandmother in you.

He got up and lumbered over to the window. On the horizon the blue had curdled into a bruise-coloured magenta: a storm was on its way. I knew I should get back to my car before the rain came. He continued talking, as if to someone on the other side of the window: *I fear that even if the technology existed to bring me back, they wouldn't do it. They think I've gone native.* He turned to address me again. *I miss your grandmother as well. She was – she is – a remarkable woman. Both you and I were the beneficiaries of this fault in our technology. We both got to spend six years with her that we weren't supposed to. So there is a part of me which will always be grateful to those brave men.*

He took something out of a drawer in the table and came to stand in front of me. *You remind me so much of your grandmother, my darling girl. She would have been so proud of you to see you like this. So proud. Thank you for coming to see me. Your grandmother always knew it was just a matter of time before they came. She wasn't afraid in the least. She was looking forward to it. Her one regret was that she wouldn't get to see you grow up. And for that I'm sorry for the role I played in all this. It may seem hypocritical for me to dissociate myself from the actions of my kind: it probably is. It's perhaps not much of a punishment but I accept this* – and he waved a hand at himself, his failing limbs, his premature infirmity – *on your behalf and on her behalf.*

He paused. *Your grandmother asked me to give you this if we should ever meet after she had gone. I'm sorry I haven't given it to you before.* He handed over the red-and-gold pot of Tiger Balm. *And to say 'jacksi packsi' to you. She said you would understand.*

The rain caught up with me about two-thirds of the way back to the car but I hardly noticed; my tears had already reduced my world to a blur. At my flat, after stripping off my soaking clothes, I collapsed into the bath, the foaming suds concealing my reclining body like cloud cover over a hidden land. I thought about Nana and hoped that her capacity for kindness was neither unusual nor underappreciated in the universe she now inhabited. That she was content: I hoped for that, too. Finally, I hoped for a place where the events represented in the black-and-white photograph of the petrified boy on her study wall did not occur.

A week later I received a call from Hilary Dutton. She told me that Professor Simovanner was dead. She'd gone to see him yesterday and found his body on the floor of his sitting room. The doctor who'd attended thought he'd been dead for no more than twenty-four hours. The exact cause had not been determined but could have been one of a number triggered by his failing body. There was an empty glass on the table by the window. Nothing else: no papers or letters had been left lying around. I listened to the news without speaking, but there must have been something about the quality of my silence which prompted Hilary to say, *You visited him, didn't you? And spoke with him. Very recently.*

I saw no point in denying it. *I did.*

And he told you, didn't he? What did he say?

I paused, not knowing how to proceed. And then I said, *You won't believe it.*

Try me, she said.

Emanation

1.

It was Monday 22nd November 1892, around six o'clock in the evening. I was standing on the steps outside my residence in Merton Square, about to hail a hansom cab to take me to the house where my fiancée lived with her parents, when an elderly man hailed me from the pavement.

'Dr Maltby,' he cried, breathing heavily through exertion, 'a message for you from Professor Hartlett.' Exhausted, he climbed the steps and held out a folded note. I recognised the bottle-green livery of the messengers at the Royal Brompton Hospital, where I was a physician-in-residence.

The note, written in Professor Hartlett's idiosyncratic scrawl (to designate it handwriting would be to confer upon his hieroglyphics a legibility they most demonstrably lacked), shed no light upon the reason for his summons. *Christopher*, it read, *there is something at the hospital you need to see. Come at once. Attend at the back entrance to the dissection rooms and ring the bell. Hurry!!* This last word underlined twice.

I groaned inwardly. I was on the way to take Helen, accompanied by her parents, to the opera. We had tickets to see Fanny Moody take on the role of Tatyana in Tchaikovsky's

Eugene Onegin, a performance I had been yearning to see ever since it had been advertised. But I could not ignore the Professor's somewhat imperious request. I handed the messenger some coins and asked him to take a cab to 36 Lisson Square and pass on my apologies to Miss Prenderville, with the request that she and her parents proceed to the opera. I would endeavour to join them once I had seen whatever it was Professor Hartlett felt it imperative that I see. With that I bent my steps in the direction of the Royal Brompton Hospital, surmising that this would be more expedient than waiting for a cab.

The evening was hard with cold. Each intake of breath sucked in an icy tendril that frost-scorched the lining of my lungs while each exhalation unleashed a wispy ectoplasm of warm breath that lingered in the air for a second before dissipating. The habitual smoggy atmosphere of the London streets had been replaced by a crisp stillness, which gave an emphatic precision to the click of my footsteps on the pavement and a crystalline purity to the electric streetlights along the Chelsea Embankment. Beyond the lights, the dark, heavy mass of the river poured itself towards the sea, black as cast iron. Ordinarily, I would have enjoyed a leisurely perambulation in such circumstances. However, my anxiety to respond to Professor Hartlett's entreaty as promptly as possible, so as to salvage something of my evening, robbed my walk of all pleasure.

As I turned the corner from the King's Road into Sydney Street, I saw the distinguished red-brick and pale stone façade of the hospital ahead of me. I cut down the side towards the rear entrance, which gave access to the autopsy examining rooms and the morgue. In my five years as a physician at the hospital I had never before visited this part of the building and I made my way uncertainly across the cobbled yard. The back door was pulled open without my having to knock and an orderly, holding a lamp to my face, bade me good evening. Asking me to follow him, he took me to a smallish wood-panelled office just off the morgue, where the Professor was sitting at a table, waiting for me.

If the hospital was a city-state, Sir Malcolm Hartlett would be our First Minister, combining his skill as a surgeon with his acumen as a hospital administrator. Possessed of a reserved, softly spoken manner, he was a solitary man, still unwed in his fifties. I believed that, for him, the hospital was his family: his fellow professors and surgeons were his younger siblings; the junior physicians and nurses, his sons and daughters; the porters, cooks and cleaners, his trusted domestic servants; the patients, his guests. When indulging such thoughts, I am embarrassed to admit I sometimes envisaged myself as his eldest son – a fancy no doubt lent force by the negligible presence in my life of my own father. Not the least of Professor Hartlett's considerable abilities was his maintenance of a calm and thoughtful disposition in all circumstances. Only a slight compression of the lips or a smoothing of his unruly eyebrows with his right forefinger (signs I congratulated myself I alone had detected) betrayed that he was in the presence of a medical emergency or a challenging diagnosis. I was therefore surprised and somewhat unnerved when the Professor greeted me full of an eager manner, excitement shimmering in his eyes.

'Sit down and read this, Christopher,' he said, thrusting a sheet of paper into my hands. It was a report from a Dr Roger Panting attached to a death certificate for a Mr Alfred Hickling:

14th November 1892

Attending Alfred Hickling (41 yrs) at home (16 Rochester Terrace, East Stepney) 7.12 pm. Patient presenting with advanced pulmonary tuberculosis. Intermittently conscious – delirious when awake. Intake of fluids negligible. Bright yellow urine. Laboured breathing, bloody expectoration. Pulse 115 bpm. BP 180/110.

16th November 1892

Attending 11.30 am. Barely conscious. Advanced haemoptysis. Large quantities of bloody sputum. Active perspiration. No intake of fluids. Pulse 121 bpm. BP 182/105. Patient in considerable discomfort. Two phials of prescribed morphine solution to be administered every two hours by spouse.

18th November 1892

Attending Mr Hickling for issue of death certificate (attached). Mrs Hickling put death at 2.18 am, which I confirmed. Cause of death tuberculosis. Mr Hickling survived by spouse and five children, two boys and three girls, all under the age of ten. May God have mercy on them all.

20th November 1892

Contacted by Mr Hargreaves of undertakers, Culsome Fanshawe & Sons of 18–20 Norbury Parade, Stepney.

Requested I attend premises to reconfirm the death of Mr Hickling as his body continued to exhibit signs of life (e.g. transmission of bodily warmth, visible movement of organs below skin, gradual clouding of eyes).

Attending corpse of Mr Hickling at the undertakers' premises, 3.20 pm. No heartbeat, pulse or motor function. But: rectal temperature of 101.5°F. Absence of rigor mortis: in fact, swelling and undulation of organs detected below subcutaneous fat layer. No discolouration of skin or apparent decomposition of organs. Sudden appearance of cataracts over eyes. Phenomena entirely novel to me – evidence of a residuary infection or parasitical infestation that has delayed process of bodily decomposition?

Asked Mr Hargreaves to keep me informed.

22nd November 1892

Attending body of Mr Hickling at the undertakers' premises, 11.10 am. Rectal temperature 101.6°F. Still no sign of rigor mortis or decomposition. Continued twitching and rippling motion of organs and ligaments below the flesh. Slight swelling around abdomen. Cataracts fully formed, eyes like white marbles.

Mr Hargreaves declined to store the body on their premises anymore and insisted it be removed.

Resolved to contact Sir Malcolm Hartlett at the Royal Brompton Hospital.

I put down the sheet of paper. The Professor was sitting on the other side of the table, directly below an engraving of Sir Joseph Lister on the wall. In place of his usual tranquillity, he exuded restlessness, drumming his fingers on the table as if tapping the sounder of a Morse telegraph.

'I taught Roger Panting many years ago,' he said. 'Not a man to flap unnecessarily. When he told me what was happening to Mr Hickling's corpse, I agreed he could have it sent to me.' He checked his pocket watch. 'I examined it when it arrived just over two hours ago. And now,' he said, getting to his feet, 'you must see it too.'

I followed him out of the room and down a short passageway, stopping outside the closed door to one of the dissection rooms. He knocked softly and the door opened a crack to reveal half of Janson, one of the morgue attendants, who nodded at the Professor and admitted us into the room. The strong electric light glimmered on the cream and green tiles which adorned the walls in an intricate faux-Moorish pattern, and I couldn't help reflecting that the design was wasted on a goodly proportion of those persons who passed through this place. A metal table with runnels at the sides that dropped into a drain in the floor occupied the centre of the room. On top lay a body covered by a white sheet.

'Before I ask Janson to remove the sheet, I need you to remember, Christopher, that Mr Hickling died the best part of five days ago and that he has generally been stored in cool rather than frigid temperatures.' We took up position on either side of the table and Professor Hartlett nodded at Janson, who pulled back the sheet.

The human body was the focus of my professional life and the obstacles to its smooth functioning preoccupied much of my waking hours. To me, it was the most commonplace object in my world, but also the source of endless fascination and wonderment. Whatever depredations afflicted the body no longer had the capacity to surprise or shock me. Nothing, however, had prepared me for the appearance of the corpse that lay before me.

Although I did not know the shape and size of Alfred Hickling's body when alive, I was sure that in death his limbs and torso had undergone considerable swelling, as if bloated by trapped water. Instead of his flesh being a greyish white like tallow or candlewax, it was caramel in hue, stretched tight like sausage skin over his engorged frame. A web-like membrane, venous like a sycamore leaf, had grown between his arms and torso and between the length of his legs, giving him the appearance of a giant unfinished papier-mâché doll to be cut out of a cardboard frame. His groin had billowed out like a cushion in the centre of which nestled shrunken genitalia, like a twig with two pale berries attached. A faint cinnamon-like fragrance hung in the air over the body.

'Touch him,' the Professor invited.

I did so and then withdrew my hand as if jolted by an electric charge.

'The body is warm,' I said.

'It is indeed,' he said. He indicated the abdomen. 'Place your hand there.'

After a few seconds I felt a small movement, a faint undulation, pass through the organs below the stomach wall on which my palm rested. Again, I snatched my hand away and stared at the body before me in astonishment. After a while I became aware of the Professor speaking with unusual intensity.

'... I've never seen anything like this before. Perhaps some extremely rare pathogen that affects cadavers only. But, really, I'm at a complete loss to proffer an explanation. I'm going to hold off conducting an autopsy until these bodily' – he paused, not able to find the right words – 'transformations have stabilised. In the meantime, I've asked Roger whether we can meet Mr Hickling's widow tomorrow morning to ascertain his state of health and movements prior to his death. After that I suggest we undertake research in the library at the Royal College of Surgeons; there may be recorded cases of the same or similar phenomena.'

He nodded again at Janson, who covered up the body.

'Apart from the undertaker, only Dr Panting, you and I – and Janson here – know about this. Let's keep it that way until we have discovered more. So not a word to anyone for the time being, Christopher, not even Helen. The absence of a scientific explanation may encourage ill-formed speculation and superstitious interpretation to fester.'

I agreed and, leaving Janson behind us to lock the door, wished the Professor a good evening and set off to join the Prendervilles at the opera.

Sitting in the back of a cab, I mused on what I had witnessed.

What I had read and seen with my own eyes admitted no explanation that readily came to my mind. I scoured my memory in search of possible causes for the changes afflicting Hickling's corpse and could alight on nothing that could provide a rationale. I had removed from a young woman a tumour with embedded teeth and strands of hair (she survived the surgery); operated on a man to excise his second heart, a quarter-sized, tuberous, pig-pink and sickly organ that nonetheless pulsed in tandem with its more powerful sibling (he died); extracted, like a ribbon from a spool, a thirty-foot-long tapeworm from the gullet of an elderly docker (the man thrived thereafter; the tapeworm did not). Marvels, all of them and mightily strange and discombobulating at the time. Yet none of them belonged to the territory of the anatomically unprecedented or the utterly inexplicable – as the dead body I had just investigated surely did.

I had to remind myself that the misdiagnoses and irrational fears that lurked in the shadows cast by our ignorance would flee in the face of medical knowledge. Fear and dread; those insidious visitors. See them for what they are and deny them nourishment. The novel transformations to which Hickling in death was subject would prove to be an instructive case study, shining a powerful light on hitherto unresearched areas of post-mortem transmogrification. This was what I chose to believe and, having done so, I resolved to quell my churning thoughts and enjoy the remainder of the evening.

2.

The following morning I stood with Dr Panting and Professor Hartlett on the narrow pavement outside what had been Alfred

Hickling's home. Above us was a sky the grey of dirty bedsheets, from which fat flakes of snow wandered drunkenly, deferring the annihilation spelt by their landfall. Number 16 was identical to the other houses on Rochester Terrace: a small terraced dwelling, two rooms upstairs and down, net curtains in the front window and a door scrubbed free of grime. We knocked and Mrs Hickling, tall and angular, in widows' black, showed us into a parlour that struggled to contain its four armchairs, side table, upright piano and bookcase.

A sketch on the wall above the mantelpiece immediately seized my attention. There was something familiar about the drawing but I could not say why that was. It showed a young woman who lay horizontal, head back, throat exposed – perhaps in sacrificial mode, although whether she was sleeping or dead was not clear – her robes flowing in ripples of light and shade over the pedestal on which she lay. Above her on the right, the sun bathed her in its radiance. To the left, the moon presided over a night sky and, beneath, a choppy sea. A flying creature, possessed of a sharp beak and outstretched umbrella-wings, with more than a touch of the pterodactyl about it, plunged down between the two celestial orbs so that the vulturine tip of its beak was barely a foot above the supine body.

'Gentlemen, I apologise,' Mrs Hickling said, indicating the empty hearth, 'but we keep only the back room heated and my three youngest are there with my sister. At least we will be able to hear ourselves talk in here.'

If Mrs Hickling was disconcerted or burdened by the collective medical knowledge of three doctors in her house, she betrayed no sign. Instead there was intelligence, resolve and hints of anger in her composed manner and level gaze.

After Dr Panting had introduced us, and we had taken our

seats and expressed our condolences, he said, 'Mrs Hickling, I've asked these—'

'Dr Panting.' She held up her hand as if to stay him. 'When I visited Mr Hargreaves yesterday afternoon to discuss a date for my husband's funeral, he was not able to oblige as he had released my husband's body that morning to the hospital – for reasons he was not inclined to share with me. And now I'm visited by not one but three doctors—'

'I am afraid I am responsible, Mrs Hickling,' Professor Hartlett said. 'And I must apologise for you hearing in the manner you did of the removal of your husband's body to the Royal Brompton Hospital.' In conformity with the approach we had discussed on our way to East Stepney, the Professor explained that some irregularities in her husband's appearance after death had suggested the need for an autopsy. This in turn had prompted our visit, so we could question her about her late husband's illness, work and personal habits.

'But I understood he passed away with tuberculosis,' she said, looking at each of us in turn. 'What are these irregularities you talk about, sir?'

'Just some swellings and discolouration. Nothing yet that disturbs the initial diagnosis. But we do need to be sure.'

The Professor led her gently through his questions. Alfred Hickling was a London everyman: he had been born less than a quarter of a mile from the house he died in and, apart from a short spell in the army in his twenties, he had passed all the intervening years in Stepney. He had been a carpenter and metal worker, working for the Huxton & Oliver Manufacturing Company Ltd, which built the double-decked omnibuses pulled by horses through the streets of the capital. They'd married on his return from his last tour in the Punjab, just over twelve years ago, and their union had been vouchsafed five bonny children, all healthy and bright but now fatherless. A steadfast husband and loving father, he'd given his family every penny he received for his labours, apart from those amounts he retained for his books (he was a prodigious reader) and the tithes he paid the shepherds.

'The shepherds?' the Professor asked.

'That is the designation given to the elders of the spiritual community we belong to, sir. The Shepardines, we are called.'

'I have not heard of them. Church or chapel?'

'We are neither. We are a community founded by the son of the great poet and united by our shared beliefs.'

'And what are the main tenets of these beliefs?'

'Why, we believe that we are all divine, that we are within God and God is within us.'

'The great poet is Mr William Blake, is it not?' I asked.

She turned to me. Her eyes were lime green in shade – the colour of sunlit yew leaves. 'That is so, sir,' she said.

'I recognise your drawing,' I said. 'And I see many of his works in your bookcase. May I?'

She nodded and I pulled out a volume with an exquisite frontispiece displaying finely sketched and delicately coloured fairy-like creatures, resembling fusions of women and moths in various poses, around the title *Jerusalem: The Emanation of the Giant Albion*. I opened it. Inserted behind the flyleaf was a handwritten note that read *To my darling Tharmas, from your Emanation*. I had a sharp sense of intruding on something private and, as I replaced the book on the shelf, I felt both embarrassed and a little surprised at myself for inspecting such a personal item.

'Do you read the poet, sir?'

'I do, Mrs Hickling,' I said. 'He has had the run of my mind on many occasions.'

'Then much of what we hold to be true will be familiar to you.'

'Fascinating,' said Professor Hartlett. 'But if we can return to your husband, Mrs Hickling. When did he begin to demonstrate the signs of ill health?'

She explained that her husband had long been plagued by a weak chest but the cough that convulsed his frame and the blood which speckled his kerchiefs – and, more lately, his clothing and bed linen – were a matter of a month only. He had given up work and taken to his bed (and she had taken up her post adjacent to it); what small parcel of vigour that remained drained rapidly from him, so that to place his hand in hers or even open his eyelids became tasks that were utterly beyond him, as the feats of Hercules exceeded the strength of a normal man. Towards the end, each cough and breath had become an agony to him, but there had been some moments when his body had been still and he lay, eyes open, staring – not at the bright shore of eternity that must surely be hoving into view, but at the space a few feet above his head. On one of these occasions he had whispered to her that *the angels have come for me*, the last words he uttered.

Although infused with grief, she was able to describe her husband's illness with considerable equanimity. But nothing in her responses shed any light on, or provided the grounds for, the errant behaviour of her husband's corpse. We rose to our feet in preparation for our departure. Professor Hartlett thanked her again for speaking with us, renewed our sincere condolences and explained that, as soon as the autopsy had been carried out, her husband's body would be released back to the undertakers.

'When will that be, sir?' she asked.

'I will try to ensure that it is as soon as possible, Mrs Hickling,' the Professor said.

Shortly after leaving, we parted from Dr Panting, who had

visits to make in the locality, and Professor Hartlett and I walked to the Whitechapel Road to get a cab back to the hospital. While we had been inside, a breeze had stirred and the snowflakes now whirled and danced in the air like frosted midges. The branches of the elm trees in Mile End Park trembled as if shaken by a giant invisible hand.

Ensconced in my thoughts, I realised the Professor had asked me a question. 'I'm sorry, Professor, what did you say?'

'I was saying that Mrs Hickling is an impressive woman.'

'Yes, yes, indeed.'

But something she had said had scratched my mind, did not sound right to me, and that evening, after I returned home and was able to spend a few minutes in my library, I confirmed that she had been wrong on one point. William Blake's son could not have founded the spiritual community she had spoken of. William Blake had married Catherine Boucher in 1782 and, although their marriage was considered loving and harmonious, Catherine was unable to bear children. William Blake had died childless.

3.

When, later that day, Janson admitted the Professor and me to the locked dissection room that housed Hickling's body, the first thing we noticed was that his limbs and torso were much further swollen, as if some bodily liquid or gas, generated internally, was lifting and smoothing from inside his fleshy creases and folds, smothering his musculature and skeletal frame. But this was not the bloating of decomposition accompanied by the pungent odours and fluids of decay. He was still warm, his flesh firm and golden in hue, with that faint tremor, almost a vibration, which seemed to signify some inner agitation of organs at the core of his corpse, unseen and only to be surmised at. The membrane emanating from his arms and legs reminded me of fungal frills sprouting from a tree trunk, no thicker than a quarter of an inch, although they were unyielding, shell-like, rather than vegetal, to the touch. As before, a hint of cinnamon was in the air.

Approaching the body, Professor Hartlett pulled back Hickling's right eyelid, then his left: a hard white rind completely covered each eye, as if the cornea had calcified. He then made an incision an inch deep and three inches wide just below Hickling's ribs. Nothing oozed from the cut and we peered into the miniature opening in his flesh: the split-open subcutaneous layer of fat formed a tiny crevasse with a glimpse of the purple exterior of the upper stomach, glistening and quivering, at the bottom.

'There is no heartbeat,' the Professor said, 'no circulation of blood, yet the organs seem healthy. I fear to explore further at this stage, in case we disturb this ... well, this metamorphosis.'

The Professor was right: a metamorphosis. That word took tenancy of my mind over the next few days as we settled into a routine. Professor Hartlett and I alternated our visits – he, the morning; I, the afternoon – before examining the body together in the evening. The dissection room remained locked and its contents secret. Janson, who lived on the hospital premises, possessed the only key. The Professor brought one of his protégés, a junior doctor named Dawson, into his confidence. He assisted with the extensive medical records we compiled; we were conscious that meticulous scientific observation would be required to combat the widespread scepticism we anticipated on the publication of the details of this phenomenon. In this regard we were assisted also by Dawson's brother-in-law, who was a photographer. He was prevailed upon to come to the hospital each morning and take a photographic image of the phantastic changes Hickling's body had undergone over the previous twenty-four hours.

Although he spent hours amongst medical textbooks and periodicals, the Professor could find neither an explanation for, nor any previous incidences even remotely comparable to, the transformations affecting Hickling's body. Of course, there were cases of corpses being preternaturally preserved through natural or human embalming processes, but embalmment alone could not explain what was happening in Hickling's case. Only a miracle seemed to remain as an all-encompassing explanation, which elicited scorn from a man who, like many of the most eminent doctors, scientists and philosophers of the age, had attended the funeral rites for the most eminent personage of all: God himself. However, as the days passed, I witnessed the Professor's equilibrium being increasingly undermined by an excited curiosity, followed by a wary bafflement and, finally, an intense frustration.

For my part, I sensed that we were witnessing something without precedent and, with our current state of medical knowledge, inexplicable – which is not to say that I doubted we would arrive at an explanation at some future time. But I was less preoccupied with attempting to rationalise it in the here and now. Besides, I could not devote the same amount of time as the Professor could to research: I had an extensive in-patient and out-patient practice to oversee and, in my personal life, the preparations for my impending marriage to Helen to finalise. If I was perhaps a little more distracted than usual by my work commitments, or more inclined to spend time at the hospital beyond the already elongated daily span of a busy doctor, my beloved Helen said nothing of these matters, continuing to exhibit that cheerful disposition and sweet understanding that endeared her to me.

A week ticked by. The icy weather tightened its hold on London. Sheets of ice, transparent at first, then a mottled cloudy grey, inched out from the frozen mud along the banks of the Thames, like a skin congealing over the surface of the river. In the insipid, dirty light of dawn, under railway bridges, beneath the porticoed entrances to grand city buildings, huddled on the pavement grilles of the underground railway air vents, lay the bodies of the homeless souls who'd had their life frozen out of them during the night. The air had such a tingling, frigid sharpness to it, you could almost snap it between your hands, smash it into shards. Looking back at those days, the chill of the dissection room seemed inseparable from the freezing streets and alleys of the city.

And all this time, in a locked room in the Royal Brompton Hospital, a strange and wondrous mutation was occurring, perhaps for the first time, perhaps for the only time. Over the course of eight days the shell-like *thing* that fringed Hickling's torso and limbs continued to grow, expanding in diameter and fanning out from behind his head until it was a corona a foot wide that followed, in rough outline, the shape of his body. Nacreous in hue, it hardened as it expanded, until it resembled in texture the carapace of a crab. As it continued to grow it curled upwards at its edges and began to arch over the body in an elegant, sinuous curl, leaving a void of about a foot between it and the swollen body it enveloped. By the middle of the second week the edges of the carapace had fused together, leaving no trace of a join: the body was sealed as if in a sarcophagus, entirely swallowed, like an insect in a Venus flytrap, except the walls of its container were so tough and adamantine that the forceful thrust of a scalpel left barely a scratch. Whatever further extraordinary transformations lay in store for Hickling's corpse would be hidden by the human chrysalis that lay before us on the dissecting room table.

4.

Almost three weeks to the day I had first inspected Hickling's corpse, I was at my desk in my consulting room at the hospital when Miriam, my secretary, announced that a Mrs Hickling was outside in the waiting room, asking to see me although she did not have an appointment. I asked Miriam to show her in. Mrs Hickling appeared tired and somewhat drawn around the bones in her face but otherwise little different from when we had met previously; again, I was struck by the vivid green of her eyes.

'I'm sorry to prevail on you in this manner, but—'

'Please, take a seat, Mrs Hickling,' I said. 'No apology is needed.'

'I have been trying to see Dr Panting, but I haven't been able to reach him. I remember the Professor saying that both he and you were at the Royal Brompton, and this is where my husband's body is being kept. So, I thought … Well, that's what I've come about. It's been well over two weeks since you came to see me and his body still hasn't been released for burial. Why is that, sir? You do have him here, don't you?'

'Of course he's here,' I said, as kindly as I could.

'Then may I see him?'

I walked to the window. My rooms overlooked the back of the main building. To the right was the yellow-brick wall of the wing housing the hospital laundry. Knots of sparrows flitted around the vents in the laundry roof, from which warm air rose wiggling and rippling into the wintry sky. Directly ahead was the sanatorium: through its windows were rows of beds, each with its wan motionless occupant framed by white starched sheets and a pillow. I was mindful of Professor Hartlett's injunction to keep information about the state of Mr Hickling's corpse confidential. But at that moment it seemed inconceivable that I should withhold from Mrs Hickling what had happened – what was happening – to her husband's dead body.

I turned to her.

'Mrs Hickling, what I am about to tell you will sound unbelievable. I barely believe it myself. But before I do so I must ask you to promise me that you will not divulge to another person what I am about to tell you.'

She warily agreed. I outlined to her the changes her husband's body had undergone since the moment of death, without dwelling on the more confronting aspects, as I wished to minimise her distress. In fact, although surprised by the account I gave, she appeared more curious than upset, displaying no signs of perturbation. She asked me whether I was certain her husband was dead and I assured her on this point.

'May I ask you a question, sir?' she said.

'Of course,' I replied, expecting her to try to extract from me some explanation, however speculative, for what was happening to her husband's corpse.

'Do you believe the soul survives the death of the body and that we live on in spirit form?'

'Well, that's not a medical question, so I'm afraid I have no professional expertise to bring to the answer. My views are probably no more worthwhile than anyone else's – rather less so, I expect, as I am no student of scripture. But, as you ask me – no, I am sorry, I don't believe our soul or consciousness, call it what you will, survives our death.'

'Why are you sorry?'

Not knowing how to respond, I shrugged. 'What do the Shepardines believe?'

She looked at me a touch sharply, as if she thought I might be gently mocking her. But seeing, I hope, that this was not the case, she went on. 'It is only as spirits that we truly live. When we die, our spirits are liberated to take on their true corporeal form.'

'They become tethered to a body again?'

'Not a human body – a spiritual body.'

I must have seemed confused; she leant towards me in her chair, as if a degree of closer proximity could assist her in explaining herself to me.

'True spiritual exaltation is the pleasure we have, we own, in our bodies: the breath of wind on our face, the music that elevates us, a husband's touch. Our human bodies we abandon on death, but we step into our spiritual bodies. These former pleasures are not lost to us; indeed, they are intensified.'

'I see,' I said although her earnest tone and animated face could not render the ideas shaping her words any more comprehensible to me. Without thinking, I asked her what kind of a man her husband had been.

'Do you have time for me to tell you about something that he did?'

I nodded, believing that it must be beneficial for her to speak of her late spouse.

'He made some toys for the children from rough cuts lying around the workshop. As presents for Christmas. Whenever he could spare ten minutes here, gather five minutes there, without it affecting his jobs for the day. Mr Slater, the foreman, he told Alfred he didn't mind, even let him use the paints. For the oldest boy, he made a dragon in gold and black with flapping wings. If you pressed a button hidden on the dragon's body, its jaws opened and a wooden flame flicked out. He fashioned an angel for each of the girls. Jophiel, Muriel and Ariel were the angels' names. In robes of red, orange and pink, each bearing the resemblance of the girl it was made for. For Gabriel, the youngest boy, he carved a bear with outstretched arms holding a sword in one paw and a shield in the other; they clashed together at the touch of a button secreted in its back. Each of them was put in its own painted box with the child's name on the lid.

'If you could've seen the faces of the children as they opened their gifts on that Christmas Day morn. I'd forget my own name sooner than I'll forget that. But they're good children and there was no complaint when they had to put their toys away to go to our service that morning out on the frosty heath. Then, that night, while the other children slept with their toys in their arms, little Gabriel came downstairs to tell us that the bear was keeping him awake by talking to him and flashing his eyes red. After telling the bear it was time to let Gabriel rest, I lay down with him and whispered him asleep. But Gabriel couldn't sleep the next night or the night after that. The bear, he said, was murmuring evil things to him while he held him close in his bed at night, telling him that his father and mother didn't love him, that his brother and sisters were jealous of him, that he would grow up into a man with a dirty beard who roamed the streets with a pack of dogs he starved and beat. Poor boy – Alfred and I couldn't say what was going through his head but he took against his toy, kept it in its box, placed the box under his bed, wouldn't look at it or even go near it. Soon he was begging his father to take the bear away and burn it, so he would never hear its cruel mutterings or see its glowing red eyes again. Alfred was most upset to see the boy made unhappy by the toy he had so lovingly crafted.

'After a few days of this he told Gabriel that he would remove the bear from the box beneath the bed it had been banished to and burn it on the sitting room fire that evening while the boy was sleeping. Gabriel flung his arms around his father's neck and sobbed with relief. Alfred asked the boy what toy he'd wish for in replacement and was amazed when Gabriel asked for an identical bear. Except this time it should be made good and not unkind. That night, while we sat before the fire, Alfred took the bear down from the high shelf where he'd put it so Gabriel couldn't see it and made to throw it on the flames. Alfred, I said, restraining him, what are you doing? Don't destroy your handiwork like this. Tell Gabriel you burnt the toy and then give the bear back to him in a week or so and tell him this is the new one you've made. He won't know it's the same bear.

'He'll know, Alfred said to me. Nonsense, I replied, why should he doubt you'd burn the old bear? But, if you want, give it a fresh coat of paint so that it looks different. He'd still know, my husband said, going on to say that he'd told his son he would burn it and that's what he had to do regardless of whether the boy would recognise the bear if he passed it off as new. He said you couldn't lie about something like that.

'Although I persisted, telling him that he would only be humouring a little boy and that it was no more a lie than Gabriel's account of the bear's imaginary behaviour, Alfred was adamant that the toy must be destroyed. He tossed it onto the fire and we watched the blaze as the flames licked it to cinders. The new toy bear that Alfred made was identical to the old bear, and little Gabriel got on fine with it. To this day, it remains his favourite toy.'

She had been staring out of the window as she spoke as if the events she narrated were unfolding on the other side of the glass pane, like the flickering figures of a zoetrope, but as she finished she turned to me. The sunlit greenery of her eyes had lessened in intensity as if a cloud had passed over. I spoke into the silence that opened between us.

'Mr Hickling was a loving father. You, and the children, must miss him very much.'

She nodded, as if she could not permit herself the self-indulgence of a reply. Instead she asked: 'Do you have children, Doctor?'

'I do not,' I said. 'I am not married – although I am engaged to be married next month.'

'You will find our children are the best of us.' And then in a brisker but not dissatisfied tone, she went on. 'I must go, Doctor. Thank you for your time. I trust you will inform me when my husband is able to be buried. Good morning.'

After she'd gone, I stood at the window and tried to identify the feeling she had left in me – a feeling I recognised as the same one I'd experienced after visiting her with Professor Hartlett and Dr Panting the day after her husband's body had been moved to the Royal Brompton. Although I eschewed the expectation, held by many of my colleagues, of deference from those they referred to as the lower orders, indeed actively discouraged such behaviour towards me, I customarily encountered a degree of reticence or awkwardness in the tradesmen, dockers, factory workers and domestic servants who made up the bulk of my walk-in patients at the hospital. But Mrs Hickling exhibited nothing like this. She was respectful but direct, engaged and confident in conversation with me – as if we were equals. Which, in all important respects, of course we were. I was also struck by the equanimity with which she received the news of the changes affecting her husband's body. Although the information was unexpected, she made no show of being distressed. I tried to imagine myself in her shoes: how would I react if told the body of my spouse, more than three weeks after death, seemed to be undergoing a physical transformation involving the gradual secretion and growth of a hard cocoon that now completely enveloped the corpse? But this imaginative leap was quite beyond me and I sat down at my desk, pulled up my notebook and called out to Miriam to admit the next patient.

5.

Later that week, I joined the Professor for our evening inspection of what I had to tell myself was still Hickling's corpse, although the pale grey seven-foot-long chrysalis on the dissection-room table, lying motionless like a pebble fallen from the pocket of a giant, was so far removed from the form of a human body that it took a conscious effort to convince myself it was indeed one. Engagements had prevented the Professor from attending the two previous evenings' inspections and so I had not seen him since the start of the week. I was struck by his febrile, distracted manner, as if he had lost a valuable personal possession and could find no ease of mind until he had located it again. As we were leaving the hospital, he suggested I join him for dinner at his club. Since Helen was visiting relatives out of town, I accepted his invitation.

'I've something to report,' he told me as soon as we were seated and had ordered. 'I came across an article by a doctor who had, about thirty years ago, travelled extensively in Indochina, exploring local medicinal customs. He lived for a while amongst a community in the Mekong River delta and later wrote about his experiences. They were a fascinating people who resided in stilted huts built over the water where they fished and grew rice.

'While there, he observed the widespread use of a plant known in translation as Live Long Water. It grew wild in the mangrove forests and was like a small fern to look at. Ground into a paste and ingested in small doses by the dying, it appeared to defer decomposition of the organs and blood after death, enabling the corpse to retain certain vestiges of life: skin tone, flexibility of limb, body temperature. This enabled the deceased to be treated as part of the community after life had departed: placed in a sitting position in the corner of the family dwelling, they were included in family gatherings at mealtimes, village ceremonies and so on. After a period of a month or so for mourning and the show of respect, the body was removed from the hut and burnt. But here's the really fascinating aspect. The name given in the local language to this period is identical to the term the locals used for the pupal stage during which the caterpillar becomes a butterfly. As if in recognition that the body is in transition from one state to another, undergoing a metamorphosis.'

'Did these bodies grow a cocoon?' I asked.

The Professor appeared to deflate before my eyes. 'If they did, there is no mention of it. Nor any mention of cataracts over the eyes. Besides, if this plant is involved, how and why did Mr Hickling come into contact with it? The author of the article, Dr Sebastian Müller, is now a professor at Heidelberg University. Although I've written to him for further information, I don't expect anything to come from it.'

'Ships from the far east arrive at the docks on a daily basis,' I said. 'It's possible this plant has been brought here by people who have travelled from that part of the world. Maybe Mrs Hickling, wittingly or unwittingly, administered to her husband a cordial which contained extracts of it. Even if this is not the case, I cannot help thinking that an explanation lies along these lines.'

The Professor shook his head and with his right forefinger combed the bristle of his left eyebrow. 'I'm not so sure, Christopher. What is happening ... well, it's inexplicable. In truth, I feel lost, abandoned by the medical knowledge which hitherto has been my means of making sense of the world.'

He carried on in this fractious vein while we ate. While I empathised with his frustration, indeed shared it to a considerable extent, I must confess that I couldn't help but feel a sense of relief when, our meal concluded, the Professor bade me good night and climbed into his cab. Consulting my pocket watch, I saw it was barely half past eight. Although the evening was cold, it was dry and clear. I resolved to join, for a couple of hours at least, the informal association of those who walked the streets of the capital at night. *Nightwalkers* had become a synonym for those who made a living off immorality; still, while it was true that many roamed the streets after dark for scurrilous or illegal purposes, there were also those who did so devoid of any nefarious intent. For every prostitute, molly-boy, footpad or burglar, scurrying from assignation to assignation, there was a policeman, nightwatchman, dog-walker, famous novelist or eminent politician who innocently strolled the London thoroughfares at night: I added myself, a thought-clotted physician anxious to exercise his limbs and rest his mind, to their ranks.

A steady pace took me east along Piccadilly, past Covent Garden, up through Lincoln's Inn and then along the Gray's Inn Road northwards. The freezing air was a bully, forcing people indoors. I strode past shuttered grilles and padlocked doors, the ghostly white bulks of porticoed façades and empty churches, the yawning black mouths and pungent manure-breath of alleyway entrances. The moon was absent, smothered by clouds, but every few hundred yards I'd detect a yellowish tinge to the darkness ahead and hear a murmur in the distance. The light would strengthen, splash across the pavement; the noise would swell to a throaty babble underscored by the plink of a piano. And then, beside me, the hissing flare of blue gas jets, packed bodies glimpsed through the condensation on the inside of a window and the hubbub of a drunken crowd that soon receded behind me as I marched on. I had no destination in mind, imagined myself an automaton following where my mechanical legs took me. Past the grand stations of Euston, St Pancras and King's Cross, huge squatting spiders spitting out their webs of tracks in an intricate tracery of branching and converging railway lines. On to Islington and along Camden Passage, where Helen and I had, one weekend, wandered amongst the shops displaying antiquarian books and maps, canes and walking sticks, taxidermied animals, Canopic jars and Palekh lacquer boxes. Now they were all shut, doors bolted, blinds pulled down, windows dark.

Tirelessly I ploughed on, up the Essex Road, even more deserted, if that were possible, than the streets I had taken previously, enjoying the cool air on my face, stretching my legs, emptying my mind of the cocooned corpse in the hospital dissection room, thoughts of which had been swirling ceaselessly in the vortex that my mind had become. And then I stopped, suddenly overcome by fatigue. I realised I did not recognise where I was. I had strayed off the main thoroughfare into a tangle of narrow lanes lined with dilapidated cottages. Not a single lamp or candle shone behind any window: darkness enveloped me. A thick silence congealed in the air, punctuated only by the yap of a distant dog and the rasp of my breathing. Now that I was motionless, the cold pinched my face and watered my eyes. I had walked much further than I had intended; it was time to return to that part of the city where my home was.

Turning, I caught a snatch of sound in the distance. Angling my head, I heard it again: a human voice, certain words, faint but distorted as if a speaking trumpet were being used. I directed my steps towards the source of the sound, down a narrow road to my left. After a dozen steps or so I descried the flickering of lights, about twenty or thirty yards ahead of me. By now, I was on the margins of open land. For the first time that night, the moon unfurled itself from its heavy cloak and escaped into the night sky, washing the grass heath ahead with a pale luminescence which made the frost glitter and picked out a path of hard, beaten earth. I could hear the voice belonged to a man, although it was still too far away for me to discern the words he articulated. A couple of minutes down the path, a large black shape loomed before me, which I recognised as a marquee of a circumference and height sufficient to house a circus. Although no light emanated through its black canvas sides, strips of illumination leaked from the gaps where the tent was pegged to the ground and where the entry flap hung ajar. Standing next to an entrance booth, flanked by two burning braziers emitting a fierce heat, was a shortish man in a black suit, yellow waistcoat and bowler hat, proclaiming through a speaking trumpet:

'... lately travelled from the court of the Patriarch Bavantine in Mostolia, her one and only visit to this ancient land of Albion on this sojourn in our material world, lately credited with securing a lasting concord between the Holy Rosicrucians of Tlenderplatz and the Archbowmen of the Margrave of Yardley in Yorkshire, renowned for her sagacity wherever wisdom is treasured, here tonight with physical integument so that we may apprehend her and, in doing so, enjoy her presence ...'

Then he lowered his voice and, rolling his eyes in my direction, uttered in a stage whisper, 'Bharmael the Archangel,' before exclaiming, 'Ladies and gentlemen, this way please. Don't push there, don't bunch, there is room for all.'

I looked around in case I had been joined by a swift and silent flock of people, but I was still the only other person as far as I could see. As if in acknowledgement, the man removed the speaking trumpet from his mouth before addressing me.

'One ticket, sir? Free entrance for the mirror-writers amongst us, sir.' He entered the ticket booth and pushed a piece of paper and pen across the counter towards me.

'Mirror-writing,' I said. 'I know not what this is.'

'You'll not be being an engraver or compositor then, eh, sir? No matter, sir, you are still most welcome. That will be half a shilling for you.'

I hesitated. My desire to return to the warm comfort of my bed was much stronger than any curiosity to see what gimcrack nonsense this surely was. But my feet and legs ached. The thought of getting out of the freezing cold and deferring my homeward trek was not unwelcome. After exchanging a coin for a ticket, the man led me over to the entrance to the marquee and, pulling the flap aside, ushered me in.

Rows of benches stretched away from me towards a curtained-off stage at the far end of the tent. The inside was warm and lit by oil lamps hanging in clusters from the poles at the entrance but thinning out towards the back so that the stage was shrouded in shadow. A goodly number of persons, well over fifty souls, occupied the benches, their backs to me: most surprising in light of the inclement weather, the isolated location and the fact that I'd seen no one in the vicinity other than the man who'd sold me my ticket. I lowered myself onto a bench around four rows from the back, next to an elderly, luxuriantly white-whiskered gentleman. He nodded and smiled at me and made a show of drawing himself in as if to give me more space, although the gap between us would have accommodated a rhinoceros. Removing my hat and gloves, I nodded back at him, and he leant towards me.

'Good evening, sir. Well, this is a fair old treat, isn't it? I was not expecting to see Bharmael in this lifetime, I wasn't, I can tell you. I saw Her Most Eminent Sandobar about this time last year and that was like a pinnacle, an absolute pinnacle. I said to my wife, if they come for me tonight or if they come for me in twenty years (if I live that long, of course) I'd be able to say to 'em, guess who I've seen, eh? None other than Sandobar. How many of you can say that? Did you see her when she came to London, sir?'

I was rescued from a response for at that moment, as if at an invisible signal, the rustling and chatter shushed to silence while, with a stroke, the oil lamps were shut off. When the curtains were pulled back the stage was bare except for four hanging lamps that gave off a wavering blue light. A distinguished-looking man, wearing an antiquated frockcoat, came on to a smattering of applause and began to address the audience, in a scholarly manner, on the importance of angels to the great Abrahamic faiths by reference to their appearances in the Talmud, the Kabbalah and the Old and New Testaments. His voice had a high-pitched, reedy quality but his intonation was unvarying and the arcane vocabulary of the angelic ranks (Malakim, Elohim, Seraphim) and the sources he referenced (the Book of Malachi, the Midrashim, the Merkabah and so on) bewildered me. This, no doubt assisted by the length of the day, made me drowsy. I must have slipped into a doze for I came to consciousness with a jolt when my neighbour shook my arm gently, whispering, 'Begging your pardon, sir, but you'll not want to miss this.'

I don't know how long I had been slumbering but the stage was now empty. The angel-lore man was nowhere to be seen. The blue light had intensified to a hue that reminded me of visits to Greece as a young man, although the temperature in the tent was far from Mediterranean. There was a pronounced chill in the air that had not been present before I had closed my eyes. An expectant, almost reverential, atmosphere hung in the tent. My neighbour was leaning forward in anticipation, mouth ajar, eyes fixed hungrily on the stage.

A pool of black liquid, like a slick of oil, appeared on the stage floor. I wasn't conscious of its arrival – it was simply there one moment when, the moment before, it hadn't been. The pool spread and seemed to undulate and bubble, as if it were tar simmering in a pan on a stove. A large bald head – its wide cheekbones, aquiline nose and closed eyes discernible beneath the black liquid that coated it – emerged from the centre of the pool, as if rising through the floorboards of the stage. I barely had time to register its dimensions – the cranium alone must have been at least three feet wide – before it was followed by giant shoulders, torso and arms, thrusting up into the air like a pillar rising from the ground, covered by the dark viscous fluid which dripped to the floor as the body rose higher still, its female sex appearing next, followed by legs the circumference of tree trunks, until, with the final emergence of her feet, she stood no less than thirty feet high, towering over the spellbound witnesses to this extraordinary sight, motionless as a statue, the blueish lamplight gleaming off the caul-like substance coating her.

An infrequent patron of the popular theatre or music hall (the playhouse or opera being more to my taste), I had nevertheless, in my time, seen productions that made great use of impressive stage effects. But I had seen nothing to rival the stagecraft enacted before me. I searched in vain for the crack that betrays a papier-mâché façade or the ropes and pulleys, trip wires and hidden mirrors that can often be glimpsed attending on even the most superior illusion. But no matter how thoroughly my eyes scoured this spectacle, any evidence of its man-made fabrication remained elusive. And I had not yet seen the crowning spectacle, the *pièce de résistance*. With a sound like the wind-blown skittering of dry leaves across the ground, two enormous wings emerged from behind the figure's back and fanned out in two giant arcs until their upper tips were pointing skyward, coming to rest a full three or four feet above the massive head of the angel (for that was clearly what it was meant to be). At their widest, the wings must have been twenty-five feet across, made of tiny scales the hue of burnished gold that rippled and glimmered like the thousands of minuscule mirrors that speckle the surface of the sea as it reflects the rays of the setting sun.

Wild applause from the audience greeted the unfurling of the wings. Then all was activity. A dozen persons rushed onto the stage, carrying buckets of water which they sloshed over the monumental figure to sluice away the residue of the black liquid she had seemingly arisen from. Others transported stepladders and brushes to finish the job. Within a minute she had been rinsed clean; her flesh gleamed dully like polished ivory. From a platform suspended by ropes just below the apex of the marquee, two persons dropped a large swathe of cream linen, which was wound loosely around the giant angel's torso and legs by the persons on stepladders. The angel remained stationary; I assumed the technology, having, so to speak, *conjured* this spectacle from the bowels of the earth, did not extend to conferring animation to her limbs. But in this assumption I was proved wrong: at this juncture, the angel held out her hands, palms up, raising her arms to shoulder height in a gesture of welcome. When her eyes remained closed, I thought that they must surely give the game away, for which master puppeteer has ever convincingly captured that portal to our soul, that conduit of human intelligence? But then her eyes finally opened to disclose vibrant violet pupils in saucers of brilliant white, like dollops of jam in dishes of cream, and I, along, I'm sure, with the others inhabiting the circus tent, felt *seen*, and not just seen, felt *assessed* by the eyes of a superior being. At that moment I abandoned any lingering reservations regarding the artistic ingenuity of the spectacle I was witnessing.

'Welcome, great Bharmael, welcome,' cried the ticket-man and the angel-lore man, who'd now appeared in front of the giant creature. Turning, they invited the audience to ascend the stage one by one to 'receive Bharmael's blessing' and to 'listen with your inner vision to Bharmael's message for you'. Jettisoning the amiable courtesy he had hitherto shown me, my neighbour bustled past me in a frenzied jillywop to be one of the first in the queue forming in the aisle. I followed more sedately and watched as each audience member knelt at the feet of the giant angel, whose right hand was lowered to a few feet above the head of the supplicant.

'Astonishing puppet-craft: are the marionettists from the Continent?' I asked as I passed the angel-lore man, who briefly clasped my hand and smiled benignly at me, but said nothing in response.

In the light of what happened in the following days, I have often asked myself if I did, in fact, receive a message when my turn came and I placed one knee and then the other, side by side, on the gritty wooden planks of the stage before Bharmael's towering presence. I have a recollection, which grew stronger as the days passed, that, kneeling, I had been overwhelmed by an appreciation of Helen's physicality in all its fine-grained particularity. A curl of hair, damp with sweet-smelling sweat, at the nape of her neck. Her habit of blinking when introduced to a stranger. The thinness of her wrists which accentuated the protuberance at the end of her ulna. Above all, a realisation that she fizzed with the innumerable thoughts and sensations of consciousness as I did, that her emotional life was as rich as mine and that her waking and night-time dreams and the self-composed narrative of her life were as meaningful, or as meaningless, as my own. In short, she was as real as I was, and at that moment I understood that in binding myself to her I owed her more than my contractual promise of devotion and material support. I needed to dismantle, piece by piece, the inner ramparts of my immense self-worth and privilege and unreservedly share my soul with her. I could commence, I realised, by liberating myself from my incessant preoccupation with the fate of Alfred Hickling's corpse. I remember having these thoughts, and although I indulge my belief that they occurred that evening and were tied up with, were perhaps a response to, the extraordinary spectacle I had witnessed, I couldn't, in truth, be absolutely certain this was the case.

6.

It was sometime between midnight and the half-hour thereafter when I hauled myself wearily up my steps and unlocked the front door.

It might have been later still had it not been for the hansom cab, wandering down Essex Road like a lonely spectre, that stopped to pick me up and convey me to Merton Square. A rug over my knees and a drop of brandy, both kindly provided by the driver, induced in me a somnolent stupor, no doubt assisted by the gentle swaying of the cab. My memories of the evening were eidetic: a series of vivid tableaux, not least that afforded by my parting look at Bharmael before I passed through the flap of the tent. After the last kneeler had received her blessing, the two men had thanked Bharmael for 'cramming her ineffable majesty into a material shell and gracing us with her sublime presence' before calling time on the evening's proceedings. As we filed out, the blue lamps were extinguished one by one. Just before the cavernous tent was plunged into darkness, I looked back to see the towering effigy, its outstretched wings vast shadows against its flesh in the ghostly blue of the remaining illuminated lamp. The show, initiated in such commanding fashion by the spectacular emergence of the giant angel *as if from the very earth itself*, had ended in a minor key with the mighty Bharmael being abandoned in an empty circus tent.

I, too, was done with the night. But it seemed the night was not done with me. As I parted company with my greatcoat, gloves and muffler and made to ascend the stairs to my bedchamber, I noticed an envelope on the side table in the entrance hall. With a start I recognised the lines and loops that passed for my name as having been rendered by Professor Hartlett. The envelope contained a note he'd written in a series of blots, whorls and strokes that suggested mental derangement if not congenital blindness. He'd had it delivered to me after we had parted earlier in the evening.

Christopher, momentous and important news! Arrived back at my rooms after dinner to find two letters had been hand-delivered while I had been out.

The first from a Dr Tanner, written earlier today, asking for my advice in connection with the corpse of the wife of the postmaster of the village of Effingham near Guildford, whom he had been attending before she died from typhus. The cadaver, he informs me, remains warm, shews no sign of decomposition or other features of a body post-death and, he can now hardly believe, is growing a hard outer membrane.

The other letter contained an article clipped from last week's *Inverness Courier and General Advertiser*, sent to me by Dawson's brother-in-law. (His mother is from that part of Scotland and has the paper mailed to her.) It contains a story about a fisherman from Findhorn, a village about thirty miles east of Inverness. A solitary and dour individual, in the final stages of consumption, he rarely left his cottage and, after he hadn't been seen for a couple of weeks, a neighbour called to see what assistance he could offer. He had to force open the door, which had been bolted from the inside. No sign of the fisherman within but he found on the bed, in his words, a giant five-foot-long white slug with a hard outer rind like a shell.

Our corpse is not unique! There are others; how many, we don't know at this stage. But we have much more to investigate now. Let us discuss in the morning. Good evening, Christopher.

I read the note again as I ascended the stairs. The fog of my exhausted brain had dissipated as if blown away by a stiff wind. It appeared the fantastic change to our corpse was not unique; there were two others at least. But what if there were more corpses, many more corpses, undergoing similar changes? At this moment, in undertakers' and hospital rooms, in bedrooms and morgues, up and down the country – wherever the corpses of the recently deceased were laid to rest – these bodies were perhaps being slowly transformed. But not transformed by that familiar decomposition whereby our *sensible warm motion* becomes *a kneaded clod*, that decay that rots our tissues and organs, consumes them over time to leave behind nothing but the lattice of our bones. They were transformed instead by a mysterious mutation that shucks off consciousness and shuts down the bodily engine that gives propulsion and sense, but allows some residual form of life to survive and causes the body to undergo a metamorphosis into – what exactly? *Something rich and strange?* And who could say how many there were? And what was the cause of this aberrant phenomenon? I shook my head. There was so much I, *we*, didn't know. I felt my ignorance like a weight, pressing down on me.

With my thoughts chasing themselves round and round in my head, like swallows tumbling in the air, I did not expect to sleep when I finally laid my head on the pillow. But I must have passed out, for the next thing I remember was a faint hammering sound. My sleeping brain at first tried to pass it off as an event in my dream, but the noise persisted and grew louder so that I was catapulted awake. It was twenty past four in the morning. The fire had gone out in the bedroom grate and my room was cold and dark. Someone was banging on the front door downstairs. I lit a lamp and descended the stairs while the knocking continued, now accompanied by a familiar voice calling my name.

'I'm sorry to be calling on you at this hour, sir,' said a breathless and flustered Janson when I opened the door. 'But I thought both you and the Professor would want to see it straightaway, sir, what's happened to the Hickling body.' There was a cab waiting at the kerb behind him. The cab window nearest to me was yanked down and Professor Hartlett stuck his head through the aperture. 'Christopher, as quickly as you can now,' he called. 'Janson came for me first. He can explain what's happening once you've joined us in the carriage. Hurry please, Christopher!'

I dressed as hastily as I could and flew into the carriage, followed by Janson, who called up to the driver to proceed to the hospital with all the speed he could muster. Once I was sitting in the cab, the Professor asked Janson to repeat for my benefit his account of what had transpired that night at the hospital.

'After both you gentlemen had carried out your evening inspection, I locked up the room after you and went to my rooms, where I fried a bit of liver and onion for my dinner. Then a sitdown and a smoke of my pipe before I did my last round at ten. I looked in on the room then and all was quiet, although I thought I heard faint noises coming from inside the shell what's covering Mr Hickling. Like a glugging or plopping noise, but very quiet. Anyways, I listened again, but couldn't hear anything so thought no more about it. Then I retired to my bed for the night. Next thing I knew it was just after two in the morning. I don't think I heard no noise, so I don't know what it was woke me up. As I told the Professor, I just felt something in the air, like you know when there has been a death in the family. Something was different. After a while I thought I better take a quick look and check on things, so I picked up the lamp and went to the room. First thing I noticed was how warm it was in there, like a laundry room it was – much warmer than when you gentlemen were in there yesterday evening. And there was a sweet smell, like the star jasmine my sister got climbing on her garden wall. But the thing was the lights in the room weren't working. I tried the switch. Up, down, up, down. Nothing.'

He broke off and rubbed his eyes before continuing.

'So I lift my lamp and the first thing I see is that the shell, the chrysalis-thing as you call it, was split right down its entire length top to bottom and yawning open like a razor clam that's been cooked. It's empty. Whatever was in there has gone. I see the inner walls of the shell, white and wet, but inside there's just a big space. And then I see a movement out of the side of my eye, and I get a fright and stupidly I drop the lamp and it smashes and goes out. But just before it all goes dark, I see something in the corner of the room, a dark shape, like somebody standing there, not moving. I knew then that I needed to let both you and the Professor know what had happened without delay.'

'How tall was the thing you saw?' I asked.

'I just got the briefest glimpse, sir. But I'd say about the height of a normal person, five foot five or six, something like that.'

I looked out the window, and in that instant I had the sensation the cab was stationary and the streets and squares were in motion around us. I imagined the outward wall of each building folding back, disclosing its inhabitants, lying in bed or huddled together on the floor, asleep, or already awake, about to start their trudge through the day. None of them knew what we knew, that we were on the cusp of a new and startling knowledge. These moments when the universe holds its breath: before Galileo lifts his telescope to his eye to see for the first time in history the cratered surface of the moon and the shimmering orbs of the planets, or before Leeuwenhoek looks through his microscope at the fantastical creatures, bustling with life, in a drop of water. The weight of our accumulated understanding up to this point trembles before it explodes, blown apart by what is discovered. Our perception of the world, and our relationship to it, will be permanently enlarged: we may, perhaps, even know what we are in the throes of becoming.

Professor Hartlett scribbled on a page torn from his notebook and handed it, together with some coins from his pocket, to Janson.

'When we get to the hospital,' said the Professor, 'tell the driver to wait. Go to the duty sister. Ask her, on my behalf, to spare a couple of nurses to accompany you to Mrs Hickling. When you get there, give Mrs Hickling this note. If Mrs Hickling wishes to return to the hospital with you, leave one nurse there to stay with the children while you and the other nurse bring her back here. The address is in the note.'

Janson nodded. The Professor seemed as if he was about to say something to me but then appeared to think better of it. A few seconds later, he spoke again.

'Christopher, what if we are wrong about this – about God, the afterlife, all that. Have you ever thought that?' When I didn't say anything, he turned to the window. 'I hope,' he murmured, 'I am worthy of what happens next.'

I didn't have time to assure him on this point, for with a jangle of harness and growl from the driver the cab had drawn to a halt in the cobbled yard at the back of the hospital, in front of the door I had entered to see Mr Hickling's dead body just over eight weeks ago. There was a flurry of activity as we disembarked and passed the horses gently steaming in the frigid air and shaking their heads as if in disbelief. Then Janson unlocked the door, fetched us lamps and handed over his keys. Finally, Professor Hartlett and I stood in front of the dissection room where Mr Hickling's body had lain. No sound came from inside. I unlocked the door and, hesitating for a moment, knocked on it. Silence. I pushed the door open into the dark space beyond and heard, or thought I heard, an intake of breath and a fluttery sound. Without thinking, my hand reached out and held the Professor's as we lifted our lamps and entered the room together.

The Wolf-boy of Ruggianto

his sows) and a knot of woodworm from Palermo (for infesting the Holy Icon of Joseph the Father of God on the High Altar in the cathedral there) had further burnished an already lustrous reputation. Her recent prosecutorial accomplishments were but a garnish to a life that was feast enough for communal discussion and digestion.

A French aristocrat by birth, she had, it was said, become transfixed at the age of sixteen by the virtue of a beautiful peasant boy who worked as a swineherd on her mother's estates. Convinced that she would never be worthy of such beatific goodness, she took holy orders and became a Clementine Sister, joining the mother house in Rouen where huge sums of money were expended by her family on keeping her in a life of pristine poverty. Partaking of a scholastic inclination, she went to Paris to study, attaining joint doctorates at the Sorbonne in theology and canon law at the unheard-of age of twenty-one. Her much-admired study of the teachings of the Desert Mothers secured her an audience with Mater Catherine VII in Rome, who so delighted in the sparkling intelligence and moral nourishment of her company that they became close friends, separated only by age, geography, outlook and taste. The Mater introduced her in turn to her fellow ecclesiastical potentates, Alexis III, Metropolitan of Kiev and all Rus, and Helen the Unbidden, the Matriarch of Constantinople; she became an *éminence mauve* to, and something of a go-between amongst, each of these spiritual mothers.

Mother Simona wore a shapeless mud-coloured woollen tunic and possessed eyes of such a limpid aquamarine that more than one of her interlocutors had felt quite at sea under her penetrating gaze. It was said her daily diet was a grapefruit (breakfast), a piece of bread (lunch) and a walnut (supper) and she could recite word-perfectly, from memory, the entire Gospel of St Joan the Evangelist in its original Greek. Her alarm at the rising tide of heretical beliefs, wizardcraft and lycanthropic transformations and her consequent adoption of magisterial responsibilities were common knowledge and widely respected. When Joco, who owned the taverna, growled that *the sooner Mother Simona arrives and we smell the scent of roasting wolf-boy flesh the better*, he was giving voice to a sentiment that many others held, the anticipatory nature of which was undisturbed by the news that Bishop Cadenza had appointed a cleric no one had previously heard of to defend the boy.

It was common practice for the preliminary interview of the charged to be conducted in the presence of both magistrates together, and the village was afforded its first glimpse of the boy's canonical defender when the two clerics, clutching the villagers' depositions, traversed the sunbaked wheel ruts of the dusty village piazza. They were making their way to the presbytery from the taverna, where they had dined and slept the previous evening after arriving in Ruggianto earlier in the day. Mother Clodagh of Ballytundle presented a stark contrast to her co-inquisitor: short, stout and round-faced where the other was tall, attenuated and aquiline-featured. It was said she came from Hibernia, a wild, little-known country far to the west, and this accounted for her execrable Italian (although Mother Simona later averred she had never heard anyone speak Latin – the language of any conversation not involving a villager – so beautifully). Mother Clodagh's orangey-red hair and vestments of shimmering emerald green (the flow of which set many of the men's tongues wagging) gave her the look of an inverted and trimmed carrot. The village's prompt and pervasive impression was that she was unlikely to impede the smooth execution of justice at Mother Simona's hands.

At the presbytery the two clerics met Mother Currochio and

her bailiff, Gennaro, and followed them inside to find the boy cowering in the corner of the cellar, face to the wall, a foetid odour emanating from his grimy body and filthy rags. Mother Simona gave instructions to Gennaro for the boy to be washed and given clean garments at the conclusion of the colloquy and, ignoring the bailiff's protestations, she ordered the boy to be unchained. Kneeling beside him, and placing her hand gently on the back of his head, she stroked his jet-black curls. *My brave boy,* she said kindly, *your ordeal is over. Look at me,* and she lifted his face so that his frightened and tear-glazed eyes gazed into hers, *it is too late to snatch your body from the flames of perdition but there is time enough for you to save your soul. Acknowledge the Satanic origins of your transmogrification and beg forgiveness of Our Holy Mother, who yearns for you to return to the warmth of Her motherly embrace.*

The boy looked down, saying nothing. After muttering a brief prayer, Mother Simona stood up and gestured at Mother Clodagh to indicate that it was her turn to speak. Keeping her distance from the boy, Mother Clodagh asked him how he had come to be found by Tronto in the midst of such slaughter, but her accent was so indecipherable that the boy was confused and Mother Simona had to translate certain words and phrases before he could respond.

He explained in a heavily accented mumble that he came from Sottolino, two valleys to the west; his mother having died giving birth to him, he had been brought up by his father, a farm labourer, until consumption had taken him around a month ago. Since then, the boy had wandered the lower slopes of the mountains alone, like a solitary tick on the flank of a cow, foraging for sustenance, sleeping beneath the slowly revolving arc of the summer constellations. The day before he had been found by Tronto, he had smuggled himself into an empty shepherd's hut for warmth and gorged himself on a goatskin of barely fermented red wine he had found there. When dusk had fallen, just as the boy himself was about to slip into his own personal twilight, two men had rushed into the hut and bundled him into a sack. The next he remembered was waking up with Tronto kneeling on his chest, pulling a rope over his head. It was wine rather than blood that stained his mouth; grape skins and not sheep integument stuck between his teeth. And while he had been naked this was because someone had unclothed him while he was sleeping; his garments lay discarded a few feet away.

He is most wily, Mother Simona murmured to Mother Clodagh, who appeared to be very much in awe of her celebrated fellow jurist and smiled uncertainly. Then, after checking something in the depositions she carried, Mother Clodagh asked the boy to remove his tunic and face the cellar wall. Both Mothers stared at the skin that covered his narrow jutting shoulder blades and the knobbly column of his spine.

There are no hairs on his back, said Mother Clodagh, very much in the tone of one commenting on the number of kittens in a freshly spawned litter.

They gradually disappear in the days following the wolf's resumption of human shape, replied Mother Simona and then, not unkindly, *Have you not studied the Tractatus Lycanthropus of Saint Eva?* Noticing the other cleric's hesitation, she added, *You may borrow my copy; I will bring it to supper tonight.*

That evening, in the back room of the taverna, Joco served the Mothers nettle soup with wizened nuggets of rabbit followed by stringy stewed eel, although only Mother Clodagh ate, Mother Simona having taken her frugal supper in her room before joining her counterpart. *So simple, so good*, Mother Simona said as she entered, peering around at the sacks of meal and barrels of ale against the walls, the freshly excavated joints of beef and sheep hanging from ceiling hooks like a row of pennants emblazoned in purple, red and white, and the scarlet tableclothed bench on which their food had been laid out.

As Mother Clodagh ate, Mother Simona regaled her with a selection of curated anecdotes: the time she walked the pilgrimage route from the French Pyrénées to Jacquelina de Compostela in Galicia with nothing but a vixen and a talking mare for company; the case of the girls' choir in Aachen who, one morning in August of the previous year, had begun singing the votive masses for Sophielagrande, the former Holy Roman Empress, in raspy discordant voices, as if the choir had become possessed by an army of bullfrogs (the choristers were indeed possessed, not by bullfrogs but by a legion of demons that took a noisy and exhausting morning to exorcise); the trip to Cairo to affirm the authenticity of a gospel written on papyrus scrolls sealed in a stone jar discovered in the crypt of the Basilica of St Barbara (after washing the still-damp ink from her hands, she had had to disappoint the expectant, and rather unruly, crowd gathered in front of the basilica door).

For her part, Mother Clodagh appeared awkward and shy; she spoke little, as if conscious she had little to say that would be of interest to her more illustrious and sophisticated companion. She was asked about Hibernia and the Order of St Patricia, where she had taken her vows, but her replies were brief and uninformative as if her words had taken leave of her. Except at the end of the meal, just before Mother Simona rose to take her leave, Mother Clodagh looked her in the eyes for the first time and asked, *What if the people here have made a mistake? There is much superstition in these remote villages.*

Mother Simona leant forward, placed her hand on that of the

other Mother (who winced at the touch as if her hand had been injured) and said, *The Roman Empress Juliana the Apostate said that all religion is superstition and yet here we are. Who are we to say where true belief ends and erroneous belief begins?*

But, Mother, there is no mention of werewolves in the Gospel.

Indeed there are not, for there were no wolves in Judea at the time of Our Saviour.

Mother Simona stood up and gazed down at the other. *Your empathy for the boy is much to your credit, Mother. But you must be strong. Assume he is found guilty: if the boy is, in fact, innocent, God will scoop him to Her breast the moment of his death, but if he is the Devil's and he repents, his immolation will rescue him from her clutches and deliver him to God. Either way, it will be a few minutes of agony in exchange for an eternity of bliss. Good night, Mother.*

A few feet away, on the other side of the wall, Gennaro was impersonating Mother Clodagh's bizarre accent to a select audience over the rat's piss Joco sold as ale. While likening it to speaking with a cow's bladder lodged in one's mouth, he made sure to imbue his observations with affectionate respect: it did not do to openly mock a clergywoman, even such an unprepossessing specimen as the Hibernian Mother. *The little bastard couldn't understand her questions,* he said. *Mother Simona had to translate.*

What did he have to say for himself? asked Joco.

He claimed he had been drinking and then taken by two men and fell asleep and only woke when Tronto here was tying him up.

Little shit, said Joco. *Do you know how many animals have been lost since that abomination has been locked up?*

Four, said One-Eyed Jacopo.

Joco glared at him.

Two, said One-Eyed Jacopo.

or other features of a body post-death and, he can now hardly believe, is growing a hard outer membrane.

The other letter contained an article clipped from last week's *Inverness Courier and General Advertiser*, sent to me by Dawson's brother-in-law. (His mother is from that part of Scotland and has the paper mailed to her.) It contains a story about a fisherman from Findhorn, a village about thirty miles east of Inverness. A solitary and dour individual, in the final stages of consumption, he rarely left his cottage and, after he hadn't been seen for a couple of weeks, a neighbour called to see what assistance he could offer. He had to force open the door, which had been bolted from the inside. No sign of the fisherman within but he found on the bed, in his words, a giant five-foot-long white slug with a hard outer rind like a shell.

Our corpse is not unique! There are others; how many, we don't know at this stage. But we have much more to investigate now. Let us discuss in the morning. Good evening, Christopher.

I read the note again as I ascended the stairs. The fog of my exhausted brain had dissipated as if blown away by a stiff wind. It appeared the fantastic change to our corpse was not unique; there were two others at least. But what if there were more corpses, many more corpses, undergoing similar changes? At this moment, in undertakers' and hospital rooms, in bedrooms and morgues, up and down the country – wherever the corpses of the recently deceased were laid to rest – these bodies were perhaps being slowly transformed. But not transformed by that familiar decomposition whereby our *sensible warm motion* becomes *a kneaded clod*, that decay that rots our tissues and organs, consumes them over time to leave behind nothing but the lattice of our bones. They were transformed instead by a mysterious mutation that shucks off consciousness and shuts down the bodily engine that gives propulsion and sense, but allows some residual form of life to survive and causes the body to undergo a metamorphosis into – what exactly? *Something rich and strange?* And who could say how many there were? And what was the cause of this aberrant phenomenon? I shook my head. There was so much I, *we*, didn't know. I felt my ignorance like a weight, pressing down on me.

With my thoughts chasing themselves round and round in my head, like swallows tumbling in the air, I did not expect to sleep when I finally laid my head on the pillow. But I must have passed out, for the next thing I remember was a faint hammering sound. My sleeping brain at first tried to pass it off as an event in my dream, but the noise persisted and grew louder so that I was catapulted awake. It was twenty past four in the morning. The fire had gone out in the bedroom grate and my room was cold and dark. Someone was banging on the front door downstairs. I lit a lamp and descended the stairs while the knocking continued, now accompanied by a familiar voice calling my name.

'I'm sorry to be calling on you at this hour, sir,' said a breathless and flustered Janson when I opened the door. 'But I thought both you and the Professor would want to see it straightaway, sir, what's happened to the Hickling body.' There was a cab waiting at the kerb behind him. The cab window nearest to me was yanked down and Professor Hartlett stuck his head through the aperture. 'Christopher, as quickly as you can now,' he called. 'Janson came for me first. He can explain what's happening once you've joined us in the carriage. Hurry please, Christopher!'

I dressed as hastily as I could and flew into the carriage, followed by Janson, who called up to the driver to proceed to the hospital with all the speed he could muster. Once I was sitting in

In February 1266 in the village of Ruggianto, located in the Aosta Valley of the Italian Alps, a ten-year-old boy, name unknown, was charged for taking on the form of a wolf and killing and partly devouring an Alpine goat, a lamb and Old Siddalato's Alsatian. The village community entertained little doubt of the boy's guilt. They had all heard repeatedly, and not just in the fug of the taverna, Tronto the Shepherd's account. Between matins and lauds on the feast day of Saints Alpig and Conda, beneath a night sky of black damask pinpricked by the celestial blaze and woven with wisps of phosphorescence, Tronto had discovered in the frozen lower field by the river, surrounded by the steaming carcasses of the beasts it had eviscerated, a wolf. It was lying on its side, whimpering in pain, its front right paw shredded to the bone. When Tronto had returned at dawn with reinforcements and ropes, the stricken wolf had disappeared, its place taken by a skinny, naked, sleeping boy, shivering in the frost. The boy's mouth was smeared with blood, and strips of sheep flesh were caught between his teeth, but there was no wound to his hands or feet. He seemed incapable, absent his metamorphosis, of the multiple dismemberments strewn around him.

The boy was a stranger and, on waking, had cried piteously and professed ignorance of the reasons for his incriminating condition. Tronto had recognised the fur adhering to some of the torn flesh discarded next to the boy and, on informing Siddalato of his trusty companion's demise, it had taken both the old man's bull-chested nephews to restrain him from thrashing the little fiend, who was dragged by a rope around his neck to the chapel. If Tronto's account was not damning enough, it was said that a filigree of black down coated the boy's upper arms and back, incongruous in one so young. And now other villagers reported that the preceding weeks had seen many of their sheep and cattle taken during the night. One-Eyed Jacopo said that, three days ago, the boy had appeared at his cottage door, begging for food. On being shooed away, the boy had cursed him before returning that very night, when One-Eyed Jacopo had with his own eye witnessed the boy transform into a wolf and then piss on his marrows. Which had subsequently turned into stones.

The penalty for being a werewolf was to be cooked on your own bonfire until your organs and muscles shrivelled more speedily than a salted snail and your bones calcified into white brittle twigs (although it was anticipated that, with not much fat on him, the bones of the wolf-boy might merely blacken and shrink instead). But first the boy had to be tried before the visiting episcopal court, which was next due to attend Barisolo, the town nearest Ruggianto, in a few weeks' time. Until then the boy was kept, in chains of iron admixed with a trickle of silver, in the cellar of Mother Currochio's presbytery, where neither the rays of the sun nor, more importantly, the light of the moon penetrated.

There was considerable excitement amongst the villagers when the news spread that the prosecuting magistrate would be Mother Simona de Curloville. Her recent successful convictions of a coven of wizards in Perpignan (for sorcery and playing the hurdy-gurdy on the Sabbath), a scrivener from Bologna (for marrying one of

No, you imbecile, not one!

Joco turned to Old Siddalato. *Will you be going to Barisolo for the burning?*

Will I? growled Siddalato. *I'm going to light the faggots myself if they let me, my farts will fan the flames and I'll be dancing the tarantella while he sizzles, whether they let me or not.*

As for the boy, still shivering from the buckets of icy water Gennaro had doused him with, but now dressed in the clean altar girl's tunic fetched by Mother Currochio, he lay in the corner of the cellar, his limbs folded in on themselves like an albino bat, whimpering and jerking in his sleep.

He dreamt that he bounded in great flying leaps through the night, so swiftly that the smatter of lights from the village (candlelight through the chinks in shutters, firelight behind sagging doors) receded behind him like a firebrand tossed down a well. As he sliced through the icy darkness, past the spindly olive trees, the hay ricks, the dilapidated huts and shacks, he inhaled a palimpsest of aromas: deep down, like a bass note, the fusty odour of mycorrhizal fungi gluing root to root; further up, the mouldering bouquet of soil and leaf litter, the blandness of sap-mottled wood; above that, the perfumes of leaves and plants – pine, citrus, mint; and, higher still, the gamey, feral scent of boar and the fishy tang of fox that hovered in the night air, like spectral presences, interlaced with a whiff of something that was so faint it was like a note pitched beyond his hearing but which thrilled him deep inside, made him want to piss.

He was barely touching the ground, and the sense of his own velocity was a pulse of joy that swelled and caught in his throat as he raced propulsively towards the horizon, where a glimmer of light oozed at the frayed edge of the heavy cloak of night – a horizon he never reached, for Gennaro woke him with a kick to his ribs and the boy cried out, either in pain or at the sudden ejection from his dreams.

After breakfast a small party made its way along the track from Ruggianto to Barisolo. The wheels of Gennaro's cart crunched through runnels of ice the colour of congealed pig fat; on its back a cage had been constructed, in which the boy huddled for warmth. A few paces ahead of the cart, the two Mothers rode side by side, Mother Simona in an ecstasy of appreciation as she surveyed the ice draped over bare branches, the fields dusted with frost like icing sugar on struffoli, and a sky whose blue reminded her, she informed Mother Clodagh, of the interior of the dome of the Church of Hagia Sophia in Constantinople. For her part, Mother Clodagh kept her eyes on the road ahead and seemed in silent communion with her thoughts. Before mounting her horse she had passed two slices of cheese and half a sausage, leftovers from breakfast, through the bars of the cage to the boy; he had said nothing but had nodded almost imperceptibly in gratitude, an interaction noticed by Mother Simona, who had smiled indulgently. At the head of the party rode Signora Francesca, a member of Bishop Cadenza's diocesan staff, who had come to escort them to Barisolo.

The journey took just over five hours and no sooner had they arrived than Signora Francesca, once she had given orders for the boy to be taken to the town's dungeon for the night, took the two clerics to one side to explain that rooms had been provided for them in the episcopal residence just off the main square. The Signora added that although the Bishop was dining with local dignitaries that evening she hoped to have lunch with both of them tomorrow after the trial and burning, which the Bishop expected to be concluded by sext (noon) at the latest, as she needed to be in Milan by vespers that day.

Mother Clodagh frowned. *But that is hardly enough time for a proper trial of the matter, surely.*

Signora Francesca's neutral, if rather brisk, tone hardened. *Is there going to be a problem here?*

Not at all, Signora, not at all, said Mother Simona, taking the other Mother by the arm and leading her away while whispering in her ear, *Don't worry, Mother, I will only need ten minutes for my submission tomorrow: the rest of the time is yours.*

And, the following day, Mother Clodagh had to admit that Mother Simona was as good as her word. The court hearing had commenced at terce, squeezed into the chapter house of the Church of the Holy Family: Bishop Cadenza, enthroned on her dais, resplendent in a shimmering chasuble of pearl-studded burgundy silk; Signora Francesca and the clerk, in black court robes, sitting below her; standing facing the Bishop, at lecterns, Mother Simona on one side, Mother Clodagh the other; between them, manacled to a post, the boy, still in the white robe of an altar girl; and, shuffling in a rough semi-circle around them, coughing and muttering, spectators and witnesses from the town and those who had trekked from Ruggianto, Tronto, Joco, One-Eyed Jacopo and Siddalato included. Through the yellow stained-glass windows, all could see the final bales of wood being deposited at the foot of the stake. The air in the court seemed to simmer with excitement, which almost boiled over when the Bishop called on Mother Simona to speak.

It was agreed afterwards that her performance had entwined the elegance of simplicity with the simplicity of elegance. The bare facts of the matter were laid out and what the eyewitnesses had seen was briefly summarised. She made no apologies for not devoting more time to proving that the boy was a werewolf: *We all know it to be true in our hearts in the same way that we know that we would give our lives for our children and that God loves us.* It gave her no pleasure, she said, to see one so young consigned to fire but burn he must if he was to be saved to the life eternal. *Let us pray,* she exhorted those around her as she stood by the boy, burrowing her fingers into his black curls, *that on the cusp of his immolation this boy begs God for forgiveness, for then the Kingdom of Heaven will truly be his, for if he does not repent, the flames that devour him will be but a pinprick next to the everlasting torment that awaits him in Hell.*

In contrast, the consensus was that Mother Clodagh made rather heavy weather of her presentation. Her interrogation of the principal witnesses was thorough rather than inspired, and some of those questioned (the questioning was in Italian whereas the proceedings generally were in Latin) had some jollity on account of her accent. Nevertheless, some of the information she elicited (for example, that most of the cattle supposedly lost to the werewolf must have been imaginary, for an investigation of the bailiff's records revealed the disappearance of only two sheep and one goat during the previous two months; or that the interval between Tronto's discovery of the injured and trapped wolf and his return to find the boy in its place had been five or six times longer than Tronto had originally indicated) had raised some eyebrows. Also, it was generally conceded that her inquisition of One-Eyed Jacopo had been particularly effective. Standing the same distance from him as the boy had been when One-Eyed Jacopo saw him transform into a wolf, she removed from beneath her vestments the skull of an ox and held it above her head.

What am I holding in my hand?

One-Eyed Jacopo squinted his eye. *A Bible?*

No, try again.

A flagon of ale?

Again, please.

The holy staff of St Petronella?

And when she asked him to produce one of the marrows petrified by the werewolf's piss, which he had been requested to bring with him to court, he admitted he had lost them.

What, all of them? All the dozen marrows you said were turned to stone, you lost them all?

Yes, I'm afraid so, Holy Mother.

He ate them, called out Joco to widespread guffaws.

The clerk brought the proceedings to an end after that and asked Bishop Cadenza to pronounce the sentence. The Bishop thanked both Mothers for their advocacy and drew attention to the deeply humane and powerful conclusions of Mother Simona. *Her presence,* she announced, *dignifies all who have been caught up in these tragic circumstances and all those present who are anxious to see the execution of both divine and earthly justice.*

Mother Simona placed her hand on her chest and bowed to the Bishop.

The Bishop then pronounced the boy guilty of being an instrument of the Devil whose particular wickedness was to transform himself into a wolf and indulge that savage beast's monstrous proclivities. He would be punished by being taken outside and burnt alive forthwith.

As the Bishop's personal guard seized the boy, who seemed oblivious to his imminent fate, and dragged him outside, the chapter house emptied as rapidly as the bowels of someone with the bloody flux, as its occupants rushed to claim those prized spots that afforded an up-close view of the stake. Nobody noticed Mother Clodagh head the other way, through the door that opened onto the deserted nave of the church, where she sat on a pew towards the back. She withdrew from her robes a leather-bound psalter and two small phials, one containing earth, the other containing a clear liquid more viscous than water. She poured two thimblefuls of each substance onto the cover of the psalter and then kneaded them together into a paste using only the thumbs of each hand. As she did so, she closed her eyes and a frown of concentration descended on her features as she muttered some Latin words over and over. As her thumbs flickered faster and faster, the words tumbled from her more and more quickly.

A huge cracking sound followed by a thunderous boom sounded from somewhere beyond the high vaulted spaces of the church. Letting the psalter fall to the floor, Mother Clodagh got to her feet, dizzy from her mental absorption, and walked to the doors of the church. Clouds, like dirty bulging sacks, hung low over the town, and tiny coronas sprang from fat globes of rain that had flung themselves against the ground. Before her eyes, outposts of damp earth expanded into wet islands that reached out to form soaked continents. Within seconds, the saturated soil fizzed and foamed under the onslaught of rain that, sizzling and hissing, swept across the town square in a series of diaphanous curtains as far as she could see.

Mother Simona materialised at her side, her tunic black and sagging from the downpour. *There you are, Mother. This came on very quickly, didn't it? Has it set in for the day, do you think?*

Oh, I would say so.

Yes, I feared as much. The burning will have to be delayed until the morning. That is most unfortunate. I am due to baptise Ottoline of Bavaria's firstborn tomorrow. Still, God's will be done. Shall we join the Bishop for lunch?

Mother Clodagh explained that she was feeling unwell and wished to retire to her room to rest, and asked the other to convey her sincere apologies to the Bishop. Once back in her room, she sat on the bench by the door, listening to the rain, her eyes closed.

As soon as night had fallen, she slipped out and crossed the square towards the dungeons. The town was deserted, washed clean by the rain, except for a bedraggled cleric, leading a donkey and heading for the episcopal residence, who said a weary good evening as she passed Mother Clodagh in the square. When she arrived at the residence, this priest, drenched through to her horsehair undergarments (which she wore adjacent to her skin in perpetual mortification of her flesh) introduced herself to Signora Francesca as Mother Clodagh. She was most apologetic; she had encountered floods near Bradanto d'Aretto; these had closed the Viona Pass and the alternative route had delayed her arrival in Barisolo by five days. Now that she was here, she was most anxious to meet the boy she was defending, although perhaps she might avail herself of a seat by the fire and a bowl of hot soup first? A startled and confused Signora Francesca brought her to the room where the first Mother Clodagh to arrive had been staying but, when they got there, the room was of course empty.

By then both the flame-haired woman and the boy were gone from Barisolo. The town jailer had gone outside for a piss; when he returned, the door to the dungeon was open, the boy's chains coiled on the floor like the shucked-off skin of a snake. The two of them moved through the darkness like a ripple across dark water, an eddy through black smoke, a disturbance in the dank, cool air, something sensed rather than seen. They raced through the orchards, past the brewery and the farmhouses and then up the slopes, flitting between the trunks of birch and mountain ash. By the time the alarm had been raised in town and a party, brandishing flaming torches, had set off in pursuit, they were above the tree line, beginning to traverse the fingers of ice and snow reaching down from the upper slopes, two silent, sleek shadows. There they stopped to rest, jointed knots of muscle flexing and stretching beneath quivering haunches, flanks gleaming with sweat, the raw air burning their throats. As she panted, she heard then the howls – and as always, when she heard them after a long absence, she felt a longing, one that seemed to flare in her stomach rather than her heart, for that lost time long ago when woman and wolf lived together in friendship and cooperation.

Come, she said to the boy, *we still have far to go before dawn.*

The Malumbra

1.

The man had been brought in after he'd turned violent following a routine ID check. He left the officer who'd stopped him with a trauma-induced cerebral oedema. It took three officers to eventually subdue him, face down on the road, arms behind his back, wrist-twined and ankle-twined. Car keys had been found in his pocket; when the unlock button had been pressed, a black saloon, twenty metres down the street, had sprung into life, headlights on, the mist coming off the marsh adjacent to the road twisting in the yellowish beams as if it was alive. They found fifty kilograms of nitroglycerin-rich explosive, looking like slabs of sweaty cheese, in the boot of the car. The man had been taken to KarzakH4D, where he was put into solitary. No record of his face, iris, fingerprints or DNA anywhere. He said his name was Manzy. He was interrogated around the clock for three days, and on the evening of the third day they called me in.

I had just returned from attending a poetry workshop. Eight aspiring poets, sitting in a circle, seven of them parsing the verses offered by the eighth. A troop of squabbling baboons would treat each other with more courtesy. The consensus of the group was that the work under analysis (not mine) was 'performative' and 'lacking in authenticity'. 'Not authentic to who?' the woman whose poem it was kept saying. Back home, I'd taken my dinner out onto the deck and ate it while the sunset smouldered above the ridge on the other side of the valley – it looked like the trees hidden below the skyline were ablaze. Handel's *Samson* was coming through the outdoor speakers. Scene I of Act III: the Chorus of Israelites were thundering through 'With Thunder Arm'd, Great God, Arise!' when the phone rang.

The caller introduced herself as Ritter and asked if I was Penton. She sounded flat, tired. There was a hint of distaste in the way she said my name, but I was tired too; I could have imagined it.

'That's me.'

'Hugh Penton?'

'That's still me.'

'We need you to come in and help us.' She told me about Manzy's arrest and incarceration in a karzak and the questioning he had been subject to on account of the explosives deposited in his car. But the situation had escalated: earlier that day, he'd been moved to a high-security facility. 'A couple of the officers were reviewing parts of the interview on tape, and they noticed ... well, they noticed some irregularities in his behaviour, let's put it that way.' She paused, as if expecting me to ask what those irregularities might be, but I didn't say anything.

'Look,' she continued, 'it's probably nothing, just a tic or something, and we know it's been a long, long time but we thought we'd better get one of you guys in to review it. We searched the data fold and your details came up as the nearest rontogen.' Now she sounded bored. It wasn't her idea to call me. Or, if it was, she was adhering to protocol; personally, she didn't think I was required.

'It's been, what, over fifteen years since the last one. Is this necessary?'

'I'm as enthused about it as you are.' She was really biting down on her words now. 'But, yes, it's necessary.'

I sighed. 'Okay, okay, I'll drive over tomorrow morning.'

'We need you tonight. We sent a car. It's already there. I'll see you in a couple of hours.'

I walked through to the front. The light had almost leached away but a faint milkiness still hung to a strip of sky above the encroaching dark mass of the trees. Sure enough, a large black saloon was waiting for me in the gloom of the yard. The only road to my place is visible from the deck and I hadn't seen the car drive in. It must have arrived earlier and parked up behind the trees, waiting for my return. As I opened the door and appeared in the doorway, the engine growled and two blazing white headlights flicked on, flooding the hallway, blinding me. Shielding my eyes, I just about made out someone holding open the back door on the passenger side of the car.

After the two guys in the front introduced themselves, they were silent, their shapes silhouetted against the globes of beam-lit road rushing towards us. Security Ministry goons. Hired for neither their conversational ability nor their easy charm: in my previous life, I'd been surrounded by them. We headed west in vain pursuit of a dwindling dab of pink sky, driving first through the suburbs – empty, dimly lit streets interspersed by the oblong shapes of community bars, encrusted with neon strips and whorls, and the red façades of urban karzaks – and then we were crossing the agricultural belt. Vast fields, invisible in the dark, radiating in either direction across the plain – only the distant twinkle of the lights of a farmstead to show that this stretch of land was not entirely uninhabited. They grew cotton, soybean and wheat for the most part out here. The farmed land petered out and finally we were in the bush, a realm of utter blackness that began at the limit of the headlights and absorbed and echoed the emptiness of the night sky. On we travelled, a tiny bubble of light, into the dark vastness of the endless interior that stretched away from us.

We hadn't seen a car travelling in either direction for well over an hour, and the road had dwindled to a strip of jagged-edged tarmac, when we finally slowed and turned left onto a rough track scratched through the scrub. After ten minutes juddering and jolting along this track, the headlights veering from side to side like a lamp held by a drunk, we came to a checkpoint in a fortified wire fence. The beam of a torch thrust into the back of the car by an officer temporarily blinded me for the second time that evening – and then we were through. We came to a stop on a square of open earth bordered on three sides by single-storey buildings.

As I unfolded my limbs out of the back seat, a woman, who'd clearly been waiting, came forward. She was my height, looked grave but composed. 'Jean Ritter,' she said. She indicated the woman standing next to her. 'Dr Michaela Santorini.'

Santorini gave me a small box and a bottle of water. 'If there's any possibility we're going to be using dipthalon shortly, you'd better start taking these. As you know, ideally you should take two tablets every four hours for a full day to protect against any accidental exposure. And the same for two days after.'

'Thanks, Doc,' I said. 'But let's not get ahead of ourselves here. I said to Ritter when she called, it's been fifteen years.'

'Sure, of course. But no harm in being prepared, right?'

I took a couple of the pills and then followed the two women down a short corridor into a conference room. There were about eight or nine persons, sitting at laptops around a U-shaped table or standing conversing. Harsh fluorescent lighting: the faint aroma of dried-out takeaway food, coffee breath and nervous sweat. On the far wall, a large screen showed a man sitting at a table in an interrogation cell; a live video feed, I assumed. As I entered, voices stilled and everyone looked over.

One of the men, whose face I recognised from way back, said, 'Fuck me. Penton.' He embarked on this little performance, turning to the other people in the room, his look saying: *do you know who this guy is?* His eyes settled on Ritter and he spoke. 'You didn't tell me you'd called in Penton.'

'He was the closest one who answered the phone.' She was stone-faced, resolutely unimpressed. 'What?' she asked the man. 'Am I missing something here?'

Somebody from the other side of the table piped up. 'Penton's one of only a handful of rontogens with a one hundred per cent successful detection rate. He wrote the fucking manual.'

'Bully for him,' Ritter said. 'Let's hope that means we all get to go home sooner.'

I smiled to myself; I was beginning to quite like Ritter. I nodded at the screen. 'That's Manzy?'

'That's Manzy,' she said. 'You need anything before we start running the tape for you? There's coffee over there if you want it.'

I declined and sat at a chair in front of the screen. Those who were standing took their seats. A man who introduced himself as Fennard brought me up to date. Manzy had been brought in around 10.30 on Monday evening. Detonators were found next to the explosives in the boot of his car. On the back seat they discovered a roll of silver foil, an empty bottle of bourbon and a battered copy of Milton's *Paradise Lost*. There was a small local primary school a quarter-mile down the road. They were working on the assumption that he'd planned to leave the car parked nearby before it opened the following morning, with the explosives primed to go off shortly after lessons had commenced. Or he'd intended to park the car in front of the post office or the council offices in what passed as the centre of town.

Shackled to a table in a karzak cell, he'd given nothing away for the first couple of days, sitting impassively, ignoring all questions, as if his interrogators were voicing a language that held no meaning for him. He took water but refused food.

So far, so normal. But then on Thursday morning he'd done something which had caused Manzy, and then me, to be ferried out here to this isolated facility, hundreds of kilometres inland. The unit had been established over twenty-five years ago to assist with the waves of malumbra assaults crashing over us – and then, fifteen years ago, when the attacks abruptly stopped, it was mothballed. Until earlier today that is, when the facility had been brought back to life.

2.

'The first potential manifestation occurred at 9.47,' said Fennard, as the live feed on the large screen was replaced by the digital recording of that morning's session running on fast forward. There was that flickering, jerky, comic effect of sped-up film: water glasses on the table instantaneously appearing then just as rapidly disappearing; the back of the shoulders and heads of the interviewing officers repeatedly bobbing in and out of view, twitching this way and that; the legs and feet of the two guards standing at the back of the cell – all that could be seen of them on the video – doing a jitterbug shuffle. Through it all, Manzy remained motionless at the centre of the frame as if composed of granite: not a tremor disturbed his outline as he sat at the table, each manacled hand lying palm down on its surface, his blue eyes staring at the camera. But as I examined the footage, I saw that wasn't quite right. His eyes occasionally dropped to regard the officers sitting across the table, disposing a look of utter indifference on them, before flicking back up to the camera.

Are you waiting for me? I thought.

The fast forward suddenly switched to normal replay and a voice I recognised as Ritter's said, '—that what you like? Knowing that you've been responsible for so much death? Kids, eh? Is that what excites you, Manzy, exercising the power to snuff out their young lives?'

A pause. Manzy was ignoring her, staring at the camera.

'This is it,' Ritter said from her seat a few places behind me. 'The reference to Milton seems to have triggered it.'

I leant forward, sensing the weight of expectation in the room like an alteration in atmospheric pressure. The last fifteen years had evaporated like the tattered, flimsy recollections of a dream on waking. I was back in front of a screen: watching, assessing, calculating, trying to decipher whether there was a pattern or meaning to movements that, on the surface, appeared random or unconnected. My right hand curled instinctively, expecting my habitual coffee mug, and I started when my hand closed on empty air. I'd given up coffee, one of the many lifestyle changes I'd implemented over the past decade and a half. Just at that moment, it seemed a bizarre thing to have done.

'You know I studied Milton at uni,' Ritter was saying on the recording (Had she? I hadn't pegged her as a student of English literature), 'and I always thought Satan, as portrayed by Milton, was a shouty pub-boor. The real hero of *Paradise Lost*? Romantic rubbish, if you ask me. "The mind is its own place, and in itself can make a heaven of hell, a hell of heaven", and all that. Spare me. I don't think Milton was that simplistic, do you? Or have you sucked in all that "Better to reign in hell than serve in heaven" crap?'

At this, Manzy did look at her. His head twitched slightly, like a ripple had run through the digital recording.

'There,' Ritter said, behind me, 'did you see it? I didn't notice it in the room but Fennard picked it up on review.'

'Back it up,' I said. 'Run it at twelve fps.'

In the replay Ritter's voice drawled an octave lower. After the word 'crap', Manzy continued to stare at the camera for a long pause before his eyes swivelled slowly to look at Ritter's. Again, a long pause.

'Run it again.' I leant forward, holding my breath, willing my eyes to see. And this time, I saw it. While he was looking at Ritter his head twitched imperceptibly. If anything, it twitched to his right.

'Re-run it at six fps from him looking at Ritter,' I said. 'Full frame focus on his face. And cut the sound.'

At this speed, it was clear that Manzy turned his head to the right astonishingly quickly, slightly lifting it as he did so.

'How long did that take?'

'Six point seven six centiseconds,' said Fennard.

'Fuck, that's quick,' I said. 'Malumbra or not, it was a good call, Fennard. Re-run it at one fps. Expand the focus to the half-metre above his right shoulder. We need to see what he's looking at.'

Even with the film slowed down to this extent, Manzy swung his head in a series of three sudden jerks: the first frame, the start of the pivot; the second frame, his head almost in profile and raised as if looking at something just beyond his right shoulder; the third frame, his eyes back at the camera.

'Freeze on the second frame. Map the coordinates in his head and calculate a horizontal axis from the retinal optic nerve ingress through the lens in both eyes.'

Computer-generated white dots appeared on the screen, extending out in a line from that sliver of left eye which was all that could be seen from the side-on view of Manzy's head. A second line of dots, originating from Manzy's unseen right eye, converged with the first line at a point about a half-metre beyond his right shoulder and two metres above the ground.

I stared at the empty space in the interrogation cell that Manzy's eyes had focused on. Nothing to see. But if Manzy had been captured by a malumbra, that's where it was standing: just to the right and one step behind him. Invisible to me but not to Manzy.

'How many other potential manifestations?' I asked.

'Three more,' Fennard said.

'Let's see them.'

The second was time-stamped at 13.12, the third at 15.48 and the fourth at 19.32 (after I'd been called). The second and fourth potential manifestations were similar to the first. A twitch of Manzy's head to his right, seemingly prompted by a change in the line of questioning, which, when reviewed at three fps or less, revealed itself as a glance by Manzy, executed with preternatural rapidity, at the space above and to the side of his right shoulder as if he was communicating with something there, perhaps seeking guidance or simply sharing a look. The third manifestation was different. Manzy flicked his head to his right as he had done before but then swivelled it all the way to his left, as if glancing at something behind him on that side too.

'Okay, extract and run the PMs together and play them again.'

I watched the spliced-together freeze-framed digital recordings another three or four times, searching for that indefinable tell, that core instinct, without which there was no certainty. Did I sense the beginning of an impatience amongst those around the table or was I projecting it? I closed my eyes, tried to inhabit my breathing. I couldn't decide who was more deluded – me or them – thinking that you could just pick this up where you'd left off after fifteen years.

'Penton, what are you thinking?' If Ritter was impatient, there was no trace of it in her voice; she still gave the impression she couldn't have been less invested in my reply than if she'd asked me if I'd seen yesterday's cricket.

I turned to Santorini, who was seated behind me.

'Doc, does that look like an anxiety tic to you?'

She stood up and massaged the back of her neck. 'There are as many different varieties of tic disorder as there are people. But, what, four tics over a ten-hour period while the rest of the time he's sitting like a block of quartzite? Unlikely. What interests me is what precipitates his head movement.'

'Yeah,' I said. 'It's invariably in response to a question that seems to irritate or amuse him. Is it an involuntary reaction to what he's heard, or is he sharing his reaction with the malumbra standing behind him?'

I got to my feet. 'If he is a captive, I've not encountered one like this before. The injuries he inflicted when he was arrested. The speed with which he can turn his head. Can a drug do that, Doc?'

'God only knows what they – what we – are cooking up these days,' she said. 'But I'm not familiar with a narcotic that could produce such extraordinary muscular rapidity.'

I looked at Ritter. 'Give me a moment, I'm going to get some air.' I headed to the door but stopped just before leaving, turned and said to her, 'The Milton thing. That was good. I'd never have thought of that.'

Outside, the air was cool on my skin. I walked away from the brightly lit compound and carried on until I came to the perimeter fence. I lay down on the ground; it was my decided opinion that this was the only way to look at the stars. Above me, the pale phosphorescence of the Milky Way stained the night sky, like a bucket of cream poured into a tank of ink. I nestled the back of my head against the sandy rock. In other continents the earth had been twisted and folded like plasticine, stabbed into airy steeples, rent with savage gashes, blistered by a molten heart simmering below its surface crust. Geology as vaudeville. But here we dwelled on a vast anvil of ancient rock, inert for aeons, hammered only by the sun. Cloaked, other than its fringes and extremities, in desert so vast our comprehension quailed before the immensity. *We're preposterous*, I thought, *it's preposterous.*

After a while I became conscious of someone standing next to me.

'Doc,' I said.

'Let me get this straight,' she said. 'I wasn't around last time. Just now, when they were saying you had a one hundred per cent detection rate. So you interviewed someone who'd behaved oddly after committing, or trying to commit, an atrocity and determined whether that person had been captured by a malumbra or not. If you judged they had, that person was executed – strapped to a chair in a berbelian chamber and poisoned with dipthalon. If you were right, once the person was dead the malumbra gradually took shape, solidified out of the air to stand sentinel over the body of its captive for a few seconds. The only time we'd ever be able to see one of those fuckers. We don't know why – something to do with the dipthalon. And then the malumbra would fade away, itself perishing or returning to wherever the fuck it came from. Right?'

'Right.'

'And that happened every time? Every time you made the call, it proved correct – a malumbra always materialised and then disappeared?'

'Correct. I always stayed for the execution. Felt I had to.'

'Sure. But what about those people you judged hadn't been taken by a malumbra, were just normal criminals – well, you know what I mean – and so weren't executed? There was no way of testing whether you were right. How do we know there weren't a bunch of malumbras escaping undetected?'

'We don't. All we could do was keep an eye on those persons, see whether they ever gave any indication of malumbra capture in the future. I guess there must have been some captives who were able to keep it hidden.'

'Although you think that was rare?'

'I do. I think, as a general rule, captives can't help but give their malumbras away. But maybe some did slip through the net. But I don't think many did.'

I rubbed my eyes.

'A woman called Barton, convicted of going crazy with a knife in a betting shop twenty years ago, was sent to a high-security facility not far from here after I'd failed to detect a malumbra presence. She'd only been there six months when she made a salad out of the organs of her cellmates. They overruled me and sent her to the berbelian chamber. Still no malumbra. Same story with another guy out west who killed his wife and children and then, later, after he'd been convicted, half the inmates in his prison wing. No malumbra appeared after he'd been executed either.'

There was a pause. I noticed Santorini staring at the sky.

'Why were you so good at this – so much better than the others?'

'I used to get asked this a lot and my answer was always the same. I don't know. I just get this sense, instinct, whatever.'

'Do you have this sense with Manzy?'

'I think I'm going to have to talk to him.'

'You're not certain about him?'

I got to my feet and began to brush the dirt from my clothes.

'That's not it. It's because I've never spoken to someone with two malumbras before.'

3.

'The sniffer-boy,' Manzy said, staring at me, as I dropped into the chair across the table from him.

His voice was soft and flat. I sensed the dropping jaws of the team watching the live feed. Malumbra captives were universally uncommunicative. As Manzy had been – until now.

'Do you know who I am?' I asked.

'Well, let's say we all know what you are.'

'You say "we". Who do you mean?'

His teeth chattered, as if caught by an ice-cold-induced spasm, but he said nothing.

'You have two of them,' I said quietly.

'That I do, sniffer-boy. This one on my right side' – he tilted his head to his right, without breaking his stare at me – 'I call Mr Gently-puss. The one on my left' – again, a slight movement of the head in that direction – 'is Mr Finger-mole.'

I'd never heard a captive acknowledge their malumbra before. I don't think anybody had. I reflected on Manzy's admission for a while before asking, 'When did you become aware of them?'

'Must have been about two weeks ago. I'd gone fishing with Raymond out at Ledgerville and we'd gone back to his place for dinner. Roast quail, new potatoes, parsnips in a mint sauce. And a bottle of Chateau Margaux 1982. Dining room dressed in sombre teak and red brocade: like the inside of a coffin. We'd finished eating and were feeling replete, you might surmise. And then I became conscious of these two, standing behind me on either side. Realised they weren't there to clear the table when it became obvious that Raymond couldn't see 'em.'

'What did they offer you, Manzy?'

His head flipped back on his neck with unbelievable speed as if a hinged desk had been thrown open. I saw the underside of his jaw convulsing and heard his upper and lower teeth clattering together. And then his head dropped back abruptly as he resumed staring at me. Had he been laughing?

'I think you have misinformed yourself, sniffer-boy. It's not a question of them controlling me. Rather it's I control them.'

'Of course. That's what I'd expect you to say. Let me change the question. Why did they come to you and why then?'

'I summoned them.'

'Oh?'

'That's right, sniffer-boy, that's what I did.'

'Where did you summon them from?'

'Your colleague would no doubt want me to say Pandæmonium, but actually they came from a very nice place.'

'What is this place?'

'Why do you care? You going to summon yours?'

'Maybe. But where do they come from? Do you know, Manzy? I don't think you do.'

His teeth chattered together again, sounding like ivory dice dashed against a marble floor, and then stopped.

Doc, I typed on my phone, *what's with the jaw movements? I haven't seen this with previous captives.*

'They come from a place—' Manzy paused and, for a fleeting moment, seemed confused. He then shook his head, as if he doubted he could explain – or I would understand – where the malumbras originated.

'Why do you have two of them?' I asked.

'They're not both mine. One of them is yours.'

'Mine?' I was surprised – I hadn't been expecting this. 'He's not going to get very far with me.'

'You say that now, sniffer-boy, but when you leave this room, Mr Finger-mole is going to be following you. A match made in heaven. Pretty soon it'll be like "with him all deaths I could endure, without him live no life".'

His lips pulled back and he smashed his jaws together again in a sudden paroxysm as if trying to splinter his teeth.

There was an insectile buzz in my pocket. It was Santorini responding to my text. *I've not seen this before either. Looks like some sort of muscular spasm. If he's not careful he's going to bite his tongue off.*

'Why now?' I asked. 'Why have they come back after all this time?'

'All what time? Time's not the same for them as it is for you.'

'The explosives,' I said. 'What were they for? Were they for the school? Why would you do that?'

'To help the children on their way. Such honey and laughter and, let us not forget, contentment awaits them.'

'What do you mean? You seem to forget you were going to slaughter them.'

'Such an emotive term. That's okay, I don't blame you. No way you understand that the fleeting spasm of extinguishment is the vehicle that takes you to a place where there's a whole lotta love – *and* a whole lotta these guys as well. Now that's enough from me. Enough from you, too. You goin' to kill me, sniffer-boy, get the fuck on with it.'

He leant back. The chains attaching his manacles to the table clanked as he crossed his arms against his chest. His head seemed to wobble for a fraction of a second as if he was settling it on his shoulders. Later, the freeze-frame analysis of the recording showed that, again, he'd turned his head to glance over each shoulder.

I asked him a couple more questions but he ignored both them and me, ostentatiously resuming his expressionless stare at the camera behind my head. I'd lost him; he'd retreated to the barbican in his head and barricaded himself inside. I stood, nodded at those watching the live feed in the adjoining room and, after the door had been unlocked, left the cell without looking back.

4.

Manzy was put to death fifty-four minutes after the door to the interrogation cell closed behind me. I'd forgotten how swiftly the mechanics of execution were implemented once an adjudication had been made. Fifteen years since they had last been relied on, the protocols were still in place. In this case, two signatures (mine and Ritter's) triggered a tightly choreographed series of actions. Four officers poured into the interrogation room and, gripping Manzy's arms and shoulders, held him steady while Dr Santorini injected him in the right upper arm with a compound of dimethoxyethane and fluothane. His unconscious body was washed, dried and dressed in a loose-fitting biodegradable garment and then strapped to a gurney, which was rolled into a lift and taken thirty metres below ground level, to the berbelian chamber.

They told me it had taken no more than an hour for the berbelian chamber at the facility to be readied for use. Lined with a chromium, cobalt and nickel alloy, the chamber had a single door. Once it had been closed and sealed, the only apertures were a series of grilles that formed part of a sophisticated filtration system through which the dipthalon was pumped into, and then sucked out of, the room. The gas chamber had also been fitted with a battery of video cameras so that both the execution of the captive and the materialisation, followed by the disappearance, of the capturing malumbra could be recorded for subsequent study and analysis. While we had been interviewing Manzy the scientific team had also extracted a canister of dipthalon from the underground vault where it was stored. They'd run a test on it. Any degradation in its lethal potency since the last time it had been deployed was too minute for the instruments to detect.

At 4.04 am Manzy was wheeled into the berbelian chamber, lifted from the gurney and strapped into a straight-backed metal chair with two wide armrests, the only piece of furniture in the room. Santorini administered by injection into his neck a solution whose principal ingredients were a stimulant to partially revive his consciousness and a barbiturate that relaxed his muscular and nervous systems. The object was to wake him enough so that the malumbra conjured by his death would appear with as much form and outline as possible (we had learnt from experience that the more conscious a captive immediately prior to his or her death, the more emphatic the appearance of the malumbra) but not to the full consciousness that would have magnified the agonising effects of dipthalon on his body. Once Manzy was sitting upright,

Santorini and the officers left the chamber and the air-lock mechanism clicked as the room was sealed.

The video feed from the cameras in the berbelian chamber appeared on the same large screen in the conference room. As Manzy woke up, his eyes searched the chamber until they found the wall-mounted camera and then they locked onto it with the same intensity they had stared at the interrogation-room camera. For a few seconds, through the agency of a digital camera, the twelve of us looked at a single person bound to a chair in the middle of an otherwise-empty room thirty metres below us, while he looked back at us.

At 4.15 am Ritter called out, 'Okay, good to go?' after which she gave the order for the dipthalon to be released. For a gas so viciously lethal, it had an anodyne, even benign, appearance – billowing out in pale milky puffs like dry ice from the ventilation grilles. But there was nothing benign about its effects on Manzy. As soon as the first wisps of dipthalon reached him, his jaws clamped and he began to thrash his head from side to side, in a vain attempt to avoid breathing any of it in. The second he ingested the smallest particle he began to convulse, his arms and legs became rigid, and his back arched. He seemed to lift from the chair, straining against his bonds, as if attempting to levitate. The tendons in his cheeks and neck swelled, like bars and cylinders of steel crouching beneath the surface of his skin. He closed his eyes. And then, like air erupting from a burst balloon, he collapsed back onto the chair, his limbs flopping, his head lolling back on his neck.

The first time I'd seen a malumbra appear I had been fascinated and unnerved in equal proportion. I'd since watched it dozens of times, and a trace of that initial reaction endured, although the primary emotion had become a bathetic weariness tinged with mild disgust. Prior to my initial sighting, I had been expecting a tall, wraith-like figure, a shadowy spectre, possessed of a palpable malevolence. Instead I saw a grey shape that resembled a half-metre-wide, two-and-a-half-metre-high plant stalk, with a bulbous crown in which a cloacal-like indentation quivered. And now, as I stared at the spot just behind Manzy's right shoulder, the familiar outline, no more than a vague suggestion at first, gradually assumed a distinct shape in the mist. And then for a few seconds I could see it quite clearly. It seemed to lean forward over Manzy's dead body and then, in the reverse of the process that had seen it materialise, it began to blur, waver in the billows of gas and fade away completely. Manzy was again alone in the berbelian chamber.

There was a silence in the conference room. Ritter turned to me. 'So what do you think happened?'

I thought for a moment. 'He played me. Made me think there was a second malumbra, when all the time there was only one.'

'Why would he do that?'

'To confuse us. To make us have this conversation.'

'Can we discount the other option?'

'Well, if the second one has attached itself to me, I can't see it.'

'Yet.'

'Sure, sure … yet. If I feel the urge to wreak indiscriminate carnage, I'll be handing myself in, you can count on it.'

Ritter looked away from me and spoke to no one in particular: 'We all heard what he said, that's all I'm saying.'

'He was bullshitting me, you, all of us. Trust me.'

She met my eyes again. 'I do,' she said. 'Anyway, thank you. Good job. The guys will drive you back. I'll see you again shortly, no doubt, at the debrief.'

I fell asleep in the car that drove me back. I climbed into the back seat to an apricot-pink glow that revealed the hard edge of the horizon to the east. I woke up to a cerulean sky dominated by a bullying sun, although it was not yet six in the morning. The first thing I did once I arrived home was switch on the pump for the artesian bore that supplied the sprinklers in the paddocks. I watched shawls of glittering drops being catapulted with metronomic regularity over the garden, causing the azaleas, lillipillies and viburnum to sparkle and the freshly strung spider webs to glisten. As I headed back to the kitchen to make some tea, my phone vibrated. It was an email with electronic plane tickets attached for the meeting later today in the capital, convened to discuss the very real possibility a new wave of malumbra attacks had commenced. I prepared breakfast to Ravel's Sonata for Violin and Cello (I wasn't in the mood for Handel) and ate my porridge and fruit on the deck, considering my options.

The email was inauthentic, of course. I didn't doubt that there would be such a meeting either later today or tomorrow – but I knew I wouldn't be attending it. They wanted me here for the next hour, focused on the trip, perhaps preparing an overnight bag. I knew how they worked. A conversation had been had after my car had departed last night, and a decision reached – the only decision possible in the circumstances, tenuous and indecisive though those circumstances were. I didn't blame Ritter: I would have done the same myself. They wouldn't send a car for me; that would take too long. Besides, the road up the valley was visible from the deck, like a piece of thread across green baize. They would come by a helicopter, six or seven of them, dropped off on the other side of the ridge, proceeding on foot, through the ironbarks, grey gums and pines. If I wasn't expecting them, the first I'd hear would be the metallic click of the safety catch on the gun behind me. Now I fancied that I'd sensed, rather than heard, while boiling water in the kitchen, a faint thrum with a different pitch from the usual background susurration of the warming insects. I reckoned I had about twenty minutes before they were here. Just long enough to prepare for them. And now that my course of action took shape in my mind, I wondered whether I might not prefer, after all, to listen to some Handel while I went about my business.

Acknowledgements

I'd like to extend my gratitude to the following people:

First of all, to Aviva Tuffield, my publisher at University of Queensland Press, who has done so much to shape these stories and without whom you, the reader, would not be holding this book. Thank you, Aviva, for giving me this opportunity.

To Ian See, my wonderful editor, whose alchemical skills have transformed and improved these stories.

To everyone at UQP who has assisted with such professionalism and expertise in preparing, producing and promoting this collection.

To Josh Durham for the inspired cover design.

To Kristina Olsson and Emily O'Grady for their advice and guidance during their expert teaching of the 2021 Faber Writing Academy 'Writing a Novel' course in Brisbane.

To my fellow writers on that course – John Arnold, Amanda Lay, India Lynn, Christine Ong, Kristine MacDonald, Leeann Nolan, Malcolm Steele and Jeanne Taylor – for their friendship and insightful advice. They stoically made repeated forays into early versions of *The Gorgon Flower* and endured more references to frothing maggots than anybody has a right to expect.

To the judges of the 2021 Elizabeth Jolley Short Story Prize and the 2022 Glendower Award for an Emerging Queensland Writer for shortlisting my writing.

To Amanda O'Callaghan and (again) Emily O'Grady for their encouragement and endorsement.

To my old friend John Clancy, who forty years ago asked me, as regards my writing, what I was waiting for. Here it is, John, sorry it took a while.

To Fiona Duncan, for her insightful comments on early versions of the stories.

To Pauline, David, Kevin, Joyce, Anne, Martyn, Kieran, Bridget, Brendan and Shelley for their interest and support, and all the other members of my family and my friends for their love and encouragement.

I am sorry that my parents are not alive to read this book. Fred and Sheila instilled in me a passion for reading and enjoyed a good story. Would these tales have cut the mustard? I'll never know, but I'm certain they would have been proud of me.

To you, the reader, for taking a punt on a first-time writer. As my wife often says, a book is only a book if someone reads it.

Finally, thank you to Tim, Matt, Ben and Joey, who are my reasons for being, and to Dominique, who has added the positions of first reader, mentor and editor to her existing essential roles in my life – I could not have parted with these stories without Dominique having improved them immeasurably first. I dedicate this book to them with gratitude and love.